AI

Well, here's a bi … can have some idea who the hell I am…

I was born in England in 1969, the son of a preacher, and often attribute my rebellious nature and outstanding talent for getting into trouble to the fact that I'm the repressed son of a priest. But to be perfectly honest I probably would have been the same regardless.

I developed a passion for martial arts which led to a British karate title and a place on the national team. My sporting commitments took me around Europe and the US and finally landed me in a sports science course.

After a distressing period of family turmoil, my father announced his intention to emigrate to Australia (yes, Anglican priests can get divorced as well as married).

Once in the land down under I began working as a personal trainer. I also embarked on two part-time occupations—modelling and nightclub bouncer—what a mixture. Several wild years of nightclub adventures and as 'Australia's Hottest Centrefold' inspired me to put pen to paper. Read on for the results.

SEX DRUGS AND KNUCKLEDUSTERS

MATT DUNK

ARROW

I would like to dedicate this, my first book, to my father and all the boys back in Perth . . . take care lads.

An Arrow Book
published by
Random House Australia Pty Ltd
20 Alfred Street, Milsons Point, NSW 2061

http://www.randomhouse.com.au

Sydney New York Toronto
London Auckland Johannesburg
and agencies throughout the world

First published 1997

National Library of Australia
Cataloguing-in-Publication Data

Dunk, Matt.
Sex, drugs and knuckledusters.

ISBN 0 09 183497 X.

I. Title.

A.823.3

Designed by Rockin' Doodles
Typeset by Midland Typesetters, Maryborough, Victoria
Printed by Griffin Paperbacks, Adelaide, South Australia

10 9 8 7 6 5 4 3 2 1

SEX

'Fuck it.'

The milky white fluid had been going in just fine until a small piece of sediment had got stuck in the base of the needle.

'Come on, you bastard, get in there.'

Jason applied more pressure to the syringe plunger. Really, he should have withdrawn the needle from his deltoid and relocated the injection to another area but his shoulder already felt like a pincushion from the previous failed attempts. He pushed against the plunger until his hand was shaking with the effort.

'Come on you fuc—'

At that moment the needle separated from the syringe, and with a dull popping sound, the two mls of white liquid exploded upwards and outwards splattering a startled Jason in the face and chest.

He sat on his bed motionless, shocked at what had just happened, with the now empty syringe in his right hand and a needle buried in his left shoulder just hanging there. The highly toxic liquid began to sting his eyes, bringing him painfully back to reality.

'Shit.'

He threw the syringe on the floor and pulled the needle out of his shoulder, placing it quickly on the bedside table so that he could rub his burning eyes. Standing up, he held them until the pain subsided.

'Fucking Stanazol, I'm never using that shit again.'

Jason looked down at his blue skin-tight T-shirt now covered with white spots, then at the wall next to his bed which was also pebble-dashed.

'Jesus Christ, how much damage can two fucking mls cause?'

Jason looked at his shoulder, a rose-red line of blood trailed from the injection site down to his elbow and had begun to form a drip. Jason picked up an old T-shirt from the floor and vigorously wiped the blood away, then rolled the sleeve down over his pincushion delt. Cursing under his breath, Jason grabbed the discarded needle and syringe and went to the kitchen to get a damp cloth to clean up the aftermath of the failed steroid injection.

Jason had just turned twenty-four. He was a touch under six foot tall with semi-long sandy coloured hair which he tied back in a ponytail. Looks-wise Jason rated an eleven out of ten, a kind of cross between Brad Pitt and Nick Testoni. Ironically, most of the trouble that he often found himself in was due to the fact that he was too good-looking.

This caused problems with jealous boyfriends who wanted to take his head off because the insecure fuck's girlfriend was looking at him. Problems every day of his life with people who assumed that a guy who looked like this has got to be an arsehole and so they treated him accordingly.

Sarcastic lesbians, insecure bosses, girls who only saw him as a handbag or a toy and, of course, gay men bestowing him with unwanted attention. Jason was far from homophobic, he had many homosexual friends, but nevertheless he had taken to wearing a gold ring on his wedding finger in an attempt to ward off any undesirable advances; sometimes it worked, sometimes it didn't.

Jason lived with Max, a massive, psychotic white bull-terrier with a scar above his left eye and a shocking craving for bananas and cats. As Jason rinsed the Stanazol out of his T-shirt, Max was undertaking the important task of licking his bollocks while he lay in his bed between the kitchen and the lounge.

'Stop that, Max, you dirty bastard,' Jason said as he slapped the dog playfully on the side of his massive head.

Max gave him a look that said, 'What's your fucking problem? They're mine, leave me alone.'

Jason made his way to the bathroom to shower and get ready for work, while Max returned to his important preening.

Jason had acquired Max when he moved to Perth from the Gold Coast nearly two years ago. The move was prompted by the traumatic break-up of his family. After sticking it out for twelve months he had the choice of either moving to England with his father or staying on the Gold Coast with his mother and sister. So what's a boy to do? He packed a rucksack, gave up his job at the local gym and left for Western Australia, as far from Queensland as possible without leaving his beloved country.

Showered, shaved and relieved, Jason went to his room and put a black tie in his pocket, along with a mouthguard and a handkerchief.

Back in the kitchen he sat with a cup of coffee and read the cartoon section of the newspaper as Max snuffled and snorted, his head between Jason's knees searching for signs of affection.

When the time hit 10.30 pm, Jason drained his cup, put on his black leather jacket and stuffed a pair of brass knuckledusters and a cricket box into his pockets. Then he grabbed his crash helmet and made his way out the door, affectionately slapping Max on the rump as he went.

Mike was standing halfway up the stairs between the bar area above and the large dance floor below.

Fucking hell, I've only just started and I'm bored shitless, he thought to himself.

Mike, a burly thirty-year-old pommy plumber with a Mancunian accent which drove girls silly, worked down drains during the day and at weekends was one of the five security staff at Davinchi's. It was here that he had met Jason and the other lads who had become his closest friends and partners in several crimes.

On the stairs on the other side of the club was

Grant, a six foot four violent psychopath with a baby face and a shaven blond flat top.

Although it wasn't even eleven o'clock yet, the club was pumping, it was a typical Friday at one of Perth's most popular night spots. The short-skirt brigade was out in force, as were the heavy drinking boys on their 'Lads'' nights out.

Mike was watching a rather cute, big breasted redhead at the upstairs bar who was wearing the obligatory short, tight dress when a movement on the dance floor below caught his eye.

'Fuck, it's too early for this shit,' he said as he launched himself down the stairs towards the dance floor.

As Mike charged through the crowd he shoved in his mouthguard and watched the various flailing arms and legs in front of him. In a clearing in the middle of the dance floor, four lads were beating the shit out of each other. Mike noticed out of the corner of his eye that Grant was no longer on the stairs.

Entering the messy brawl, he grabbed the nearest guy in a headlock from behind and gave the one he was fighting with a solid shove in the chest, sending him back into the other two brawlers.

Grant arrived on the scene and took hold of the two lads nearest to him by the scruff of their necks and with one swift movement crashed their heads together with a sound that would have been quite sickening if the music hadn't been so loud. One of them fell to his knees while the other stayed on his feet, dazed and bleeding.

The one Mike had in a headlock began to struggle

so violently that he had to put a sleeper-hold on him, restricting the blood and oxygen flow to his brain until he passed out. This took a little over four seconds and the guy was now lying on the dance floor 'sleeping'.

The last brawler, seeing the futility in going any further, attempted to flee the scene and lose himself in the throng of people at the bar, but two strong hands closed around his shoulders and Mike proceeded to frog-march him to the front door, closely followed by a beaming Grant with two very dazed and battered casualties.

Jason had parked his pride and joy motorbike, or his 'horny, fuck-off muscle machine' as he liked to call it, around the back of Davinchi's and was walking to the front of the club. He could see Eddie, the head doorman, and Steve, a modern day 'Conan the Barbarian', standing at the door when one body, followed by two more, was launched out into the street. Then Mike and Grant appeared at the doorway. Jason arrived and smiled at the four bouncers in front of him—his friends.

'What's happening, boys?'

'Oh you know, the usual. How are you, mate?' replied Mike.

'Good, dude. Let me guess—your handiwork, Grant?' Jason said, nodding in the direction of the bloodied battle victims.

'No, wasn't me mate,' Grant said with a cheeky smile on his guilty face.

'There's one more inside. I need some help to get him out, though,' said Mike.

'Oh, not again, Mike. It looks so fucking bad when they're carried out unconscious by two doormen,' moaned Eddie.

'Sorry mate, but I had to.'

Jason and Grant laughed and pushed Mike back into the club as he continued to protest his innocence. Jason dumped his gear in the cloakroom while the two boys went back for the remaining brawler who was just coming round and sitting up groggily on the dance floor.

Within four minutes of the fight erupting, peace was once again temporarily restored to Davinchi's.

Eddie and Conan were organising the growing queue out the front while Grant cruised around inside like the Terminator on a seek and destroy mission. Jason and Mike stood on the stairs watching, waiting and perving.

It was almost 2 am when Jason saw her. She was five foot nine of sex on legs. Her long brown hair lightly touched the top of her tight arse which was clad in a very short, tight, gold sequined dress.

Jason stopped in his tracks as he spotted her ordering a drink. Her large breasts seemed to be resting on the bar.

'Fuck me,' he said rather loudly.

Sensing that someone was watching her, she looked straight over at Jason who was by this time almost salivating at the mouth. With large, red lips she smiled and gave him a well-rehearsed look that said a hundred things at once. One of them being a very sultry, 'I want you.'

Jason smiled back and was just about to walk over to her when the DJ's voice boomed over the intercom.

'Security to bar two, security to bar two.'

His smile vanished as the girl in the golden dress shrugged, gave a little wave and trotted off to her friends.

Typical, fucking typical, Jason thought as he ran downstairs to join his partners in the 'fun and games' that had erupted at bar two.

'So where is she?' asked Mike.

'I don't know, I was just about to go and talk to her when that last fucking fight kicked off,' Jason said as he examined the splattering of blood on his white shirt.

'Big tits, eh?' Mike's shirt too was a little bit redder now than when he started work. He looked at a spot on his sleeve.

'That Grant, he's a fucking nutter, no wonder he's got so many assault charges against him. Did you see him headbutt that dickhead in the red jacket?'

'Yes and I—'

Mike cut him off, slapping him on the arm and pointing. Coming down the stairs was the girl in the gold dress with two of her friends, chatting, laughing and glancing mischievously at Mike and Jason.

The first thing Jason noticed as the girl approached (apart from her massive cleavage) was her perfume, it was beautiful. He later learned that it was Armirage de Givenchy.

'You are gorgeous, what's your name?'

'Caroline, what's yours?'

Jason took her hand and led her into the lounge room. It was dark except for the two candles that he had placed by the stereo. A track from UB40 was softly pulsing out a smooth reggae rhythm. Jason put their glasses of red wine on the coffee table, then pulled her against him, saying nothing, and they began to dance gently. She smelt so good. Her breasts pushed provocatively against him, they were large and soft. With his left hand Jason held Caroline's, his right was on the small of her back, holding her tight against him. She rested her head against his cheek, and her long hair softly brushed against the top of his hand.

Jason lowered his head and kissed her neck, it was soft and warm. He kissed it again and she let out a quiet moan. He was so turned on, his pulse was racing and his cock, by this time, was very hard.

Caroline looked him straight in the eyes and they kissed. She had the most voluptuous, softest lips Jason had ever kissed in his life. She pushed her warm, wet tongue deep into his mouth, making him dizzy with lust.

Jason disengaged himself from Caroline's mouth.

'Fuck, I want you.'

'I want you too,' she replied.

With that they kissed again, deeper and harder. Jason began to pull the straps of her dress over her shoulders while she unbuttoned his shirt. Her breathing was loud and passionate and every time Jason kissed her she would moan in response. This girl was sexual chemistry with a pulse rate. Jason pulled her dress down over her large, soft cleavage, she wore no bra.

He couldn't help looking down at her breasts.

'They are beautiful,' he said as he pulled her close to him, this time feeling the hot soft flesh of her chest pushed against his own.

'Take your dress off.'

Their eyes stayed locked as Caroline began to wriggle her tight dress down her curvy body. Jason kicked off his shoes and fumbled with his pants.

They pressed against each other, naked except for their underwear, kissing, touching and breathing hard.

Jason held her shoulders and kissed her as he guided her down onto a large beanbag on the floor. He wanted this girl so badly, she was gorgeous and had him so horny he was shaking with excitement.

As she lay there, Jason took her delicate, white G-string in his hand and began to pull it down over her hips. Caroline raised her arse slightly to allow the lacy underwear to be removed. Fuck, that was a turn-on in itself, Jason thought.

He knelt in front of her, Caroline's legs were either side of him as he ran his hands up the inside of her thighs. She moaned softly as his fingers reached her pussy.

'Oh my god, you are so wet.'

'That's the effect you have on me.'

Jason played with her soft, wet pussy, slowly pushing his fingers inside her. The sounds she was making were driving him crazy, she lifted her head.

'For god's sake, fuck me.'

'Not just yet.'

Jason placed his hands on her narrow hips and kissed her stomach, then licked it. Then did the same to the inside of her thigh, right next to her pussy. Caroline was gripping the beanbag tightly.

'Stop teasing me.'

'OK.'

With that Jason licked from the base of her pussy just above her arse right up to the top of her clitoris where he ran his tongue in circles over it again and again. Then he took the whole of Caroline's pussy in his mouth and gently sucked on it, occasionally dipping his tongue right inside her.

'Oh my god,' Caroline crooned as her hips gyrated in the slowest, sexiest way imaginable.

That was it, he had to have her. Standing up, Jason pulled off his jocks to reveal his ultra-hard cock. Caroline looked at it hungrily. He lay down on top of her and she grabbed his face and kissed him, a sense of urgency in her passion. She tasted herself on Jason's mouth and liked it.

'Do you want me to fuck you?'

'You know I do.'

Jason took his cock in his hand and rubbed the head over and around her saturated pussy. Then with one slow, strong movement, he pushed himself deep inside her. They both moaned loudly and kissed.

'My god, you feel fucking amazing.'

Jason began to withdraw his cock only to push it back inside her again. Caroline's mouth was open and she was gasping with passion. Jason looked at her perfect mouth as he squeezed her breasts. Their bodies moved well together, making wet, fucking noises.

Caroline loved to be tongue kissed which was fine by Jason. He started to push harder and faster into her, and she responded with a loud moan.

'Oh, you like that, huh?'

'Yes, yes I do, I'm going to come. Oh my god, I'm coming.'

And boy did she come, again and again and again.

Jason lost count of how many orgasms she had, she was incredible. Dripping with sweat he told her to turn over.

'Get on your hands and knees for me, stick your little arse out, I'm going to fuck the shit out of you.'

'Oh, you are so nasty. I love it.'

Jason slid his cock inside her from behind and began to fuck her. He reached around and fondled her soft swinging breasts, then ran his hand to her dripping pussy and tickled her clitoris.

Another orgasm ripped through her gorgeous body.

'I want you to come for me,' she cried.

'Oh you want it, do you?'

'Yes, come for me.'

'Where do you want it?'

'Anywhere, I don't care.'

'Come for me again and I'll blow for you.'

Jason fucked her as hard as he could, which was pretty goddamn hard, until she was almost screaming with desire, then she came again.

Jason withdrew his wet cock and taking it into his hand he wanked all over her. His hot come jetted out over her back and arse as he threw his head back in total fucking ecstasy.

They were both sweating, panting and covered in come. Jason lay down next to her and they cuddled up, kissing, touching, and recovering.

'That was unbelievable,' Jason said. 'Have you studied sex at uni or something?'

She giggled.

'No, medicine.'

'Serious?'

'Yeah, I study part-time at uni and work part-time as a medical assistant at a surgery.'

'No shit. So you want to be a doctor, huh?'

'A surgeon, actually.'

'I like that. If I ever get bashed up I can come and get you to fix me up.'

Caroline smiled cheekily.

'I'll fix you up all right.'

Eventually Jason got up and grabbed the doona from his bedroom then went back to the lounge where he and Caroline fell asleep on the beanbag.

Thankful that the screaming and shouting had finally subsided, Max closed his eyes and with a loud snorting sigh fell asleep in his bed.

It was just after 11.00 am and Jason was still sleeping; a slight smile of contentment across his face.

Drifting out of his unconscious state he stirred as something touched his cheek. He felt it again, a warm wet tongue, on his mouth this time. His smile broadened as the memories of the previous night flooded his groggy mind. Opening his eyes wearily to gaze on the buxom goddess next to him, Jason was confronted with the massive white head of Max just as the bull-terrier licked his mouth again.

'Oh fuck, you dirty, disgusting bastard. Get the fuck off me, you fat git.'

Max wagged his tail and tried to lick Jason's face some more.

'Yuck.'

Jason stood up, wrapped the doona around his waist and shuffled out to the kitchen, wiping his mouth with his hand. Max hopped into the warm beanbag, satisfied that his master had appreciated his morning greeting.

Caroline turned to Jason with two cups of tea in her hands.

'Good morning, I didn't know whether you take sugar or not so I put one in anyway.'

She was wearing his white shirt over her underwear, it hung off her like a tent. She looked so cute.

Jason smiled.

'Perfect,' he said taking his tea from her.

'I borrowed your shirt, I hope you don't mind. What are these little dark spots all over it?'

The blood on the shirt had dried and turned a muddy brown colour.

'Oh, nothing just er . . .'

The phone rang and saved him from having to lie to her.

'Hello.'

'Hey, Jase, it's Mike.'

'Hey, mate, how's it going?'

'Good, I just called to see if you shagged that bird with the big tits last night?'

Caroline stood against the kitchen sink about eight feet away from him, sipping her tea. Jason hoped to god she couldn't hear Mike.

'Er yeah, good mate, I start at eleven tonight.'

'What? I know you start at eleven. Did you fuck her or not?'

'Yeah that'll be great, let's meet later on today for coffee.'

'Oh, OK. She's there is she?' Mike started to laugh. 'All right Jase, I'll see you tonight at work, you lucky fucker.'

'No worries mate, catch you later.'

Jason put the phone down, unsure of whether Caroline had heard or not.

'So, can you give me a ride home on that mean machine of yours?'

'Sure, would you like a shower first?'

'I'd love one.'

Caroline trotted past him toward the bathroom, running her hands through his long hair as she went. Jason gave her a playful slap on her arse and she giggled off into the shower.

'Max, come here.'

Max appeared at the doorway.

'Come here, you daft bugger.'

The dog plodded over to his master, happy to be summoned.

'What am I going to do with you, eh, you crazy dog?' Jason patted the dog's head and lovingly manhandled his best friend.

The phone rang again.

'Hello.'

'Jason, I'm pissing fucking razor blades,' a distressed voice exclaimed.

'Grant, is that you?'

'Yeah, listen, I woke up this morning and went to the loo and it felt like someone was pouring acid on my nob.'

Jason fought hard against the overwhelming urge to laugh and managed to keep his reaction down to a broad grin.

'Just calm down, mate, it sounds like you've picked up a dose of the clap, that's all.'

'What the fuck do you mean that's all, it feels like my jocks have been sabotaged with Dencorub.'

Suppressing a slight chuckle, Jason couldn't believe that such a large and violent young man could be scared of anything, let alone this.

'Grant, are you telling me that with all the women you've slept with you've never had an STD?'

'What the fuck has a phone call got to do with this?'

'No, sexually transmitted disease, dickhead.'

'Oh right—no, I've just been lucky I guess.'

'Lucky, that's an understatement—fucking miraculous looking at the monsters you take home, and you never use condoms, either.'

A flash of guilt swept over Jason as he remembered the events of the previous night—condomless. Oh well, he was pissed and everyone knows you can't catch an STD when you're drunk!

'Listen, if I'd wanted a lecture on the clap I'd ask my mum. You've had this shit before, what am I supposed to do?'

'OK, just make an appointment at the local quack, get your sorry arse down there and he'll put you on a course of antibiotics, all right?'

'That's it, that's all it takes, a course of tablets?'

'Well yes, if it's just the clap that is; if it's something more serious they'll probably have to amputate or wait until it turns green and drops off.'

'What the fu—'

'See you mate, good luck.'

Jason put down the phone and roared with the laughter he had been holding back, tears crept into the corner of his eyes.

Caroline returned to the kitchen, dressed and fresh.

'What's so funny?'

'Oh nothing, just a mate of mine, that's all.'

Jason reduced his laughter to a smile and looked at Caroline.

'You are gorgeous.'

FOUR HARD-BOILED EGGS

Grant put the phone down.

'Bastard.'

Grant still lived with his parents—well, his mother anyway—and they got on pretty well together. But this was something that he couldn't go to his mum with. He remembered hearing once that it took about fourteen days for the symptoms to appear, and he had certainly had unprotected sex two weeks ago. Fuck, he had unprotected sex every weekend.

He was twenty-two years old and not afraid of any man he'd ever met, not even the boss of the security company he worked for, and that was a scary man. But the thought of losing his best friend, Mr Wriggly, scared him shitless.

He thumbed through the telephone book and found the address of the doctor he'd gone to see when he broke one of his knuckles. He had told the doctor that he'd jammed his hand in a car door, but of course that was bullshit; he'd done it punching someone into unconsciousness during a brawl at the club.

Grant dialled the number.

'Hello, East Perth surgery.'

'Hi, I'd like to make an appointment for today, please.'

'Certainly, how's two o'clock?'

Grant was sure that the receptionist was telepathic and knew exactly what he was going there for.

'That's fine, thanks.'

'Your name?'

'Grant Johnson.'

'Thanks Mr Johnson, see you at 2.00 pm.'

He put the phone down. It was twelve-thirty, he would watch TV for an hour then go and see the quack. He just prayed that he didn't need to go to the toilet again.

The rev counter of Jason's motorbike hit 9000 rpms and the powerful 750 cc engine hurtled the bike along at just over 120 km/h in a 60 km/h zone. Caroline was holding onto Jason far tighter than she really needed to.

God what a slut, she thought. I only went out last night to celebrate Tammy's birthday and ended up sleeping with one of the bouncers, but fuck he's cute. It was that cheeky, boyish smile that did it. Oh, who am I kidding, it was the whole delicious package. She snuggled in even closer behind Jason. Her golden dress was almost up around her hips by now, causing several double takes from pedestrians as the blur of black leather, gold and long tanned legs flashed by.

Within ten minutes of leaving Jason's place they arrived at Caroline's apartment, which she shared with Tammy and another girl, Rosie. Ordinarily it would have been a twenty-minute car ride, but Jason was no ordinary road user.

Caroline clambered off the bike and returned Jason's spare helmet.

'Well, I might see you later on tonight then.'

Caroline gave Jason a kiss on the cheek and happily sauntered off, greatly exaggerating the wiggle of her arse for Jason's benefit, who she knew would be watching.

He shook his head as Caroline disappeared into the building.

'Fuck, that's hot.'

Jason clicked the bike into first and disappeared. He was home in less time than it took to get to Caroline's place.

'Next please—Grant Johnson.'

Grant rose from his seat where he'd been reading an article in *Cosmopolitan*, 'Why Women Fake Orgasms'. He put the magazine down and followed what was thankfully a male doctor into the room beyond.

'Take a seat, Grant, I'm Dr Edwards, what can I do for you today?'

Dr Edwards was of average height, average build,

glasses and, well, just average, except for a gap between his teeth.

'Well, it's a bit . . .'

Grant struggled to find the right words to describe his delicate situation.

'I shagged this tart two weeks ago and I think she's given me the clap.'

There, that was easy. Grant felt he'd expressed himself very well indeed. Now he half expected the quack to shriek in disgust and run from the room waving little bells shouting, 'Unclean, unclean.' However, to his surprise the doctor casually asked, 'OK, have you been experiencing any symptoms such as pain when urinating or any discharge at all?'

'Yes, definitely a pain when I piss but no discharge, I don't think.'

'Very well, I'll take a swab from you and put you on a course of antibiotics for ten days, it sounds like chlamydia, nothing to worry about.'

'Chlamydia, that's the same as the clap, right?'

'Exactly,' the doctor said, a barely noticeable smirk creeping over his face.

'Now if you could just hop up onto the examining bed and take your pants down, I'll take a swab from you.'

'You'll take a what?'

'A swab, it's pretty routine. We send it off to a pathology lab and they run tests on it.'

Grant sheepishly made his way onto the bed, not quite sure what was going on or what a swab was.

If he tries anything funny I'll take his fucking head

off, he thought as he unbuckled his belt.

Dr Edwards pulled on a pair of white surgical rubber gloves and removed a thin metal rod, about six inches long with a cotton tip, from its plastic wrapping.

'What's that for?'

'This is the swab. I'm going to insert it about one inch into the eye of your penis to obtain a sample.'

'YOU'RE GOING TO FUCKING WHAT?'

'Now hold onto something, this will feel a bit uncomfortable.'

It was almost four o'clock. Jason and Max were both lying on the beanbag watching TV, Max was on his back, his legs in the air, while Jason rubbed the top of his head. How happy could one dog be? They'd just come back from a walk along the beach where he'd urinated on someone's towel, drunk salt water and got into a fight with a black Alsatian, and now was hanging out with his beloved master—what a life.

Jason, too, was happy. Usually being called 'a fucking cunt' as his dog savaged another would have ticked him off somewhat. Several times since he'd acquired Max, he'd found himself in a brawl with the owner of another dog that Max was bashing up, dog fighting dog, owner fighting owner—what a team.

This time, however, he'd dragged the bull-terrier away (which is not an easy task) and offered his apologies to the Alsatian's furious owner who was going through his extensive vocabulary of insults.

Back at his place, Jason was on cloud nine, sipping on a cup of coffee, chilling out with his mad dog and watching taped episodes of his favourite show, 'The Gladiators', which he kept secret, of course. Commando had just severely injured one of the contestants during a heavy clash in the 'Powerball' game when Jason's phone rang. It was Grant.

'Hey bro, how did you go at the quack's?'

'How did I go? He skewered my penis with a steel rod and you knew didn't you, you bastard?'

Jason burst out laughing.

'Yeah, sorry mate, but I didn't think I should tell you about that part, you probably wouldn't have gone.'

'You're fucking right I wouldn't have gone, no alcohol and no sex for ten days, I'll die.'

'Well, just look at it as a learning experience. Maybe you'll stick a johnny on that lethal weapon of yours in the future.'

'No way, I'm never having sex again in my life, I'm going fucking celibate, I am.'

'So do you know who you caught it off?'

'No.'

'What about the cute brunette?'

'Which one?'

'Never mind, listen I've got to bail, I'll see you later at the club.'

Jason didn't really have to go but Delta had just appeared on the screen and she was, well, cute. Also, Jason had lost interest in talking about Grant's diseased member.

Delta was swinging her taut figure across a series of suspended rings towards her terrified opponent when a loud farting sound resounded from the kitchen.

'Oh Max, you dirty bastard!' Jason yelled.

Max appeared at the door with a silly bull-terrier grin on his face and a wagging tail.

'Don't you come near me, you fat smelly git. That's it, no more bananas for you.'

Max plodded over and dropped his head on Jason's leg. Jason looked lovingly at his dog. How could such an ugly, brutish animal with no social graces whatsoever be so appealing? Mind you, that also described most of his best mates. Jason smiled as he patted Max's heavy head.

The phone rang, waking Jason. He'd been asleep in the beanbag for over three and a half hours.

'Hello,' Jason said, groggily.

'Hi Jase, it's Eddie. Listen, can you start at ten? I'm putting Steve on the late shift, he's not in the best of shape at the moment so I'm reducing his hours just until the comp's over.'

'Yeah, no worries mate, see you at 10.00 pm.'

Jason put the phone down. Steve worked as a freelance personal trainer by day and as a bouncer by night, and was one of Jason's closest friends. He had been dieting severely for his second body-building competition after winning his first one ten months ago. Although Jason had never competed himself, he was well aware of the effects of the insane dieting programme, not to mention pumping yourself full of testosterone at the same time. Add to that a gruelling training schedule and you end up with a bad tempered and potentially violent human being. Steve was no exception. With one week to go before the state titles he was a six foot, 100 kilogram liability and not the most ideal person to have on the front door of a club supposedly 'being nice' to drunken patrons as they tried to push past and step on your toes.

Jason called Steve.

'What.'

'Hey smiley, it's Jason.'

'Hi Jase, what's up?'

'Eddie just called, it must be getting pretty tough, huh?'

'Yeah, that's an understatement. It's probably for the best to cut my hours down a little bit, I'm so fucking moody at the moment.'

'Hang in there, mate. Hey, can you get me some Deca-Durabolin next week, I'm not using that fucking Stanazol again, it's got too much shit in it. I almost blew myself up with it yesterday.'

'Yeah, no worries, bring in the cash tonight and I'll organise it.'

'You're a legend. Stay cool mate, I'll catch you tonight.'

Jason put the phone down. Poor bastard, he sounded so depressed. Mind you, eight weeks on tuna, rice cakes and egg whites and I'd be pretty fucking depressed too, he thought.

'Shit, it's eight-thirty now, I've got just over an hour to eat and get ready.'

Jason got up and walked briskly out of the lounge, promptly collided with Max and fell over the top of him, landing heavily on the floor.

'Oh, you fat bastard,' moaned Jason, slightly winded.

Max wagged his tail and licked Jason's face.

Arriving at Davinchi's, Jason was greeted with a smile and a handshake from Eddie.

'Thanks for coming in early, Jase.'

'No worries boss, I'll dump my gear in the cloakroom.'

He went into the club and turned right into the cloakroom where Amanda, the door girl, let him through.

'Hi gorgeous, have you been waiting for me long?' quipped Jason with a cheeky grin on his face.

'Waiting for you, that will be the day.'

Amanda was a typical door girl, a twenty-one year-old student working in the club to help pay her way through university. She was one intelligent girl and, as Jason had verbalised, 'gorgeous', but to the disgust of all the doormen, Amanda was one of those highly annoying females who had a long-term boyfriend and was pathetically faithful to him. She was the girl every guy at the club wanted, simply because she was the girl that no-one seemed to be able to get.

'Come on, Amanda, why fight it, you know you want me,' Jason said on his way out, giving her one of his best 'come and get it' smiles.

'Don't look at me like that, Jason. What's that they say about dogs and their owners?'

'Oh, that's cold, that's really cold.'

Amanda giggled cheekily as Jason left to join Eddie.

God, I've got such a crush on him and he doesn't even know it, Amanda thought to herself. Oh well, maybe one day.

The club was about a quarter full and people were beginning to roll up to the front door.

'We'll let the next ten in and then we'll form a queue with these fine upstanding citizens,' said Eddie.

'Yo,' acknowledged Jason.

Eddie was the oldest and most vaguely sensible of the doormen who worked at Davinchi's. At thirty-two, he was a successful sales representative for a computer company and moonlighted as a doorman, primarily for a social life but also to add a splash of adventure to his often mundane routine, and working as the head doorman at Davinchi's certainly did that.

By the time Steve arrived at the club just before eleven there was a long queue, the music was blaring into the street and, as usual, the place was going off.

I'm not in the mood for this shit, Steve thought.

'Hey Conan, how y'doin' buddy,' said Jason.

Steve had earned the nickname because of his long brown hair and his huge muscular build, and on top of all that he was a very good-looking dude.

'Good, mate,' he said, forcing a rather unconvincing smile.

'What's in the box?' Eddie nodded at a white plastic container under Steve's arm.

'Just some eggs. I get to eat one hard-boiled egg every hour and a half. Lucky me, eh?'

'You're fucking kidding me,' said Eddie.

'I wish I was. Still, only a week to go.'

Steve placed his coat and the box containing his four prized eggs in the cloakroom. Without so much as a word to the gorgeous Amanda, he made his way into the club and positioned himself on the stairs overlooking the crowded dance floor. The diet was driving him mad, all he could think about were his four hard-boiled eggs as his stomach began to rumble. No-one could possibly understand what he was going through, the pain, the self-denial. Those four eggs sitting in the cloakroom meant more to Steve than anything in the world at this particular time.

Grant arrived at ten past eleven.

'You're late, arsehole,' welcomed Eddie.

'Fuck off,' he replied politely. 'You pussies are hopeless without me, ten minutes and you're shitting yourselves.'

'He's right, you know,' Jason turned to Eddie, 'potential troublemakers take one look at Grant and think, "Shit, I don't want to get thrown out by the big bald fuck with the face like a bulldog pissing on a thistle," and behave themselves.'

Eddie burst out laughing as did a couple of the people waiting in the queue. Jason grinned at Grant. The large doorman gritted his teeth and clenched his fists.

'That's it, pretty boy, I'm gonna kick your arse,' and he charged at Jason in the doorway. Jason laughed as

Grant made a playful attempt at a headlock and the two friends began to mock wrestle.

'That's enough, girls, piss off inside and send Mike out,' Eddie said as he kicked Grant up the arse.

'OK, boss,' replied Jason, and the two 'girls' disappeared inside.

'So how's Mr Wriggly?' he shouted into Grant's ear.

'What?'

'How's . . . your . . . dick?'

Grant winced, not pleased to be reminded of the day's painful events.

'Still a bit sore but I'll survive, probably emotionally scarred for life, though.'

'I didn't think you had any emotions.'

'What?'

'Never mind, I'm going to take a cruise around.'

Grant gave Jason the thumbs-up as he climbed the stairs for a spot of 'seek and destroy'.

Upstairs the bar was packed, as was the entire club. A group of four body builders were seated in one corner. Jason recognised a couple of them from around the traps but didn't really know them.

Big fuckers, he thought, hope they don't kick it off. What a nightmare trying to throw those monsters out.

Jason had just started to wonder whether Caroline would make an appearance that evening when the inevitable announcement came over the speakers. 'Security to front bar, security to front bar.'

He raised his eyebrows and barged his way through the crowd. A brawl had erupted when a large drunken scumbag had punched a girl in the mouth after she had refused his advances by telling him to 'Fuck off and die.'

Her boyfriend was just returning from the toilets with two of his mates and naturally was not amused. In an instant it was on. The three lads rushed towards the scumbag but were intercepted by two of his mates and all shit broke loose.

Eddie and Mike were the first to get there, closely followed by Grant and Steve. As Jason descended the stairs he put in his mouthguard. The scene was chaotic, arms, legs, fists and all other body parts were lashing out in all directions.

He reached the fight just as Mike was dragging a guy out of the melee by his hair towards the front door, blood splattered across his chest. Jason grabbed one guy from behind in a headlock and proceeded to drag him viciously towards the door, but the brawler began to struggle violently and was in danger of breaking free.

Fucking hell, thought Jason, right, have some of this. And he increased the pressure around the guy's neck until he felt it crack and his victim began to splutter and choke.

'You like that, motherfucker?' spat Jason. As he reached the front door Mike was on his way back to collect another body but stopped dead and stared at the now semiconscious human being in Jason's stranglehold.

Mike looked at Jason, horrified, and pointed at the body. Puzzled, Jason peered around the front of his arm to see that he was holding Eddie, boggle eyed and gasping for air.

Back inside, the scene in front of the bar resembled

a bizarre, violent game of Twister with Grant and Steve in the thick of it. With one hand, Grant had pinned the woman-basher to the floor by his throat and was fending off kicks to his mid-section with the other. Steve had received a flailing elbow in the mouth which had upset him, to say the least. He grabbed the body that the elbow belonged to by the front of its shirt and pulled the offender roughly towards him, at the same time lowering his head so that the brawler's nose went crashing into the top of Steve's skull, instantly smashing it in and to the right. Blood splattered from the man's nostrils onto Grant below, and Steve's new friend fell to his knees holding his broken face.

The woman-basher had passed out under Grant's hand which left the bouncer free to Rugby tackle the guy kicking him. As the kicker crashed to the floor, he attempted to punch Grant in the back of the head. This had little effect and was returned with three hard open-handed strikes to his face, bloodying his nose and smashing his lips against his teeth, splitting the top one in two.

Steve's mouth was also bleeding, he could taste it. Grabbing the two remaining brawlers by the scruff of their necks, he pushed and bundled them through the swinging doors that divided the bar from the entrance hallway.

Outside, Jason had released the head doorman who was now leaning unsteadily against the wall holding his neck.

'Just get the fuck back inside and help the boys,' rasped Eddie.

The swing doors burst open as Steve came through

with the two struggling fighters. Mike took one from him and they launched the brawlers out onto the street. Jason returned inside to see one body lying prostrate on the floor and Grant standing over another bleeding heavily from the nose and mouth. Jason lifted the unconscious body under the arms and dragged the man towards the door. Grant picked up his last victim and frogmarched him in the same direction.

Out the front of Davinchi's the five doormen stood, breathing heavily, mouthguards in and shirts splattered with blood. The scumbag responsible for the brawl in the first place had regained consciousness and his mates were helping him up. The two parties were yelling abuse at each other and at the bouncers.

'That big cunt there punched my girlfriend in the mouth and I end up being fucking hit and thrown out by you arseholes,' one of them screamed into Eddie's face, who had by now regained his composure.

'Listen mate, I don't know anything about your girlfriend so just back off, OK.'

The boyfriend was bleary eyed and half crazed with frustration as he shouted abuse and waved his arms around. Blood from his smashed nose was pouring into his mouth and he spat it out everywhere as he rambled on. Some hit Grant's chest, adding more to the already ruined shirt.

'Fuck off, dickhead,' growled Grant through his mouthguard as he gave the boyfriend a shove so hard that more blood shot from his nose hitting Grant in the forearm. Grant began to advance on him with a murderous look in his eye, but Eddie put his arm across to stop him.

'Chill out, back inside, you too, Steve. Hit the stairs.'

They grudgingly moved inside, leaving the other three bouncers to stay and face the enraged drunken brawlers.

As Steve and Grant pushed their way through the crowd they found the girlfriend sitting on a chair, bleeding and crying, and being comforted by a girlfriend, a barmaid and Dominic, the manager of the club.

'You fucking arseholes threw out the wrong blokes,' he yelled.

'What?' shouted Grant, pretending not to hear.

'This girl got a smack in the mouth,' he continued, 'and then when her boyfriend and his mates went to help her, you fuckheads bashed them and then threw them out.'

Without waiting for an explanation, Dominic barged past the boys and made his way to the front door.

Steve and Grant looked at each other.

'One of these days,' shouted Steve into the blond giant's ear, 'I'm going to hit that smart little fucker so hard he'll be in a coma for a month.'

'It wasn't our fault,' Grant shouted in reply. 'I feel sorry for the tart but fuck, all we saw was an all-in brawl when we got there, how the fuck are we supposed to know what went on before that? We're not mind readers.'

'Fuck him, little twat, he doesn't know his arse from his elbow. C'mon, let's get on the stairs.'

Dominic was not too impressed by the scene outside the club. Bodies lay strewn and bleeding over the wide footpath, and the boyfriend and his mates were still screaming violent abuse at the doormen and their opponents. Meanwhile, Eddie, Jason and Mike were telling everyone to calm down.

Dominic looked at the bloodied doormen and tapped Eddie on the back. He wheeled around raising his left hand in defence and pulled back his right fist. Dominic moved back abruptly and gave the head doorman a look that could have melted nails.

'My office, five minutes,' Dominic said through gritted teeth.

Eddie lowered his hands. The instigators of the brawl had seen fit to leave the scene and the battered girl was being helped out of the club. At her mouth she held a red handkerchief that had originally been white.

'Uh-oh,' Jason said when he saw her.

'No shit,' replied Eddie. 'Listen, you and Mike stay here, I've got to go and face Dominic.'

'Just tell the little prick to stick it up his arse.'

'Jason,' said Eddie, glancing at his blond, ponytailed mate.

'I know, I know, he's the manager and we should respect that, still it doesn't mean we have to like him.'

'I know, mate.' Eddie slapped Jason on the shoulder and stepped inside.

Within minutes of the bashed girlfriend's party leaving, a buxom Caroline bounced up to Jason with her two gorgeous flatmates by her side.

'Well hello, beautiful,' Jason said, flashing one of his 'to die for' smiles. 'Fancy seeing you here.'

'Well, I wasn't going to come out tonight but the girls wanted to, so I thought I'd tag along,' she said as she gave him the sexiest wink he had ever seen.

'This is Tammy and this is Rosie,' she continued. The girls introduced themselves to Mike and Jason. Tammy was a very good-looking, bubbly blonde with impossibly white teeth and a smile to match Jason's. She was clad in a short, very short, black dress that did little to hide her almost perfect body. Rosie's body was perfect, and so was her face. Jason was trying desperately not to blatantly perv on her, however Mike wasn't holding back, and was almost dribbling as he gawped at the Cindy Crawford look-alike standing in front of him, oozing sex.

'In you go then girls, we'll see you in there soon.' Jason waved them past Amanda, ensuring that she didn't hit them for the ten dollar cover charge. Amanda raised her eyebrows and pulled a face at him.

'I want her,' babbled Mike.

'Which one?'

'What's her name? Rosie, she's a goddess, does she have a boyfriend?'

'How the fuck should I know? Anyway, since when has that ever stopped you?' Jason said.

The two bouncers let a few more people into the club and chatted about doing a foursome date later in the week.

Eddie returned looking dejected.

'Took an ear-bashing, mate?' said Mike.

'Yeah, the fuckers are glowing red by now aren't

they? Oh well, Jase you go inside for a bit of S & D, and while you're at it tell the boys to put on their jackets to cover their shirts.'

'No worries, boss.'

He left Eddie and Mike to supervise the many impatient partygoers in the line.

Jason reached the stairs where Steve was arguing with two drunken idiots intent on being quarrelsome.

'But we're only having a look at the tarts on the dance floor,' slurred one of them.

'Listen, I've asked you nicely two fucking times now, move off the stairway.' Jason noticed that Conan's right fist was clenched and he was holding his mouthguard in the other.

'What's the problem, fellers?' said Jason, placing a calming hand on Steve's shoulder.

'Nothing mate, we're going,' drawled the other idiot as he unsteadily pulled his cohort up the stairs. Although they were very drunk, the two burly young men realised that arguing with two burlier doormen was probably not a good idea, especially as they were both covered in what was obviously someone else's blood.

'Yo, Conan!' said Jason, thumping Steve on his rock-hard thigh, snapping him out of his evil stare. 'Eddie says to put jackets on.'

'What?'

'Jackets,' Jason shouted.

'Righto,' Steve nodded, 'I'll get Grant's, too.'

He disappeared into the crowd leaving Jason on the stairs. He looked over to the other side of the club where

Grant smiled and affectionately gave him the middle finger. Jason returned the gesture with the wanker sign.

In the cloakroom Steve grabbed the jackets, but before he left he opened his lunch box, peeled two of his eggs with trembling hands and wolfed them down in seconds.

Fuck, he thought, now I know what a junkie feels like when they get a hit.

He paused for a moment, looking hungrily at the two remaining chicken ovulations, but then snapped the lid shut and returned to the packed nightclub.

Jason was watching Caroline, Tammy and Rosie on the dance floor as they danced together, and boy were they dancing together. When they had arrived, he had assumed that the smiling, affectionate threesome were just high on life and having a good time, but now as he watched them he knew differently. They were gyrating and sliding up and down each other, running their fingers through each other's hair and over their bodies, all the while looking at each other and smiling ecstatically.

Es, Jason thought, they're on fucking Es.

Steve handed Grant his jacket and pointed to where a large group of hormone-crazed guys had gathered to watch the all-girl floor show.

'What's going on over there?'

'Fuck knows,' he replied. 'I'm going for a piss and a cruise around.'

Steve nonchalantly gave Grant a thumb but was far more interested in the gathering on the dance floor just below Jason.

Jason was not impressed with what was happening in front of him, or rather, why it was happening. His last girlfriend had almost died when she'd taken a bad E given to her by an ex-boyfriend at a twenty-first birthday party. She and her ex-boyfriend both ended up in hospital that evening, although it wasn't drug abuse that put him there. It was Jason. He was also unimpressed with himself because no matter how much he disapproved of hard drugs, the scene on the dance floor had given him a throbbing hard-on that was pushing against his cricket box and making life very uncomfortable indeed.

Caroline, Tammy and Rosie, however, were blissfully unaware of Jason's views on Ecstasy and were basking in the glory of all the attention they were receiving. Caroline took Rosie's face softly into her hands and stared up at Jason with her big sultry eyes, giving him a look that would have steamed up Clark Kent's glasses. Then she slowly tilted her head and kissed Rosie fully on the lips. Rosie ran her delicate hands down Caroline's torso and rested them on her hips. Jason's jaw dropped as he watched the two girls kiss. Caroline's tongue glistened as it pushed into Rosie's open mouth, and for a moment time seemed to stand still. Jason had never seen anything so sensual in his life, it was mesmerising, their kissing was so soft and loving but at the same time it was hot and dangerously sexy.

'Fuck me, look at those two dirty sluts,' said Grant as he elbowed Jason in the arm. Jason, who was on another planet at this point in time, lost his footing on the stairs and stumbled down four of them. He just managed to save himself from falling down all together. Grant grabbed Jason's arm and pulled him back up. Giggling and starry eyed, the girls left the dance floor and made their way to the toilets, leaving almost twenty guys boggle eyed and dribbling into their beer.

The next two hours passed by fairly uneventfully. Eddie and Mike moved inside onto the stairs and were replaced on the front door by Jason and Grant. Steve was on seek and destroy.

As he patrolled the upstairs bar his empty belly rumbled with a fierceness that was bordering on being painful.

'Right, boiled-egg time,' he said to himself.

It was 2.30 am and the club was in full swing as he descended the back stairs that led to the cloakroom. Once inside, Steve impatiently took the lunch box from its resting place, pulled off the lid and reached in for the two hard-boiled eggs.

He froze. His expression as he looked down into the box was as if he'd just found a dead body. At the bottom of the lunch box were the scattered remains of broken eggshells.

'Who ate my eggs?' Steve said in a quiet monotone voice.

'What did you say?' Amanda said chirpily.

Steve looked at her with hate in his eyes as he felt his whole body begin to tremble with anger.

'Who ate my fucking eggs?'

'Oh, I saw Grant eating some eggs about ten minutes ago.' Amanda smiled, totally unaware that she was standing dangerously close to a volcano. 'Why, were they yours? Don't worry about it, come and have some pizza with us after work.'

Krakatoa erupted. Steve threw the lunch box to the floor and stormed out of the cloakroom, red faced with thick blue veins pumping visibly in his forehead. He strode towards the front door where Grant and Jason had their backs to him. Grant was halfway through telling Jason for the third time just how cool and together he was at the doctor's when a force hit him viciously from behind, sending him lurching forwards a good four feet.

Jason spun around as he reached for his mouthguard, ready to hammer whoever it was that had pushed his mate. Steve stood on the top of the steps, his eyes blazing, looking like a huge possessed killing machine.

'What's your fucking problem?' Jason said.

Steve's murderous stare never left Grant. The huge doorman turned around to face his assailant.

'You ate my two boiled eggs, you shitbag.'

'Your fucking what?' replied a confused Grant. 'You fucking psycho, you're lucky I don't take your head off your shoulders.'

Grant advanced on him. Even though the two behemoths were the best of mates, no-one pushed Grant Johnson around.

The two solid months of dieting, training and mental torment filled Steve's head and materialised as the featureless form moved towards him.

With what sounded like an attacking growl from a

werewolf, Steve launched his 100 kilogram frame at the 120 kilogram Grant, grabbing him by the throat. Grant began to spin to his left in an attempt to deflect the blow and get Steve in a headlock. The two bouncers stumbled backwards and hit the deck, hard.

A crowd of people stood shocked and gawping at the security officers while they viciously punched, elbowed, kneed and kicked each other as they grappled on the ground. Jason also stood in amazement. He was watching two of his closest mates bashing each other senseless over a . . . a . . . boiled egg?

He snapped out of his trance and dashed forward, grabbing Steve who had just smashed Grant in the mouth with a strike from his open hand causing a nasty cut which now streamed with crimson. Steve's face was also covered with blood from a small but deep cut over his left eye.

Coincidentally, it was at this precise moment that Eddie decided to rotate his boys and he now stood at the door open-mouthed as he watched three of Perth's finest bouncers brawling right in front of him.

'Break it up, you dumb mutherfuckers,' Jason yelled as he struggled to wrench them apart. Realising what was going on, Eddie helped Jason to separate the two crazed doormen, which was no easy task to say the least.

Finally, with all his strength Jason managed to restrain Steve in a full nelson, and Eddie pulled back Grant who was totally enraged and still a little confused.

'What the fuck is going on with you two arseholes?' Eddie snapped.

'He ate my eggs,' answered a breathless Steve.

'He what?' Eddie said.

'He ate my boiled eggs.'

'He's a fucking psycho,' shouted Grant.

'Grant, back inside. You wait here Mr Boiled-fucking-Egg.' Grant lumbered off into the club.

Steve began to relax and his head dropped slightly as waves of reality swept over him.

'Now, I don't know what the problem is here and right now I don't have the time to play amateur psychologist. Steve, go home, get your shit together and call me tomorrow afternoon.'

'Chill out, dude,' Jason said. 'I know what you're going through, mate, after the comp I'll take you out and buy you as many eggs as you can eat.' Jason smiled at Steve and gave him a sympathetic slap on the back.

Steve smiled, nodded and walked off towards his car as he held a handkerchief to his swollen, bloodied eye.

Eddie looked at Jason and shook his head. 'Un-fucking-believable,' then turned towards the club.

Standing at the door, hands on hips and grinding his teeth, stood Dominic.

'My office . . . NOW!'

CONDOMS

Jason woke at the sound of Max barking at his bedroom door.

'Shut the fuck up, ugly, it's Sunday, leave me alone,' Jason croaked.

He looked at his bedside clock. It was eleven-thirty in the morning. Max gave two more loud barks and jumped onto Jason's bed.

'Oww, you heavy bastard.' Jason let fly with a loosely aimed slap at the bull-terrier's head, but missed completely. 'All right, get off me and I'll let you out.'

Jason groggily rose from his bed and followed Max to the front door where he let the dog out to 'water the garden'.

Jason went into the kitchen, put the kettle on, and thought about the events of the previous evening. Caroline and her friends, the poor girl who copped a smack in the mouth and, of course, Steve and Grant's brawl over two boiled eggs.

Max returned from the garden with a happy look

on his scarred face and lapped noisily at his water, sloshing more over the sides of the bowl than he actually got in his mouth. Jason shook his head and smiled as he watched his dog.

The phone rang.

'Hi Jason, it's Caroline.' Jason tensed a little.

'Hi, how are you?'

'What's wrong with you, you were avoiding me like the plague last night. What did I do?'

'Oh . . . nothing . . . everything's cool.'

'Don't give me that, what's the problem?'

'Look, I had a really horrible experience with my ex-girlfriend when she was given a bad E and ended up in hospital. So I'm a bit anti-drugs, OK.'

'Oh, I'm sorry but I didn't know. Anyway, how do you know we were on Es?'

Jason laughed and relaxed a little.

'Oh come on, give me a break. Firstly, I see people on Es every week, shit, I can tell you who's on what just by watching them for a minute. Secondly, I know that you're an incredibly sexy girl, but what you and your girlfriends were doing on the dance floor almost started a riot.'

'Were we that bad?'

Jason laughed again.

'Put it this way, it's a good job I don't have a weak heart, otherwise I'd be another coronary statistic by now.'

Caroline giggled.

'Hey listen, if I'm not still in your bad books, do you want to do something tonight?'

'I'd love to, but I promised Mike I'd hang with him tonight.'

'Why don't you both come round here and we'll get a video? Tammy's going out. Rosie thinks Mike's really cute, we can all hang together.'

'OK, I'll call Mike and see what he wants to do, then I'll call you back.'

Jason paused before he lifted the receiver again. He was really keen on Caroline, but the drug thing had kind of burst his little bubble for her. When it came to girls, Jason was hardly the 'let's settle down and have lots of kids' type, but he was genuinely in search of a soul mate. A beautiful woman to fall in love with. Since joining the security team at Davinchi's, Jason had many girls chasing him and, more often than not, well and truly catching him. Caroline, however, was the first girl in over a year to penetrate at least some of his barriers and touch his heart.

Jason snapped out of his trance and called Mike.

'Well, I think I know what his answer will be, eh dog?' Jason said to Max as he waited for Mike to answer the phone.

Max wagged his tail and a globule of saliva dropped from the corner of his mouth and plopped on the floor in the kitchen.

'Hello, Mike speaking.'

'Mike, you ugly pommy twat, it's Jason.'

'Fuck off, you kangaroo shagging Aussie bastard, what do you want?'

'I've got a really tough decision for you to make. Do

you want to come round my place tonight and watch Max lick his nuts or would you rather go to Caroline and Rosie's place and watch a video?'

'Ooh, now let me see, that's a fucking tough one that is . . . oh OK, I guess we can go and see the girls. What's the story, is Rosie in for it?'

'Yeah, by the sound of it she is. Right, well I'm going to get my arse down to the gym before it shuts. Come round to my place any time after two o'clock and we'll have a couple of beers before we go over.'

Steve swallowed his last mouthful of tuna and boiled rice with a face that looked as if he was swallowing live maggots. He then washed it down with a glass of delicious, flavoursome water.

Five more days, just five more days, he thought to himself.

He sat in front of the TV. His massive legs hung out unnaturally from his shorts and his upper body, squeezed into a little white tank top, looked as big as a house. His every movement seemed to send ripples through his thickly muscled frame.

He looked at the tablets in front of him, thirty-six altogether. A mixture of multivitamins, fluid-reducing capsules, oral steroids and some quite dangerous thyroid tablets to turbocharge his metabolism.

Fuck, he thought, look out liver here they come.

Steve was taking a total of fifty-two tablets a day and injecting himself with up to fifteen mls of steroids per week. His balls had shrunk, his skin was fucked and his temper was atrocious, although that could be blamed mostly on his insane dieting, but in five days' time he would be on stage at the State Body-building Titles and then it would be all over. Afterwards, he intended to eat non-stop for two solid weeks: cakes, chips, pizza, chocolate and, of course, a shit load of beer.

After taking half the tablets Steve shook his head. 'This is the last comp I do.'

He thought of all the money he'd spent on his body, not only for the drugs but the tanning lotions, the cost of having one and a half minutes of music professionally mixed at a studio and the exorbitant price he paid to have a choreographer put a routine to the music. In fact, the competition was costing him more money than he was actually earning. If it hadn't been for his parents grudgingly lending him a couple of grand, he would have had to pull out of it.

'After this, I'm going to find a sport that'll make me some fucking money . . . Golf or tennis or something.'

Steve finished the last of his pills and then went to his bedroom to give himself a two ml shot of Tribolin, a veterinarian steroid designed specifically for geldings. When he had finished, he called Grant who picked up the phone, annoyed at being interrupted.

'Yeah, what.'

'Grant, it's Steve. I just wanted to apologise again for last night.'

Grant laughed. 'No worries, you fucking psycho. Pretty good palm strike you caught me with, you cunt.'

'Thanks, mate. I've got a nice black eye, not a bad elbow.'

The two bouncers chatted and laughed some more about the fight they'd had and how they were sure it would be hot gossip around the club scene by now. And they were right, it was.

They said goodbye and Grant went back to his piano. At school music was the one subject that remotely interested him and, after almost five years of lessons, the only thing that the large doorman enjoyed more than putting someone in hospital was playing the piano, particularly classical music. Often he would arrive home from work at five in the morning and bash out a Mozart concerto perfectly with his white shirt still splattered with blood and fragments of flesh and hair. His keyboard prowess remained, however, a secret from his fellow bouncers who, he was convinced, would take the piss out of him for the rest of his life.

Steve carried on watching TV. A hamburger ad came on so he quickly turned the channel only to find a pizza commercial offering him two large pizzas, garlic bread and a chocolate cheesecake for only $19.95. Steve threw the remote control at the TV with such force that it smashed into several pieces, sending the two batteries flying out in opposite directions.

He looked at the fast-food ad and then at the smashed remote control on the floor in front of him.

'Fuck.'

*

Jason pulled up outside the gym just after midday. He dismounted the bike which was pinging as it cooled down. Removing his helmet, he walked briskly into the gym and was greeted by Trudy, the gym instructor-cum-receptionist.

'Hi Jason,' she beamed, genuinely pleased to see him, 'you're not going to get much of a workout in, there's barely forty-five minutes left.'

'Who cares, I only come here to perv on you anyway, you know that.' Jason gave her a smile that actually physically made her wet. Trudy was twenty-one, with deep green eyes, brown longish hair and a body that would have made Pamela Anderson jealous. The main similarity being the quantity of silicone that both Pamela and Trudy had implanted in their breasts.

Trudy and Jason had been flirting ferociously with each other ever since Jason had begun training there, six months ago. They had never had sex together but both knew that it was inevitable, and the chemistry between them promised that it was going to be awesome.

Jason left Trudy at the reception desk a little flushed and very moist. He himself had a semi hard-on that would have become complete if he had stayed there a moment longer.

Only two other guys were in the gym and they were coming close to the end of their heavy leg workouts. Jason acknowledged his fellow gym users and began his workout, starting with a front deltoid press with two fifty-five pound dumbbells.

Jason had a physique that other guys envied and

sent women gaga. Although not blessed with a genetically huge musculature, through four years of training and intermittent 'light' steroid use, he had built himself a lean and very muscular body that Van Damme would have been proud of.

The two exercise victims hobbled out of the gym leaving Jason heaving and sweating his way through his session.

Trudy strutted through the gym nearly an hour later.

'You've only got five minutes left and then I'm going to have to throw you out.'

'Ooh yes please, as roughly as you like.'

She giggled and bounced off into the female change rooms to close everything down.

Jason finished his last exercise and replaced his weights like a good gym junkie should.

Then he leaned against a bench, panting. Beads of sweat popped from his forehead and trickled freely down the sides of his face. His skimpy white singlet was saturated and stuck to his chest and abs.

'Fuck, that was a good one,' he said to himself, looking at his bedraggled form in the mirror.

Trudy appeared from the change room and walked slowly towards him. She had a look in her gorgeous green eyes that Jason had seen before. He looked at her in the mirror, she was steaming. Without a word, Trudy reached up with her right hand to the thin strap of her peach-coloured aerobics top and pulled it down over her shapely shoulder, then she did the same to the other side. Jason watched. Trudy slowly pulled her top down over her brown breasts, revealing her erect nipples and her very full cleavage.

He turned to face her, his heart was pounding and he was aroused to a state that was clearly visible through his tracksuit pants.

Trudy moved closer. The first thing to touch him were her breasts as she pushed them against his still sweating body, and she put her arms around his waist.

They both moaned as their tongues found each other's mouths. Jason took her firmly by the back of her head with one hand and squeezed her lycra-clad arse with the other.

Shaking with lust and six months of foreplay, Trudy pulled Jason's singlet over his head to reveal his solid chest and six-pack abs, then she removed her top completely, all the while stealing hot tongue kisses.

She pulled away from him, looking hungrily into his eyes, then slowly she descended to her knees, not once taking her eyes from his. Her breasts rubbed along Jason's abs, collecting his sweat as she went down.

Taking his pants in both hands she pulled them down to his knees in one steady movement. Jason's erect cock brushed against her face, causing her mouth to open instinctively. Her hands moved over his pelvis taking the base of his cock in one hand and cupping his warm balls in the other. It was only when she slid the head of Jason's ample cock into her mouth that she took her eyes from his and closed them as she began to skilfully gorge herself on his throbbing muscle.

Jason moaned in pure ecstasy, his mind swimming

in waves of lust. Trudy's head moved slightly faster now, up and down his entire length, occasionally stopping to gently lick and suck on his testicles, all the while wanking his shaft with her delicate little hands.

By this time Jason was moaning freely, and in between mouthfuls of flesh so was Trudy. She looked up at Jason, still playing with him.

'I want your come, I want it in my mouth and all over my tits . . . come for me.'

Needing no further encouragement, Jason took Trudy firmly by the back of her head and pushed her mouth over his cock and she passionately returned to sucking him off.

'I'm going to come,' he moaned. Trudy squeezed his balls slightly as she took his creamy come into her eager mouth, then halfway through his orgasm, she pulled Jason's cock from her mouth and wanked the rest of the juice from him, which spilled out all over her surgically enhanced cleavage.

Jason moaned loudly as he watched his come hit Trudy's tits and slowly run down between them. She looked up at him with a good amount of his orgasm on the corner of her mouth, which she wiped with her hand then licked from her fingers.

'You taste good,' she said as she ran the palms of her hands down over her wet breasts, rubbing Jason's sticky come all over them.

Jason took a step back and watched lustfully as Trudy touched herself.

'Take your shorts off,' he said. 'I'm going to eat you.'

Trudy willingly complied with Jason's request and lay down on her back in front of him between two workout benches with her tanned legs apart.

Jason moved down onto his knees and ran his hands over her smooth thighs. She closed her eyes. Trudy had one of the most appetising pussies that he had ever seen, almost clean shaven save for a very thin, stubbly line of hair just above her pouting lips. As Jason kissed and licked down her legs he could see just how wet she was as the slippery film of 'lust liquid' covering her pussy glistened under the gym lights.

Trudy's hands reached Jason's hair just as he pushed his tongue into her body, causing her to moan ecstatically. She tasted good, like mildly sweet honey, he thought. He moved his head up and down over her swollen pussy, kissing, licking and occasionally probing right inside her with his hot tongue. Trudy held his head tighter now as she slowly gyrated her hips into his face and her moaning intensified.

'I'm going to come,' she blurted.

Jason cut loose on Trudy's shaven pussy, finally taking almost all of it into his mouth, firmly sucking on her until she let out a loud gasp as she came into his mouth. Jason kissed her pussy several times and licked her come from his lips, then they lay there for a while, his head resting on her thigh as she played with his hair.

Trudy's thoughts began to drift away from the ecstasy she had just experienced to her boyfriend who would have finished footy practice by now.

Jason had a faint smile on his face and his eyes

closed until, unexpectedly, a vision of Caroline swept through his mind and his smile faded.

Mike sat in his plumber's van, waiting for Jason.

'Where the fuck are you, Jason, you prick,' he wondered out loud.

It was nearly three o'clock and Mike had been waiting for over twenty minutes, although he didn't mind too much. After all, his mate was fixing him up with a filthy date for the evening.

Mike had begun his vigil outside Jason's front door but Max was so excited to see him that the bull-terrier almost smashed through the bottom pane of glass in the front door with his thickly boned head.

Seeing the glass shaking precariously for the third time, Mike thought it best to wait in the van before the dog broke the front door down completely.

Just as Mike was ejecting a tape to turn it over, Jason pulled up next to him.

'About fucking time, where have you been?'

Jason removed his helmet and gave his friend a mischievous smile.

'You've been shagging, haven't you?' said Mike.

'Come on inside mate, and I'll tell you about it over a coffee.'

'Fuck the coffee, I've got half a carton in the van.'

Jason had just begun to dismount his bike when he heard the sound of smashing glass coming from his apartment. Max had recognised his master's voice and that, combined with the previous frustration of not being able to greet Mike, was just too much for the forty-six kilo block of muscle. Max had charged straight into the front door with his head down and come out the other side, remarkably unscathed.

He now stood in front of Jason and Mike wagging his tail, sure that they were well pleased to see him.

'You dumb, fat, clumsy mutherfucker,' Jason said, as he stood with his hands on his hips looking at the bull-terrier. 'You've gone and smashed the front door again, haven't you?'

'You mean this is a regular occurrence?' said Mike.

'Regular as fucking clockwork. This bastard's making the local glazier a fortune.'

Jason knelt down and patted Max who licked his hand and snorted.

'Come on, let's have that beer,' Jason said.

Mike retrieved the carton from the van and the two friends went inside.

'. . . and so then I put my singlet back on and came home,' said Jason as he finished the story along with his second beer.

'Fucking hell, no wonder you were late, you lucky git. I wanted to shag her.'

'Go for it, I don't care.' Jason paused. 'You know . . . afterwards, I felt . . . guilty.'

'Guilty, why?'

'This is going to sound really soft but . . . I couldn't help thinking of Caroline.'

'You daft twat,' Mike said, laughing, 'you've known Caroline what, less than a week and you're getting the guilts already? Shit, you didn't even have sex with Trudy.'

'Fuck, that can only mean one thing,' Jason said with a look of horror on his face. 'I actually . . . like her.'

Mike quickly reached for two more beers.

'What time did they say they'd be here?' called Rosie from the bathroom as she finished applying her eyeliner.

'About seven,' replied Caroline, who was curled up on the sofa watching taped episodes of 'Melrose Place'.

'What's the time now?'

'Umm, nearly eight.'

'Bloody hell, how rude. How dare two guys be late for us. They should think themselves lucky to be invited round at all.'

Caroline giggled. 'Very true, anyway you're not even ready yet.'

'That's beside the point.' Rosie finished her make-up and joined Caroline on the couch.

The girls were both wearing jeans and T-shirts. Rosie's was tight and Caroline's was baggy, although it still failed to hide her large breasts. They were halfway through discussing the important question of who was cuter, Jake or Billy, when the intercom buzzed, saving the debate for another day.

Caroline answered the intercom. 'Hello, who is it?'

'It's Santa Claus and I've brought me mate Rudolf, can we come up?' Jason replied, trying not to sound too pissed. Caroline pressed the door release button, allowing the boys into the building.

'Do you think they'll realise we've been drinking?' said Mike in the lift.

'Nah mate, the two best bullshitters in Perth, we'll swing it,' Jason said then hiccupped loudly. They reached the sixth floor and knocked on the door.

'It's open,' came the reply. They entered the apartment and walked as sensibly as they could across the room.

'Hi gorgeous,' said Jason winking at Caroline.

'Hi,' said Mike. 'Where's your kitchen, I'll put these in the fridge.'

'It doesn't look like you two need any more alcohol,' said Rosie with a playful smile on her gorgeous face.

'Are you suggesting that we've been drinking? Well, I'm insulted,' replied Mike as he staggered slightly and bumped into Jason. They all laughed.

'Come here Rudolf, I'll show you where the fridge is,' said Rosie as she took Mike's hand and looked at him with what he was sure were blatant 'fuck me' eyes.

'No, I'm Santa, he's Rudolf.' Rosie and Mike disappeared into the kitchen.

'So, what movie did you get?' said Jason as he dropped down next to Caroline on the sofa.

'*While You Were Sleeping*. Have you seen it?'

'No, any juicy murders in it?'

'No, but a guy gets mugged.'

'So lots of blood then.'

'Well no, not really, it's kind of a romance story.'

'Cool, lots of hot, dirty sex.'

'No,' replied Caroline after she kissed him on the mouth, 'that comes after the movie.'

Jason felt the contents of his Calvins stirring. Mike and Rosie returned from the kitchen giggling and laughing with a bottle of wine and four glasses.

By the time the wedding scene came on, nearly an hour and a half later, all the wine was gone and both couples were heavily involved in intensive snogging. Mike and Rosie had started barely ten minutes into the movie and were now onto the 'dry rooting' stage.

'Come on, let's leave these two alone,' said Caroline as she led Jason, unprotesting, in the direction of her bedroom.

'Let me put some music on,' purred Rosie.

Mike pulled his head out from under her T-shirt. 'Good idea.'

She went to the stereo and put on a Michael Jackson CD while Mike stretched out on the floor. When she returned, Mike took her in his arms and the two libidos on legs continued rubbing and kissing and began tearing each other's clothes off. Pretty soon, articles of clothing were strewn in every direction around the room, leaving Mike and Rosie moving all over each other's naked bodies. Mike scooped her up in his strong arms and placed her gently on the couch.

She looked lustfully into his eyes, and asked, 'Do you have any protection?'

'What,' Mike said with a cheeky, drunken look on

his face, 'this is no time to be asking me about sunglasses.'

'No,' giggled Rosie, 'you know what I'm talking about, condoms.'

'Oh, right, yes I do have some extra-sensitive, naturally lubricated, big-boy prophylactics in one of my pockets, hang on.'

Fuck, I hate condoms, Mike thought as he rummaged through piles of discarded clothing in almost total darkness. Nearly ten minutes of frantic searching went by until he finally found it.

'Aha, found the little bastard,' he said.

That was the easy part, he thought, now it's time to attempt the near impossible task of putting the fucking thing on, in the dark, pissed.

Oh shit, Mike looked down, his erection had got bored and left him. So again all the rubbing and kissing was brought back into play to return Mike's impatient male organ to its original, erect splendour.

Ten minutes later and Rosie's as wet as she's ever been and Mike has a hard-on that could knock nails into a piece of four by two. He clumsily ripped open the small square package, his hands trembling in anticipation of the ecstasy that awaited.

Once open, he deftly took the teat of the condom between his thumb and forefinger to expel any air from it (he'd read the instructions, all right). Then he placed it on top of Mr Wriggly and proceeded to roll it down. Mike looked at Rosie just waiting for it on the couch, lying there naked and playing with her breasts.

Boy is she in for it, he thought, but wait, hang on,

it's inside out. Oh my god, I've managed to get it an inch and a half down my willy but the two-timing little bastard's inside out, and it's the only fucking one I have on me.

'Do you want some help over there,' crooned Rosie.

'No, it's cool,' lied Mike.

'Fuck it, you're going on buster,' he said under his breath and began to pull and stretch at the rubber saboteur which was now bone dry and in danger of breaking. 'Right, this is war.' Mike pushed his finger up inside the condom in an attempt to roll it down in reverse but only succeeded in spearing his foreskin with his nail.

'Oww, fuck.'

'What's wrong?'

'Nothing, oh god, I think I'm bleeding.'

At this point Mike knew that no amount of swearing, begging or just plain despair was going to win the battle against the condom. Battered and bruised, Mr Wriggly waved the white flag of defeat and hung limply between Mike's legs with a totally fucked-up condom hanging ridiculously from him.

Mike looked at Rosie on the couch.

'Well, you only really came round to watch a video, anyway,' said Rosie, a grin on her face.

'Fuck, I hate condoms,' replied Mike.

PARTY

The phone rang just after eleven o'clock on Monday morning, waking Jason from his sleep.

'Hello,' said a very tired sounding Jason.

'Hi, it's Caroline,' she chirped.

'How can you be so full of energy after what we did last night? I'm knackered.'

'It's because of what we did last night that I'm so energetic. You recharged my batteries.'

'Christ, I wish two hours of shagging had the same effect on me, I feel like I've been six rounds with Mike Tyson.'

Caroline giggled.

'Listen, you cheeky thing, I've got some amazing news for you, but I'll let Rosie tell you.'

She handed Rosie the phone while Jason remained on his back with his eyes closed.

'Hi Jason.'

'Hi Rosie, what's going on?'

'Would you be interested in doing a photo shoot for a magazine?'

'What, like a modelling photo shoot?'

'Yes, two and a half thousand dollars for two hours work.'

Jason's eyes opened.

'Two and a half grand, well you've certainly got my attention, but I've never done a photo shoot in my life. I think modelling is a big load of wank, to tell you the truth.'

Rosie laughed.

'A lot of the time it is, but one of my less "wanky" modelling friends is a photographer for *Australian Centrefold Magazine* and—'

'*Australian Centrefold*,' Jason said, sitting up in bed. 'You mean it's tackle out?'

'If you mean, is it nude, yes, but the pictures are done really tastefully. Haven't you ever seen the magazine before?'

Jason smiled. 'Well I've heard of it, but I can't say that I've ever actually gone out and bought one, no.'

'Well listen, let me give you Natalie's mobile number and you can call her and see what you think.'

He agreed to take the number, and after fumbling around on the floor under his bed, miraculously found a pen and wrote it down. Then he said his goodbyes to the girls.

'*Australian Centrefold*, eh.' He chuckled and fell back to sleep.

On Tuesday afternoon, Jason arrived home after a punishing leg workout. Max greeted him enthusiastically, almost pawing him in the testicles.

'Fucking hell, porky, be careful.'

Jason placed his helmet on the kitchen table, clicked the kettle on and sat down in the lounge with the telephone. He looked at it momentarily and then went to dial the photographer's number, but paused and pulled his hand away.

'Fuck, come on, call her, dickhead. Just talking to her can't hurt.'

Once more, he reached for the phone and this time he managed to dial the number.

'Hello, Natalie speaking.'

'Hi Natalie,' he began, feeling like a fish out of water. 'My name's Jason, I'm—'

'Oh, hi Jason, I've been expecting your call. From what Rosie tells me, you would make a perfect model for the magazine. That's if you're interested, of course.'

He laughed a little nervously.

'Well, it's very nice of Rosie to recommend me to you, but to be quite honest I've never actually done any modelling work before.'

'That's OK, a lot of the guys we use haven't, we go for a spunkier kind of look than the typical male model.'

'And it's like . . . nude, isn't it?'

Natalie laughed.

'Most of the shots are done semi-nude, bathers and bike pants, that kind of thing, but yes the centrefold is in the raw, so to speak.'

Jason was beginning to relax a little. Natalie had a bright, friendly voice and from the way she spoke on the phone, she was obviously used to reassuring apprehensive would-be models.

'Listen, Jason,' she continued, 'I'd love to meet you in person and discuss everything in more detail over a coffee. How are you fixed tomorrow afternoon?'

'I'll just check my diary, hang on.'

Jason covered the mouthpiece with his hand and waited for several seconds. Of course, he didn't have a diary, but a guy's got to give the impression of being booked out, hasn't he?

'Yep, mid-afternoon's not looking too bad, how about Hardie's Cafe at two?'

'Perfect, Hardie's, that's near the Brookdale Bar isn't it?'

'Yes, that's right.'

'OK, well I look forward to meeting you tomorrow,' said Natalie.

'Cool, see you then.' Jason put the phone down.

'What the fuck am I doing?' he said to himself. 'Hang on, I don't even know what this girl looks like.'

The phone rang. It was Mike.

'Hey, Captain Condom, what's happening?' said Jason, laughing.

'Very fucking funny.'

'Sorry mate, but that was a peach of a story.'

'Yeah, well tonight will be different. I'm going back there with a fucking suitcase full of johnnies and shag the knickers off her.'

'You really are the last of the true romantics, Mike. You don't give up easily do you?'

'No, not when bonking's concerned. I've got my good reputation to think of after all.'

'You've got a reputation all right, mate, but it's far from good.'

'All right, all right, enough of the abuse. I just called to see if you wanted to meet up for a coffee tomorrow afternoon and I can give you all of tonight's gory details.'

'Yeah cool. How about three-thirty?'

'Yeah sweet, what about at Hardie's?'

'No,' Jason snapped. 'How about the Brookdale next door, we can have a couple of beers and get into the really juicy bits.'

The two boys agreed and signed off.

Jason walked into Hardie's just on two o'clock, and after acknowledging Pedro, the Mexican owner, he spotted a girl who had to be Natalie seated near the window. She was impossible to miss. The table was strewn with photographs, slides, a couple of magazines and a very expensive camera was placed reverently in front of her. A cappuccino was relegated to the seat next to her as there was no room on the table for actual coffee.

Natalie looked up as Jason approached her. She smiled. Her first impression was that here was someone special, someone with amazing potential. Natalie had photographed many good-looking guys for the magazine before but the spunk now standing in front of her with the cheekiest smile she had ever seen was a godsend. He had an adventurous, hungry glint in his eyes that Natalie felt could easily draw someone in and mesmerise them. His smile was infectious, almost to the point where she actually wanted to be mischievous and naughty.

'Hi,' said Jason, 'you must be Natalie.'

'Yes, and you have to be Jason.'

She held out her hand, and he politely shook it then sat down opposite her.

'Looks like you're busy,' he said, nodding towards the table.

'Always,' replied Natalie. 'Now, I've brought along a couple of copies of the magazine for you to have a look at.' Natalie passed them over and Jason flicked through them.

She motioned to a waiter to order more coffee. Natalie was twenty-eight years old with short, dark brown hair. She had cutesie, little-girl type features and was wearing black, loose fitting pants, a white T-shirt and a black jacket. Jason thought that she probably had quite a good figure under all that shit she was wearing, but it was hard to tell.

Natalie talked and Jason listened, occasionally throwing in a question or two regarding exactly what was expected of him. She was keen to tell Jason all about the Centrefold of the Year award which was to be announced next month and how, if Jason decided to go ahead with the shoot, he would be the twelfth and final model to be included in this year's competition.

Jason, however, was far more concerned about the immediate dilemma he faced of whether posing nude for a girls' magazine was, after all, the right thing to do.

'So, how long have I got before you need an answer?' he asked.

'Well, we would have to shoot you within the next two weeks, so I'd need an answer preferably before the weekend.'

'Hmm, OK, look I'll go away and think about it, and call you before Saturday.'

They wrapped up their business and Jason rose from the table.

'Oh, before you go,' said Natalie, 'I'm sure it's a silly question but do you have good abs?'

Jason smiled and lifted up his loose fitting sweat-top and tensed his stomach.

Natalie gazed upon the six distinct square blocks of muscle, two feet in front of her face. Jason's naturally olive coloured skin covering his mid-section was pleasantly devoid of body-fat, leaving him with a hard, muscular set of abs.

Natalie had a quick vision flash through her mind of Jason's abs flexing powerfully as he thrust himself deep inside her naked body.

'Um, yes,' she said, flustered. 'It was a silly question.'

Jason pulled his top back down and, still smiling, left the coffee shop.

As Natalie watched him go, she felt a line of slippery fluid trickle down the lips of her pussy and soak into her black, lacy G-string.

Jason walked fifty yards up the street to the Brookdale Bar, a flashy new yuppie drinking hole that by day was a pleasant place to have a focaccia and on a Friday and

Saturday night was one of the busiest and trendiest places to 'be seen' in Perth.

There were only about twenty people scattered around the lavish bar and Jason immediately spotted Mike sitting at a table, stuffing his face full of fettucine carbonara.

'Hey, you fat bastard, where's mine?'

Mike looked up and beamed a devilish grin through a mouthful of pasta.

'Hey mate, grab a seat,' he said and swallowed.

'So how did you go last night, or should I ask how did Mr Wriggly go?'

'Mr Wriggly got well and truly fed last night.'

Mike had a smile on his face that suggested he was quite pleased with his efforts.

'It was brilliant, the total opposite of the other night's fucking disaster.'

'Good on you, mate, glad to hear that you didn't let the side down.'

The two doormen laughed and chatted about work and women and nothing in particular.

'So how come you're not working today, slack?' said Jason.

'RDO mate.'

'What the fuck's an RDO?'

'Rostered day off, nob-head.'

Mike's phone rang.

'Hello, Mike speaking.'

'Hi Mike, it's Steve.'

'All right mate, what's up?'

'Jo's having a bit of a relo-bash tomorrow night and she's invited me and a couple of mates along. Do you fancy it?'

'A fucking relo-bash, what the fuck do we want to go to a relo-bash for?'

'I know it sounds shit but Jo's got some cute friends that'll be there and of course there'll be a free feed and plenty of beer for you boys.'

'Well it's starting to sound better, hang on I'll ask Jase, he's right here.'

Mike covered the phone, 'It's Steve, there's a party at his girlfriend's place tomorrow night—you in?'

'Yeah, fuck it why not.'

'Yep, no worries, when and where?'

While Mike finalised the arrangements with Steve, Jason went to the bar for a Diet Coke. As he was waiting for the barman to return Jason idly scanned the bar for nothing in particular when his eyes stopped, glued to the vision at the back of the bar.

The vision was wearing a ridiculously short, tight pink miniskirt with a black aerobics top and no bra. Her breasts weren't large, in fact they were quite small, but her body was un-fucking-believable.

Jason blinked, he was staring and he knew it but he couldn't help himself.

She was bending over a pool table, taking her time with the shot. Her long wavy hair was dark brown, almost black, and cascaded down her back perfectly. As she stretched out over the table Jason noticed that she came up onto her tiptoes, causing the lean muscles in her legs to tense slightly. The vision was tanned, had to be a sunbed, Jason thought as he drank her in with his eyes. She looked like she had some Italian blood in her. Jason's loins twitched.

What a package! Her face was almost too perfect, full pink lips, small nose and her eyes . . . fuck, her eyes were incredible, dark and piercing, they almost seemed to project her intense sexuality for all to see.

She took the shot and potted a striped ball into a centre pocket. The vision stood up and smiled when she caught Jason looking at her. It took him a second or two before he realised that he was staring at her. He blinked quickly and returned her smile.

'Oi you, you walking hard-on,' said Mike.

Jason snapped out of his trance, took his drink and returned to the table.

'Fuck me, fucking, fucking dead. Have you seen that girl at the pool table?'

'Yeah, but I'd forget about her if I were you, mate, she's one of Macey's tarts.'

'Oh bollocks, that'd be right, I instantly fall in love with one of that mutherfucker's women.'

'Keep your voice down, you never know who's listening.'

Jason and Mike chatted on about more boys' talk and Mike gave a very detailed account of the previous night's activities.

Throughout Mike's rendition Jason kept stealing glimpses at the scantily clad vision as she leaned across the pool table.

She, too, made the occasional glance towards Jason's table, and several times they had some serious eye contact happening.

Fuck, I wish I was that bloody pool table, thought Jason.

Then he remembered the notorious gangster who, according to Mike, 'owned' her and decided it was time to leave before he got himself into trouble.

Jason and Mike rose from their table just as the pool game finished, and they reached the front door at exactly the same as the vision and her girlfriend.

The vision looked straight into Jason's eyes. A normal man with normal strength of character would have probably looked away and been left dumbstruck.

Jason looked back at her and smiled.

'After you,' he said, motioning to the door.

'Why, thank you,' she replied. 'It's so nice to meet a real gentleman.'

'My pleasure.'

The two girls wiggled their way through the door and walked off up the street giggling and whispering as the boys watched. Just before they turned the corner, the vision looked back, her hair flicking over her shoulder, and gave Jason a smile that truly belonged on the cover of *Vogue*.

Mike looked at Jason, shaking his head.

'You're fucking hopeless, you are!'

Jason nodded.

'I know.'

*

The three doormen pulled up outside the large, three-storey house just after 7.30 pm. There were many cars lined up along the roadside, indicating a party in full swing.

'I can't believe we're going to a fiftieth birthday party at seven-thirty on a Thursday night,' said Jason from the back of Steve's car.

'Well, fuck off home then,' replied Mike from the passenger seat, 'it'll mean more food and dirty women for me and Conan here.'

'Don't call me Conan, you pommy wanker.' Steve slapped Mike in the back of his head.

'Yeah, you pommy twat, fuck off back to England.' Jason punched Mike in the arm and the three mature doormen began fighting in the car. Laughing and giggling like schoolgirls they finished their male bonding and climbed out of the silver Mitsubishi.

As the boys walked towards the party carrying a six-pack of beer each (well, Steve had a bottle of Diet Coke) they heard loud singing emanating from behind the house.

'Fucking hell,' said Mike, 'it sounds like the old bastards are going off.'

Steve rang the doorbell and after a while it was answered by Jo, Steve's girlfriend, a short blonde with breasts that would have sunk the *Titanic* if it hadn't already hit an iceberg. It was these particular features that had prompted Grant to nickname her 'Little Miss Titanic Tits'.

'Come on inside boys, you didn't need to bring any

drinks, we've got plenty,' she said obviously halfway pissed herself.

'See, told you porky,' said Jason, kneeing Mike up the arse as they walked in.

'Fuck off, blondie,' he replied, laughing.

As they walked through the hallway to the kitchen they saw that the 'oldies' were outside in the large patio area by the pool, merrily singing away while one of their number hammered out 'Heartbreak Hotel' on his guitar, surprisingly well. The younger set were in the lounge room and kitchen, drinking heavily, playing dance music and generally fucking around. There were around forty 'oldies' and about fifteen younger partygoers, all aged in their early twenties.

Jo introduced Jason, Mike and Steve to everyone outside and in, and the boys politely said hello to the other guests, not really listening to any names except for a couple of cute girls.

The party moved up a gear, everyone was drinking freely and having a good time. The sing-song by the pool was in full swing and inside, one of Jo's friends had begun strumming out old Beatles songs on his guitar. He was good too, and a small group sat around him singing drunkenly along.

As the evening wore on, one girl, Gillian, had become a particular pain in the arse. She was currently removing CDs from their sleeves and frisbeeing them around the room.

'Look at that daft fuck,' said Mike.

'She's turned into a right dickhead since she started drinking,' returned Jason.

'She was a dickhead before she started drinking,' added Steve.

A Simple Minds CD whizzed past Mike's right ear.

'Oi, watch what you're doing over there.'

'Oh, fuck off arsehole,' drawled a drunken Gillian.

'Will you stop that please,' shouted Jo as she walked into the lounge room. The drunken girl gave Jo a sarcastic sneer and sat down with the group of singing partygoers.

The boys had just returned to their conversation of who was the toughest bouncer in Perth when they were interrupted by a grating howling noise coming from Gillian.

'Do you mind,' said the guitarist.

Gillian laughed and carried on howling.

'Hey, will you shut the hell up,' one of the girls shouted over her.

Gillian stopped, looked at the girl and pushed her off balance.

'Fuck you, mole, I'll do what I want.'

The girl went to push Gillian back but the guitarist and another guy got in between them and a shouting and swearing match followed, resulting in Gillian storming unsteadily off into the kitchen, leaving behind her the ladylike sentence of, 'Fuck you, cunts.'

The boys watched the little scene in amusement.

'She's the kind of bird you'd go out with, Mike,' Jason said.

'No, I like my girls a little rougher around the edges.'

The three friends laughed and carried on drinking.

Almost twenty minutes later the young guitarist was

bashing out a collection of early '80s tunes and Mike, Jason and Steve had taken a place on the floor next to him, singing along as only doormen can.

Halfway through a U2 song, Gillian staggered back in and promptly tripped over Steve's leg. Only the wall stopped her from falling.

Steve looked up at her disgustedly.

'What are you fucking looking at arsehole?' Gillian drawled and kicked Steve in the back.

'What's your fucking problem?' he snapped.

Female or not, Steve was in no mood to be sworn at let alone kicked. Gillian attempted to crouch down, bringing her face to within inches of Steve's.

'I said, what are you looking at arsehole?' she spat into his face. Steve tensed.

Mike put his hand on Steve's shoulder.

'Ignore her, mate.'

Steve had just begun to turn away from the foul-mouthed Gillian when she slapped him squarely in the side of his face with a force that betrayed her wiry frame.

'Fuck you, you bastard,' screamed a drunken, psychotic Gillian, and she raised her hand for a second strike. Steve, however, was a little too quick for the crazed lunatic bent over in front of him. Ordinarily he would have just pushed her away and left the room, but unfortunately these were no ordinary circumstances.

By the time Gillian's hand had begun to descend on him. Steve had spun on his knees to face her and had reached up, grabbing two large handfuls of hair. With one swift movement, he pulled Gillian down to his left and threw her heavily to the floor. Gillian yelled and screamed and lashed out at Steve who still had her by the hair. Other girls in the room began screaming. Mike and Jason looked at each other in astonishment as the bizarre scene unfolded in front of them.

'You crazy fuckhead, chill out bitch,' shouted Steve as he let go of her hair.

Gillian grabbed a bottle from the floor and began to rise to her feet.

'I'm going to fucking kill you, you cu—'

Just before Gillian could finish her sentence and before Mike and Jason could stop him, Steve let fly with a right cross which caught Gillian on the right temple. It sent her flying backwards into a display cabinet. The ornaments inside it fell and smashed.

Steve moved towards her, fists clenched and eyes blazing, but Jason and Mike managed to grab a shoulder each.

'Whoa, Steve, leave it, mate,' shouted Mike.

'Reality check, dude, let's get the fuck out of here.'

Just at that moment, Jonathan, Gillian's muso boyfriend who had seen Steve smash his beloved girlfriend, came running into the room, red with rage.

'You fucking bastard, I'm going to take your head off.'

Jonathan ran towards Steve with his hands outstretched.

Jason and Mike let go of Steve's shoulders as they knew what was coming.

Unfortunately Jonathan didn't, and ran straight into

a right handed, open palm strike which caught him in the jaw. His legs buckled underneath him and he began to sink to the floor. Steve, who by this time was getting fairly upset by people trying to assault him, caught Jonathan with a sickeningly effective knee in the face as he went down, knocking him back with such force that two of Jonathan's teeth flew straight out of his mouth and landed in the fireplace. As he landed, his head cracked against the side of the fireplace knocking him out cold; blood flowed freely from the back of his head and soaked into the beige carpet. The singing outside continued, the oldies blissfully unaware of the pandemonium inside the house.

Just as Jonathan hit the deck two things happened. First, Gillian scrambled across the room to where a foot-long fire poker lay, and was about to stab Steve in the leg with it when Mike grabbed her in a headlock and began to grapple with her on the floor, trying to avoid the flailing poker.

Secondly, Rodney, a mate of the unconscious Jonathan, arrived on the scene.

'You fucking psycho, I'm going to sue you for this, you're going to jail you fuckers,' he yelled at Steve, and pushed him in the chest. 'Come on, you want to hit someone, hit me.'

'Fuck this, I've had enough of this bullshit,' said Jason standing next to Steve who was just about to deck a third person.

'Listen mate, just back off, we didn't start this, we just want to leave,' Jason said as he began to usher Steve out. Rodney, however, had other ideas and went to grab Jason by the front of his shirt, pulling back his right hand to hit him.

Jason instinctively took Rodney by the hair and pulled him roughly towards himself, at the same time striking him in the jaw with his elbow. You could actually hear his jaw crack, just before he fell limply to the ground, where he lay unconscious.

Mike's headlock on Gillian had turned into a sleeper-hold and he now stood over her prostrate form on the floor. She was still holding the poker. The three doormen looked at each other in disbelief. Jonathan was making groaning noises so thankfully wasn't dead, and Rodney was out cold.

'Lads, I think it's about time we got the fuck out of here,' said Jason.

'Good idea,' Mike said, and the boys made their way swiftly out of the house amidst the sound of screaming girls, general pandemonium and the oldies out the back who had just started the second verse of 'Jailhouse Rock'.

They jumped into Steve's car and sped off down the street. As they turned into the main road, an ambulance and two police cars passed them in full flight.

The boys looked at each other.

'Good party,' said Mike.

DIRTY

Jason finished tying back his hair then grabbed his jacket and bike helmet. It was ten-thirty on Friday night and he was off to work, albeit with a heavy brow.

It had been a big day, beginning with a call from Steve at 10 am. Apparently, after the three desperados had left the party, the various parents of the opposing youngsters had begun arguing over the responsibility for the damage done in the lounge room. This resulted in another brawl erupting between about eight of the drunken oldies.

By the time the cops arrived, the lounge room resembled a scene from the LA riots, and the police, after separating the brawlers, weren't too sympathetic to anyone's cause, let alone the calls for various charges to be laid.

The boys from St John's had cleaned up the mess and taken several of the pissed partygoers to hospital for stitching and X-rays.

So it sounded like the three bouncers had got lucky

and thankfully they wouldn't be receiving any visits from Mr Plod.

This wasn't the only thing on Jason's mind, however. That afternoon he had called Natalie and agreed to go ahead with the photo shoot, setting a time for six-thirty on Wednesday morning, and he had been stressing out ever since.

He slapped Max on the rump and set off for work with a little black cloud above his head.

Mike stood with his back against the wall of the stairway overlooking the dance floor. Jason was on the opposite side nursing a sore hand after smacking someone during a brawl barely fifteen minutes earlier.

Grant was on seek and destroy while Steve and Eddie were out the front. Steve, although in a weakened state from the dieting, was in decidedly good spirits, and Eddie was quite hopeful that Conan wasn't going to put anyone in hospital for breathing incorrectly.

Out of the corner of Mike's eye he noticed someone descending the stairs towards him. He looked up and saw that it was the hot bleached blonde he'd been perving on before the last brawl had broken out. The black dress that she was poured into was a tad restrictive to say the least.

She had to come down the stairs almost sideways.

The girl was looking directly at Mike with mischief blazing in her eyes, and cheeks flushed from the many rum and Cokes she'd consumed.

She reached him, and he gave her an uneasy smile, not sure whether she was going to return the smile or slap him in the face for some emotional crime he'd committed against one of her friends, or maybe even herself, that he'd been too pissed to remember.

Instead, she stopped dead in her tracks.

'You are gorgeous,' she said.

'Why, thank you,' replied Mike. 'You're pretty damn cute yourself.'

He was just about to ask what the 'dead cert's' name was when she took his hand and attempted to lead him down the stairs.

'What are you doing?' he shouted, over the music.

'Come with me to the girls' toilets,' she said, swaying slightly.

'What?' Mike wasn't quite sure if he'd heard her correctly.

The bleached temptress repeated her request.

'Why?' said Mike. 'What did you have in mind?'

'A head job,' she replied, looking him straight in the eye.

Mike's jaw dropped as he felt Mr Wriggly growing in his Calvins. Was this a joke? Was there a camera somewhere? No matter, a gorgeous blonde was trying to drag him off to the ladies' room to orally abuse his manhood. That was more than good enough for him.

'Hang on,' said Mike, and he waved to Jason.

After giving him the thumbs-up, Mike allowed himself to be pulled down the stairs towards the toilets.

What the fuck's going on down there, Jason thought

to himself as he watched his mate being led through the crowd. That's the chick that Grant bonked a couple of weeks ago, or one of them anyway.

The door of the ladies' flew open and Mike was led straight past several girls preening themselves in the mirror, and into the cubicle at the end of the row.

Once inside, the blond libido on legs crushed herself against Mike, and pushed her tongue deep inside his mouth as she fumbled with his belt buckle and zipper.

As she expertly made short work of undoing his pants, Mike disentangled himself from her tongue.

'Fucking hell, you're a horny little thing, aren't you?'

She took his hand.

'Touch me, feel how wet I am,' she said, lifting her dress to reveal that she had no underwear on.

He touched her saturated pussy. A moderate amount of dark brown hair covered her swollen lips. Mike pushed two of his fingers easily inside her, he could feel the heat of her sex covering his hand. The thought of just bending her over the toilet and fucking the shit out of her there and then flashed across his mind. However, he didn't have any condoms on him, and was fairly certain that the girl in front of him with almost half of his hand inside her was definitely not a virgin.

He removed his hand.

'Sit your little arse down,' he said as he guided her down onto the toilet seat.

This girl needed no guiding. Breathing heavily now, she grabbed his hard cock and literally shoved it deep into her mouth and proceeded to fuck him with her lips.

Mike pulled her hair back out of her face so that he could get the best view possible.

She was good, real fucking good, as she licked, sucked and slurped over his hard dick, all the while playing with his balls and giving them the occasional lick, too.

Mike's hands were pushed against the cubical walls.

'Fuck me,' he closed his eyes. 'You are good.'

Without warning she stood up, turned round and bent over the toilet. She still had his cock in one hand while the other was desperately pulling up her dress.

'What the fuck are you doing?' said Mike, opening his eyes.

'Fuck me, fuck me now you bastard,' she blurted, pulling his cock towards her hot, moist pussy.

'No fucking way, I've got no condoms.'

'I don't care.'

'Well I bloody well do.'

Mike put his hands on her arse and spun her round to face him.

'Sit back down and suck my cock, I want to come in your mouth.'

'As long as you promise to fuck me when you finish work.'

'No problem, I'll invest in some johnnies and I'll fuck you so you can't walk for a week. Now sit down, I've got to get back to work.'

She eagerly returned to giving him one of the best head jobs he had ever had, and he'd had a few.

*

Grant had taken Mike's spot on the stairs and was busy picking his nose, totally unconcerned whether people saw him or not.

Steve had swapped places with Jason who was now controlling the oversized queue with Eddie when the DJ's voice came over the intercom.

'Security to upstairs bar, security to upstairs bar.'

Grant stopped picking his nose, Steve bounded up the stairs while Mike was halfway through a mind-shattering orgasm.

'Oh fuck,' he moaned, half in ecstasy of coming and half in frustration of the DJ's announcement.

Withdrawing his dripping wet cock from her mouth, he shoved his box back into his jocks, did his pants up and left his 'dead cert' sitting on the toilet with false promises of meeting her after work.

Steve and Grant arrived at the scene more or less at the same time, and were both fairly disappointed to find that it was only two drunken idiots dancing on top of the bar.

When the bar staff had asked them politely to get down they had been told to 'fuck off'. But now, faced with two massive bouncers, the drunks decided not to push their luck and were climbing down, especially as Grant had greeted them with, 'Get the fuck off the bar now, or I'll rip your fucking faces off, mutherfuckers.'

The offenders were given a stern warning and were allowed to remain intact and in the club. The two bouncers finished chastising the drunks and had turned to go back to the stairs, when Mike arrived.

'What's up lads?' he asked.

'Oh nothing,' Grant said, 'just a couple of cockheads dancing on the bar, where the fuck have you been?'

'I've just got the best head job of my life in the bogs.'

'You bastard,' said Grant. 'Who was she?'

'I don't even know her name, a heavily peroxided little bimbo in a black dress. She's a fucking sexual hooligan.'

'It's not the one that Grant shagged a couple of weeks ago, is it?' Steve asked.

Grant smiled. 'Was she wearing any underwear?'

'No, dirty bitch.'

Grant laughed.

'That's the one I rooted. I think it was her that gave me the clap, did you fuck her?'

'No, but she wants me to after work.'

'Well, if you do, make sure you stick a rubber on.'

'Mate, if I fuck her I'm going to wear a full-length wetsuit with a mask, snorkel and flippers.'

The three doormen laughed loudly and returned to work.

The scene outside the club was chaotic. The line was longer than ever and was moving very slowly, if at all, causing several disgruntled patrons to whinge and moan at Eddie and Jason.

Meanwhile, a heated argument had been gathering momentum between two scruffy scumbags who Eddie had turned away for being, well ... scruffy scumbags, and another guy who seemed to be on his own but probably had friends inside the club.

The argument had started when the two scumbags, who were yelling and screaming blue murder at Eddie for not letting them in, jostled the lone dude as he attempted to leave the club. This resulted in the ongoing battle of words which was drawing ever closer to a punch-up.

Jason and Eddie kept an eye on the proceedings, although they were far more interested in organising the restless masses in the queue. Any altercations outside the club were not legally the doormen's responsibility and any interference could result in hefty fines and assault charges. So even if a brawl were to develop outside the club (as they regularly did), the bouncers knew that they were legally obliged to keep the fuck out of it.

The lone dude was outnumbered two to one, but was slightly taller and a touch bigger than his opponents and had no intention of backing down. The scumbags were drunk and very aggressive but up to this point no physical contact had been made. That was until one of them gave the lone dude a heavy shove and all shit broke loose.

Grant appeared at the front door just in time to see one of the scumbags cop a smack in the mouth.

As the brawl developed and blood began to run freely, the three doormen stood and watched the melee in front of them as anyone else would watch TV, occasionally making comments like, 'Good punch' or

'Look, he's wide open, he should throw in a head butt or knee him in the bollocks.'

Up until now, the two women who were with the scumbags had kept fairly well out of it. But now that their men were involved in a brawl and by all appearances weren't doing too well, the girls had begun to advance on the fighting trio, shouting obscenities that would have made the devil himself wince.

'Here we go,' said Eddie. 'Those slags are going to get involved now.'

'Slags? It's not like you to refer to girls that way, Sir Eddie.'

'I know mate, but believe me, those two are slags. They've been barred from several clubs around town for all kinds of shit.'

'Like what?' enquired Jason, as one of the girls attempted to knee the lone dude in the knackers, while the other aimed punches to his face.

'Like brawling, stealing, just being too pissed, oh and I heard that they were thrown out of the Sunset Club for pissing in a glass at the bar in full view of everyone, and then daring someone to drink it.'

'What?'

'Oh yeah, real class these two.'

The lone dude had successfully knocked one of the scumbags down and was wrestling with the other one, while the girls were raining blows down onto his back and head.

'Fuck this, I'm going to pull these bitches off him,' said Jason, and took a step towards the brawl.

'Don't be stupid, it's nothing to do with us, keep out of it,' said Eddie as he put his hand up against Jason's chest.

'Aren't you going to stop that?' yelled a girl in the queue.

'We can't, it's outside the club,' Eddie said.

'But look, that guy's going to hurt those girls, you have to do something,' said someone else in the queue.

'That's not the way I see it,' said Jason, throwing a dirty look at the couple in the line.

The lone warrior had been trying desperately to avoid the blows from the overweight females and had not laid a finger on them. Unfortunately, one of them had just connected with a blow to his face and had drawn more blood from his already bleeding nose.

Pushing the scumbag away from him, he turned and caught the girl's leg just as she aimed a kick to his shin. Lifting the leg above her waist and revealing the knickers beneath her short skirt, he shoved her away with a force that well and truly dumped her on her arse. She fell with a loud thump and the slapping sound of fat flesh on concrete.

The doormen looked at each other and smiled. Grant applauded in approval.

'Well done, mate, now smack the other one.'

However, the valiant warrior was eager to leave the scene. He gave the other girl, who was by now hysterical and attempting to bite his arm, a good shove and ran off down the street.

'That's right, run away you fucking cocksucker,' screamed the hysterical female.

The girl who had been dumped on her backside was now crying as she sat on the footpath, covered in blood and dirt.

The two male scumbags had begun to walk up the street, nursing their wounds.

'Come on Shaz, leave it,' one of them shouted back to the girls.

Shaz helped her blubbering friend to her feet and sat her down on a nearby wall, then she turned her anger on the doormen.

'You fucking arseholes, why didn't you help my friends, you useless cunts?' she spat into Jason's face.

'Listen, calm the fuck down and get out of my face.'

'Fuck you, don't you help a girl when she's being beaten up in front of you?' she screamed.

Jason began to open his mouth but Grant answered for him.

'We would have helped a girl in trouble, but all I saw were two drunken, fat sluts, who got what they deserved.'

The drunken, fat slut reddened and had 'Look out I'm a total psycho' clearly written in her widened eyes.

'What the fuck did you just call us, you cunt?'

The psycho approached Grant.

'I said, all I saw were two fat, drunken sluts. Don't tell me you've never heard those names before?'

Jason and Eddie looked at each other.

'Uh oh,' said Eddie.

With a loud shriek the girl launched herself at Grant, arms flailing viciously.

Grant gave her a shove with half the force that he would usually use on a guy but enough to send her staggering back.

'Keep the fuck away from me, you crazy bitch, or you'll get a slap.'

She advanced on him again, yelling and swearing as she swung her right fist at his head.

Easily blocking the shot, Grant slapped her with both hands in the chest with all his one hundred and twenty kilos behind it. The result was quite spectacular. She flew backwards about four feet, completely airborne.

Eddie and Jason were sure that her feet were actually higher than her head when they discussed it later.

When she finally hit the ground, her whole body jolted with the impact and her face went white.

Jason noted that the vicious, foul-mouthed female sitting on the pavement with her skirt up around her waist was a true Kodak moment.

As she drunkenly rose to her feet, the doormen stared at her. Urine was running like a tap from her crotch and flowed freely down her legs, covering the pavement.

Several shouts came from the queue and passers-by condemning Grant's actions as 'bouncer brutality'.

Five or six well-meaning males had gathered in front of the three doormen shouting abuse at them, albeit from a fairly safe distance. The situation was beginning to get a little out of control. Jason and Grant had already inserted their mouthguards and were quite willing to start hurting people when a police car pulled up and two decent sized cops made their way nonchalantly over to Davinchi's.

Eddie saw them approaching.

'Officer, I'd like the girl over there charged with assaulting one of my security officers, and these gentlemen here are becoming overly aggressive and disturbing the peace.'

The small crowd, including the two girls, began hysterically shouting their story at the police officers, all at the same time.

'OK,' said the slightly taller cop, 'listen, everyone move along now. If you have a complaint, come into East Perth Station tomorrow and make a statement. If you remain here I will arrest you for public disturbance violations.'

With some complaints the crowd dispersed, not wanting to spend Friday night in a cell down at the lock-up.

As one cop took a statement from the two girls, the other went over to Eddie.

'Do you still wish to charge the young um . . . lady, sir?'

'Actually no. I think we'll just let it slide this time round. Thanks for the help.'

The officer winked at Eddie and joined his partner who was warning the girls of the trouble they were in, but he explained that if they left the area they would be let off with a caution.

Hopelessly drunk and not totally aware of what was going on, the girls agreed and staggered off down the street.

The three friends looked at each other.

'Time you went back inside, young man,' Eddie said to Grant.

'No worries,' he replied, and made his way back into the club.

Jason slapped Eddie on the back.

'Having a cop for a brother certainly comes in handy now and again, mate.'

Eddie nodded and smiled.

'Come on, let's get some of these people inside.'

The rest of the evening passed by relatively incident-free, apart from one drunken idiot who fell down the stairs and broke his arm.

At the end of the night most of the staff stayed behind for a drink and a chat. Steve told a select few people about the luxury room that he had booked at the casino's hotel on Sunday night, and invited them over for what, hopefully, would be a celebration after the competition.

Jason stretched as he walked towards his unit, shaking his head and smiling as he remembered Grant and the flying nun.

He stopped short of his front door. It was open. Wooden splinters covered the floor and the lock was hanging broken from the doorframe.

He took the knuckledusters from his pocket and slipped them over his right hand. His mind raced. If anyone was still around, they would have heard him arrive.

He peered inside. The laundry light was on as usual, so visibility wasn't a problem. No-one was in the kitchen, so Jason moved inside as quietly as he could.

Room by room, he pushed open the doors, dusters at the ready.

The house was empty.

As he walked back to the kitchen, Jason was confused, nothing had been stolen. His TV, stereo, even forty dollars that he'd left on the kitchen table were still there.

Suddenly, his heart sank to his stomach and his mouth went dry. He looked down at Max's bed. It was empty. Max was gone.

Jason had arrived home from work at about 5 am, it was now almost nine and he had just returned after four hours of screaming round the streets of Perth, searching every road and back lane that he came across, looking for his dog.

Since Jason's family had fallen apart over a year ago, Max had become the only living thing with which he truly felt a close family bond. Certainly, he had several good mates that he thought the world of, but Max, the crazy, scarred bull-terrier, was his brother, his father, his mother and sister, all in the one clumsy, muscle-bound package.

Jason called everyone he could think of to help him track down whoever had stolen Max. He phoned the police, dog pounds and all his mates, asking them to keep an eye out and an ear open for any sign of the dog. Finally, he called the newspaper and placed a reward for information or the return of his bully.

Jason finished his calls and, over a cup of coffee, wrote out the ad that he'd placed in the newspaper. Then, after draining his cup, he rode to a printing shop and had two hundred copies run off.

Armed with a roll of sticky tape, Jason hit the streets once more and plastered telegraph poles and shop windows with the reward leaflets.

By the time he returned home it was one o'clock. He sat on the bike and removed his helmet, placing it on the seat, and rubbed his eyes. He had been awake for over twenty-four hours now, and was totally exhausted.

Swamped with feelings of anger, frustration and worry, Jason lowered his head slightly. Water filled his eyes and a tear ran down his left cheek, then his right. Then Jason lowered his head a little more . . . and cried.

STACKED

Earlier in the day, after Jason had made several more phone calls, exhaustion had got the better of him and he had fallen asleep within minutes of lying down. Eight hours later, the alarm clock woke him from his restless sleep. He looked momentarily at the clock, just before hitting it heavily. It was 9.30 pm. Jason rolled out of bed and made his way to the kitchen.

He flicked on the kettle and took a cup and a tea bag from the cupboard. While the kettle boiled, he stared hopelessly at Max's empty basket.

'When I find out who's got my dog . . .' he said under his breath.

After shovelling some cold, leftover chicken pasta down his throat and drinking his tea, Jason set off for work.

'You're fucking kidding me,' said Eddie, as Steve finished telling him the news. 'Jason must be furious.'

'I don't think furious quite covers it, the guy's ready to tear people limb from limb, literally.'

While the boys discussed their mate's predicament, Caroline and Rosie arrived at the club.

'Hi Eddie, hi Steve, is Jason here yet?' chirped Caroline.

'Er, no,' said Eddie. 'Have you heard about his dog?'

'No, why, what's happened to Max?'

'Some bastard has stolen him,' Steve said.

'Oh my god, that's terrible.'

The bouncers and the two girls were discussing the missing dog when Jason appeared from around the back of the club, undoing his helmet as he walked towards them.

'Hi,' he said flatly, not looking at anyone as he walked past them into the club.

The four looked at each other.

'The poor guy,' said Rosie. 'I wonder if there's anything we can do.'

'Well, apart from returning Max along with the head of the person who took him, not much.'

Jason positioned himself on the stairs, giving Mike a half-hearted wave. It was going to be a long night.

An hour and a half later, Jason was daydreaming about what he was going to do to the person or persons responsible for Max's disappearance when the first trouble of the evening developed.

Down on the dance floor, two drunken turds had decided that they wanted to dance with two cute girls and were not going to take no for an answer.

Unfortunately for the girls, the two turds were

beginning to manhandle them. Unfortunately for the turds, the girls they were harassing just happened to be Caroline and Rosie.

One of the unsuspecting drunks grabbed Rosie by the arm and pulled her roughly towards him. 'Come and dance with us for fuck's sake, what's your problem, are you frigid or something?'

'Get your fucking hands off me and leave us alone, arsehole,' said Rosie as she attempted to break free.

Caroline went to her friend's aid and tried to push the man away.

'Oh fuck off, you stuck-up sluts,' yelled the turd as he pushed Caroline and Rosie heavily.

Rosie fell to the floor.

Jason had spotted the trouble and was now rushing down the stairs.

Mike had also seen the whole incident and was now less than six feet from the scene. As he reached the dance floor, he shoved the pusher in the chest with all his strength, sending him flying into a wall, knocking the air out of him.

'You like that, mutherfucker?' yelled Mike as he advanced on the other turd.

Turd number two had basically shit himself as he saw his mate fly across the floor, and had turned to run away through the crowd. Just as he took the first step, his head was snapped back viciously by Jason's outstretched arm in a textbook clothesline. It was just like something from a brawl in an ice-hockey movie. The turd's feet left the ground and he landed with a bone-crunching thud, hitting his head on the floor which knocked him out instantly.

Jason glanced over to make sure that Mike was doing OK. After Mike had shoved number one away, he had laid a punishing blow into the guy's stomach and was now pushing him towards the door with the man's arm well up behind his back.

Jason pulled his victim up off the floor and hoisted him over his shoulders in a fireman's lift and followed Mike through the crowd.

When Mike reached the front door, he pushed the still winded girl-basher so hard that he flew out the door and landed flat on his stomach, winding him further.

'Steady on, Mike,' said Eddie.

'Fuck him, he was roughing up the girls inside.'

Just then, Jason came out of the club with the body over his shoulders. He walked up to a low wall and gently lowered the limp form up against it. Taking him by the the front of the shirt, Jason slapped him hard in the face.

'Wake up, dickhead.'

There was no response, so he slapped him again and the drunk made a moaning noise, then rolled over and threw up in the gutter.

Jason left him there and turned to where Eddie, Mike and Steve were standing by the front door.

Eddie put his hands on his hips and stared at Jason.

'Don't look at me like that,' Jason said, as he walked back into the club. 'He's still alive, isn't he?'

Eddie turned to Mike, raising his eyebrows.

'Keep an eye on him.'

'No worries mate,' Mike replied, then winked and returned to the stairway.

Several minutes later, Dominic emerged from the club to check on the numbers.

'How many have we got?'

'Just on, maybe ten over,' replied Eddie.

Now, in reality for every 'ten over' there were actually about fifty extra people inside, but for the sake of any off-duty cops who might overhear, the numbers and several other aspects of the club's operations were discussed in code. So if there were 'thirty' extra people in the club, there were really about one hundred and fifty. Another example of club code was if Eddie told whoever was on the door with him to go and get a 'soda water' (which he never drank), it meant that the boys from the Liquor Licensing Department were here and to warn Dominic and the other doormen.

'Right, well go to twenty over, and then just one in, one out,' Dominic said.

'No worries,' winked Eddie.

'What happened to them?' Dominic said, pointing at the two women-bashers who were leaning against the wall, coughing and spluttering.

'Oh, just two drunks.'

'Why is that one bleeding?'

'I don't know,' replied an innocent-looking Eddie. 'He wasn't bleeding when he left the club.'

Dominic glared accusingly at him, but said nothing.

*

Half an hour later, Eddie sent Steve inside and replaced him with Grant.

Steve walked over to where Jason was standing guard and put a hand on his shoulder.

'How y'doin', mate?'

'I'm OK. Anyway how are you, big day tomorrow, eh?'

'Yeah, it's all over tomorrow, thank fuck. Are you still coming?'

'Of course I am, wouldn't miss it for the world. What's the competition like?'

'Well, there's some pretty good lads in it. I hear that Tommy from Warwick's gym is huge.'

'Ah, no worries, mate, I'm looking forward to watching you kick arse.'

Jason was happy to be distracted from the subject of Max, and the two doormen chatted on the stairs for a while.

Caroline and Rosie left the club and invited Jason and Mike around to their apartment after work.

At the end of the night, Steve went home to get some sleep before his body-building comp later that afternoon. Eddie also left, leaving Grant, Mike and Jason out the front of the club.

'So do you want to come and check out the Sunset Club?' said Grant.

'Yeah, fuck it,' said Jason. 'Let's go and say a quick hello to Chris and Angus.'

*

The Sunset Club was a large complex of bars, including a garden area, a band room and a nightclub upstairs with a dance floor. It was old, dirty and in desperate need of some serious renovations.

The fourteen or so doormen who worked there would joke that they were in more danger of being injured when the walls came crashing down than actually breaking up the many violent brawls that erupted regularly each night.

The Sunset Club seemed to attract more fights than anywhere else in Perth, so the doormen were hand picked to cope with the job, resulting in over a dozen of the most testosterone-crazed lunatics that ever worked security in Western Australia.

Two such lunatics were Chris and Angus who were currently positioned upstairs on either side of the dance floor, scouring the packed club hoping to spot trouble.

Chris was about five foot ten with a shaven haircut and looked like he'd swallowed a house. His extra large white shirt was stretched to tearing point across his wide back and huge deltoids.

He was in reality a nice warm person, however at four-fifteen on a Sunday morning, standing at the edge of the Sunset's dance floor, Mr Nice Guy was nowhere to be seen.

Angus on the other hand was a twenty-five year-old psychopath of truly epic proportions, and could only be loved by his mother or his best mates, three of whom were on their way to see him.

Angus was an ex-British Royal Marine, which says it all really, and by day he worked as an armed guard.

Standing six foot one, he was a touch thinner in build than Chris but had an even shorter haircut. Two small scars adorned his face, one on his left cheek and the other over his right eyebrow. All the boys were jealous of his facial war souvenirs.

Angus had been sacked from just about every other club in Perth, but for the Sunset he was perfect. His eyes narrowed slightly and a devious smile that was unnoticeable in the darkened club spread across his face. He'd spotted trouble.

As the three doormen approached the club, Mike and Jason were teasing Grant over the fact that he was one of the very few bouncers who had ever been sacked from the Sunset for excessive violence.

'I heard that you were sacked because you were just too fucking ugly, even for this shithole,' said Mike, making sure he was a safe distance away from Grant, if there was such a thing.

'Fuck off, you pommy arsehole.'

'No, I heard it was because he got beaten up by two girls when he wouldn't let them in,' said Jason.

'Fuck you, pretty boy, you wouldn't have lasted five minutes there, in the dark one of the boys would have mistaken you for a girl and tried to root you in the toilets.'

Mike laughed.

'That's a pretty good reply for such a big bald fuck like you, and what are you laughing at shithead?'

Grant grabbed Jason in a headlock and Mike took his feet. They carried him to the front door of the Sunset

Club, where the head doorman was standing with two other hired assassins.

'Sorry boys, you can't come in dressed like that. Try that dump up the road, what's it called, Davinchi's.'

'We can't,' said Jason as he was placed on his feet, 'we just got thrown out of there. Anyway what's wrong with what we're wearing?'

Jason looked at himself and his two friends who were wearing exactly the same as the Sunset doormen.

'Oh come on, look at you. You look fucking ridiculous.'

Martin, the head doorman, broke into a smile and offered his hand.

'How are you lads? Come on in and have a beer, go and see Gary, he'll fix you up with a bar card.'

The doormen said their hellos and had begun to walk inside when familiar crashing and rumbling noises caused them to back out.

Chris appeared with two guys in a headlock, one under each arm.

'Now listen, idiots, I'm going to let you go, but if you do anything silly I'm going to have to hurt you.'

The two idiots were only seconds away from passing out and were far from doing anything silly. They staggered off down the street.

Angus came out holding a large brawler by the scruff of the neck with an arm up his back. Angus saw his mates standing in front of him. With a sinister smile, he winked at them and promptly thrust the brawler's head against the doorframe, smashing his nose into his face and cutting his eyebrow.

'Watch where you're going, clumsy,' said Angus, and launched his poor victim out of the door.

'Lads!' he exclaimed, happy to see his friends. 'Come on in.'

'So, what was his crime?' Mike said.

Angus looked at them in mock disbelief.

'Didn't you see his hair? It was disgusting, he obviously hasn't washed it in weeks. I'm not having someone like that in my club.'

The doormen laughed and walked up the stairs with Chris and Angus.

It turned out that the greasy haired yobbo had attempted to break a bottle into Angus' face, so all things considered, he got off very lightly with just involuntarily headbutting the doorframe.

'This place amazes me,' shouted Jason into Mike's ear. 'It's like Beirut on a bad night, but there's always heaps of good-looking women here.'

'Beats me,' he replied. 'Fuck me, look at those two.'

Several beers and one brawl later, Mike and Jason left Beirut and headed for Caroline and Rosie's apartment.

When they arrived, the sun was just beginning to rise. The girls were still awake and watching music videos. After a round of hot chocolate, the two couples retired to their respective bedrooms.

Caroline's alarm clock woke Jason at one o'clock that afternoon. He staggered out of the bedroom, not sure whether he was suffering from a lack of sleep or an excess of sex.

'Oi, sleeping beauty,' Jason said, knocking on Rosie's door. 'Get your sorry arse out of bed, we've got to be at the Burswood at two.'

'What time is it now?' croaked Mike.

'Just gone one.'

'Fuck.'

'Exactly.'

Arriving at the grand Burswood Casino, Mike steered his plumber's van round the huge fountain into the hotel's courtyard, and parked outside the red-carpeted entrance where four valet parking dudes were working away like ants.

A doorman dressed in a top hat and tails approached the van as Mike and Jason were getting out.

'Excuse me, gentlemen, service vehicles to the rear please.'

'My good man,' said Mike, in his broad pommy accent, 'can you please get one of the lads to park my vehicle under Slater, Mike Slater?'

Mike slapped ten dollars into the palm of the confused doorman and with a broad smile disappeared into the vast Burswood complex with Jason by his side, trying not to laugh.

Once inside, they followed the signs directing them to the convention centre where the State Body-building Titles were being held.

Grant, Eddie, Angus, Chris and Martin were already at the table. The competition had been in full swing for nearly half an hour, and up on the stage were six heavily muscled females flexing and posing as several judges watched them and wrote down their various scores.

The athletes were judged on muscular density, symmetry, body-fat levels and stage presence.

Mike and Jason greeted their mates and sat down. The plush convention centre was full of body builders, health fanatics and many other people fascinated with the whole scene, and what a scene it was. In that one building were probably ninety per cent of all of Perth's bouncer population, not to mention models in impossibly tight dresses, bodyguards, businessmen, and the obligatory handful of gangsters. In fact, it looked like the entire clientele of Davinchi's Nightclub had been dressed up to the nines and transported over to the casino.

'We haven't missed him have we?' Jason asked.

'No,' said Grant, 'he's not on for about another twenty minutes yet.'

The boys ordered some drinks and settled in for the show.

The table to their right was full of huge body builders who'd done their best to dress up for the occasion. A couple of them had obviously been unable to find suits that fitted and, after giving up, came along wearing tracksuits and T-shirts.

Scattered around the convention centre were about twenty waitresses and ushers, busy serving the tables of what must have seemed to them to be extremely strange people. Every time a new batch of contestants came on stage the crowd would cheer for their favourite while the casino staff would stop and stare, boggle eyed in disbelief at the huge rippling freaks of nature battling it out for muscular supremacy.

Finally, it was time for Steve's line-up; the men's open division, the toughest and most prized category of them all. The standard was very high, especially for a state competition. One by one, the tanned and well-oiled behemoths strutted out onto the stage.

As one competitor strode out into view, the table next to Jason's burst into applause, with shouts of, 'Go, Tommy,' and, 'It's yours, Tommy.'

Tommy was huge.

'Fuck me, he's a big bastard,' said Eddie.

Thick blue veins coursed visibly across every part of Tommy's body, branching out over his bulging forearms and down his thighs. Even his stomach had veins on it.

Steve was the ninth and final contestant to walk onto the stage, and he was greeted with the same enthusiasm as Tommy, but this time by Jason, Mike and the rest of the crew.

Steve was awesome, every bit as lean as Tommy and just as big. His lats looked like wings as he stood on the stage, and his long brown hair cascaded over his massive shoulders making him look more like Conan the Barbarian than ever.

A girl in the crowd whistled in appreciation. It was clear that Tommy and Steve were the hot favourites.

'Boo, no way, give up you big girl, go home,' came from Tommy's table.

'Hey number nine, piss off and get a haircut . . . boo.'

'What the fuck did he just say?' said Mike.

Grant rose from his seat as the booing continued.

'I'm going to tear his fucking arms off.'

Jason reached over the table and grabbed Grant's shoulder.

'No, not here for fuck's sake, just let it go.'

Angus looked at Jason like a pit-bull wanting desperately to be given the order to kill.

'Chill out, Angus,' said Jason.

The six or so body builders on Tommy's table gave the doorman a few dirty looks and continued cheering for their mate as the judging rounds began.

The contestants were instructed to turn to various angles and hit certain poses while the judges compared and marked them.

Throughout the fifteen minutes of judging, the booing and snide remarks continued from the next table.

As soon as the judging rounds had finished the body builders left the stage to prepare for their individual routines which were approximately one and a half minutes long and set to music of their choice.

'I reckon we hang around afterwards and do those cocksuckers,' said Grant with hatred in his voice.

'Look, I'll go and have a word with them,' said Jason, 'just to let them know that Steve's our mate. Leave it to me.'

'Excuse me, gentlemen,' he said politely, 'but Steve, number nine, is actually a mate—'

'Fuck off, blondie, we don't want to hear it,' said one apartment block on legs.

'Listen, we don't want any trouble, we—'

Again, he was cut off, this time by a different monster.

'He said fuck off. Now I suggest you do just that before you get hurt, boy.'

Jason clenched his jaw and ground his teeth. Under any other circumstances he would have been quite happy to accommodate the dickhead in front of him, regardless of his size. However, he gave a half smile, turned and went back to his table as Tommy's mates sniggered and laughed.

'How did it go?' said Mike.

'Fine,' said Jason. 'Just fine, very reasonable, polite guys when you get to know them.'

'They told you to fuck off, didn't they?' said Chris.

The compere announced the first body builder before Jason could answer, and so began the individual routines. Here the contestants would be judged on overall presentation and stage presentation.

Tommy was number seven and was welcomed on stage by his idiotic fan club. His routine was good and he obviously loved performing in front of an audience.

Mike leaned over to Jason.

'This guy's really good, it's a pity he's got such wankers as mates.'

Jason nodded in agreement.

Number eight came and went. Then it was time for the last competitor, Steve.

'Please god, don't let this happen,' Jason said under his breath.

Steve walked on and the goon squad immediately piped up with more insults. He seemed oblivious to the noise, and began his routine as the music pumped out over the crowd. He was awesome.

'Boo, go home with your boyfriends,' shouted the original goon who had told Jason to go forth and multiply.

'Right, that's it,' said Grant as he and Angus rose to their feet.

'Wait, let me handle it,' yelled Jason, above the music.

Jason made his way over to the table once more.

'Excuse me,' he shouted, tapping one giant on the shoulder.

Now Jason was genuinely going to try to reason with the body builder, but as the guy looked up at him with a scowl on his face Jason knew that a confrontation was inevitable.

'Oh fuck it,' said Jason, pulling his arm back slightly, and quick as a flash struck the monster square in the nose with an open palm, smashing it to one side and knocking him clear off his seat.

Just as quickly, Jason spun to his right, where one of the other body builders was lunging towards him. With a snapping left kick, he connected perfectly with the body builder's testicles, bending him over.

Jason followed up with an upper-cut so vicious that one of the giant's teeth landed three tables away in the cleavage of a very lovely young model. Roots an' all.

It was on. The rest of the body builders were diving towards Jason as Mike, Grant, Angus, Chris, Martin and

Eddie began to clamber over chairs and tables to meet them.

Up on stage, Steve could tell that something was going on somewhere in the audience, but the bright lights shining down on him made it impossible to know what or where, so he happily continued flexing and posing his way through the routine, unaware that his six best mates were brawling in with a group of body builders . . . over him.

The lounge resembled a fight scene out of *Braveheart* as the two opposing tables of bouncers and body builders clashed with bone-crunching ferocity. As soon as Jason had de-toothed one of the body builders, another had swung a vicious right hook that caught him flush in his left eye, knocking him back into the table.

Within a few seconds of Jason being punched, Chris had flung himself at the attacker, landing on him a classic grid-iron style hit.

The mound of muscle went flying over several chairs, landing heavily on the floor in a flurry of punches and a medley of other blows.

The next few moments were just a confused mass of arms, legs and the occasional body hitting the deck and promptly getting back up again for more bloodshed.

The host of the competition along with half of the audience watched, horrified, as the mayhem raged on. Steve seemed to be unfazed by the pandemonium in front of him. What the hell, the show must go on as they say.

One of the duty managers in the casino had notified

hotel security over the intercom and now four young, scrawny officers were running through the gaming area towards the convention centre, unsure of why they had been summoned so urgently to a body-building show.

'Maybe someone's lost a ticket or something,' suggested one of the officers as they reached the doors of the centre.

Inside, Angus was pulling one of the steroid heads off Eddie who had received a bloody nose from an elbow.

The four security staff arrived just in time to see Angus headbutt the body builder in the face, cracking his nose bone in two. He then proceeded to plant a blow to his stomach, doubling him up. Then, taking him by the shoulders he drove his left knee hard into his jaw, lifting the huge body momentarily off the ground. The man landed on the floor, bleeding heavily and very much unconscious.

The security staff stood frozen as they watched a dozen of the biggest guys they had ever seen demolishing a large part of the room, not to mention each other. One of the casino staff could actually feel his legs shaking and was wondering if his three mates were just as scared as he was. They were.

Exhausted and battered, the two sides came to a stand-off.

The body builders had given an impressive account of themselves in the fight but had clearly come off second best as two of their party remained unconscious. Not one of them had escaped without being severely bloodied or having a bone or two smashed.

Jason and the boys weren't panting as heavily as the body builders, and were visibly in better condition all round. Even so, they were still going to have several nasty cuts and bruises to show from their clash with the muscle-heads.

Mike looked at Jason as he gasped for air.

'Just another day at the office really.'

Jason smiled.

'Come on, we'd better get the fuck out of here before casino security throw us out,' he said as he nodded towards the four pale trembling security officers.

Battered and bleeding, the six doormen backed off from the body builders who were not heartbroken to see them go.

They left, leaving an entire auditorium of gasping, shocked patrons.

Steve was currently walking off stage, a little perturbed at the lack of applause after what he felt was an admirable performance.

Tommy was waiting backstage when Steve finished. The two competitors shook hands.

'Good luck,' said Tommy, smiling genuinely.

'Yeah and you too mate,' returned Steve, 'what the fuck was going on out the front? I couldn't see anything because of the lights.'

'I don't know. I heard someone say something about a brawl.'

Steve froze.

'A brawl?' He closed his eyes and shook his head. 'Oh no, please no.'

The doormen made their way to the carpark, jumped into their cars and headed off to Mike's place to clean themselves up.

Back at the casino, the compere had announced the three finalists who were now lined up on stage. The crowd, which was back into the show, whistled and cheered in appreciation for the three awesome bodies in front of them. This time, however, there was no booing coming from table number twelve which, along with number eleven, was empty.

The third place announcement was no surprise. This left Steve and Tommy side by side awaiting the decision.

The compere looked at the results sheet in front of him.

'And taking second place in the State Body-building Titles is . . . Tommy Barnes, leaving our winner this evening, for the second year running . . . Steve Smith.'

The crowd cheered for a valiant runner-up and even more so for Steve as he raised his arms in victory.

Receiving his medal and massive trophy, Steve took his place in between Tommy and the third-place winner and the three body builders posed and smiled for the cameras.

When the photos and applause had finished, Steve left the stage with a grateful wave to the audience.

After many congratulatory handshakes and much back slapping, Steve showered, changed and walked out into the crowded auditorium with a five-foot high trophy and a smile.

As he made his way towards table number eleven,

he could see that Jason and the rest of the crew weren't there. When he saw table twelve his smile disappeared.

Three cleaners were wiping down blood from the two tables and attempting to soak up more blood from the carpet. The duty manager approached him.

'Do you know the animals responsible for this?'

Steve looked up at the poor stressed-out manager and was going to say, 'Yes I do, they're my best mates, so fuck you,' but thought better of it.

'No, no way, all my friends are either altar boys or in the church choir.'

He smiled and left a confused casino manager watching the cleaners as they finished mopping up the remains of the battle.

Back at Mike's place the boys had done their own mopping up and after raiding his wardrobe, were sitting in the lounge room drinking coffee and reliving the afternoon's events.

'But listen,' said Eddie, holding an ice-pack to his ever-swelling eye, 'the place is so big, no-one's going to recognise us. We'll go in pairs. The hotel is separate from the casino, so the chances of running into any of the staff from the convention centre are minimal.'

'Yeah, right,' said Mike sarcastically, holding his hand which he suspected might be broken.

'I wonder if the bastard won?' said Chris.

' 'Course he did,' replied Mike, 'anyway, there's one way to find out.'

Mike reached over to the phone with his good hand and called the casino. While he was waiting on hold, the five other doormen were getting impatient waiting for the result. Finally, he got through to someone who had something vaguely to do with the competition.

'Umm . . . yes . . . let me see,' said the someone. 'The winner of that category was um . . . Steve . . . oh I can't read the last name.'

That was enough for Mike. He slammed down the phone and yelled for joy.

'Yes, Stevie-boy won.'

The room erupted in shouts and yahoos as the celebrations began.

'Right, that does it,' shouted Mike over the noise, 'let's get a shit-load of grog, call some dirty women and get the fuck round to Steve's hotel room for the mother of all parties.'

This idea went down well and they began to leave the house.

'Lads, lads,' said Jason, 'let's just make sure that we keep out of trouble, OK?'

The doormen laughed and walked out to the cars.

'I'm serious,' said Jason despairingly, as he followed after them. 'I am.'

Steve was enjoying a glass of champagne with Jo and her friend Simone in his four-hundred-dollar-a-night suite when a knock at the door interrupted their conversation. He wobbled over to answer it. After two months of alcohol abstinence, the glass and a half that he'd already consumed had gone straight to his head. He opened the door to be immediately rushed by six bouncers. They dragged him into the room and threw him onto the bed, spilling his champagne.

'Stevie-boy, what a champion,' said Jason, sitting on his chest while everyone else slapped and pinched him. Steve laughed and struggled until they let him up.

'Well done, fatso, so you kicked arse, eh?' said Chris.

'Yeah mate, and talking of kicking arse, what the fuck happened in the lounge today? People were talking about it all afternoon, someone said it was like World War Three.'

The boys laughed.

'It wasn't us,' said Chris, 'but we heard about it. Bloody hooligans.' He smiled and immediately winced as a nasty cut on his lip opened slightly. Everyone laughed and Steve looked around at his mates, all of whom had similar injuries. He finally looked at Jason.

'Oh, nice black eye mate!'

'Fuck off, you should see the other guy.'

Laughing again they proceeded to pop several bottles of champagne and toasted to Steve's triumph.

'To Conan,' said Jason, as everyone raised their glasses.

'To Conan,' they repeated.

After the third bottle was empty, Jason called Caroline and her two flatmates. They agreed to be at room eight hundred and nine in half an hour. Chris then got on the phone and invited Lynda, his current girlfriend, who was also going to bring two of her friends along.

The room was fully laden with the fattiest, sugariest foods known to man. Crisps, chocolates, cakes, icecream and more assorted lollies than any local corner shop would ever have in stock. Steve was munching his way through everything. He had a family-sized block of chocolate in one hand and a large glass of champagne in the other.

'Hey, Grant!' called Jason, 'I think it's about time we gave Steve his present.'

'Oh shit, I almost forgot.' Grant reached into one of the boxes they'd carried the alcohol in, and pulled out a card and a medium sized package wrapped neatly in gold foil, with a red ribbon tied perfectly around it.

'There's no way any of you peasants wrapped this up,' said Steve, as Grant handed him the package. The peasants voiced their objections.

'Well that's fucking gratitude for you,' Chris said. 'We all put blood, sweat and tears into that present and then you question our handiwork.'

'Sorry, lads. It's very nice.'

Steve carefully removed the ribbon and unwrapped the present. As soon as he saw what was inside a grin spread across his chocolate-marked face.

'You wankers,' he said affectionately.

He held in his hands a box of twelve eggs, all of which had faces drawn on them, along with the names of his best friends written on the shells.

'I boiled them myself,' said Grant.

'Open the card, porky,' added Jason.

Steve opened it.

To the best mate a bunch of blokes could have.
Well done Steve, you kicked arse again.
Now we intend to fill you so full of piss and chocolate that you'll never be able to compete again.
Best wishes, all the boys.

PS. Sorry about Tommy's mates but the wankers deserved it.

Scrawled over the card were all six of his friends' signatures. Steve felt a slight lump in his throat, as one by one, Jason, Eddie, Mike, Angus and Chris shook his hand and gave him a slap on the back. Finally Grant approached him.

'You crazy fucker,' he said. 'It's a good job that Jason and Eddie pulled us apart when they did or I would have put you in hospital for sure.'

'Fuck off would you,' said Steve, laughing.

'Well come on then, mutherfucker, let's go now,' Grant said, with a serious look on his face.

'My pleasure, arsehole,' returned Steve.

The two doormen raised their hands and began moving around each other as boxers do just before punches are thrown.

Jo and Simone looked at the other bouncers in alarm hoping that they would stop what was about to happen, but the boys were all lying on the bed and the floor smiling, drinking and watching Steve and Grant. As if on cue, the two mates launched themselves at each other, but instead of hitting, they stretched out their arms and embraced in a big bear hug, laughing merrily. The rest of the boys laughed along as they'd seen it all before.

'You male macho arseholes,' said Jo, 'you had us worried there for a moment, honestly.'

Steve grabbed Jo with one arm and pulled her towards him, kissing her forehead.

'Do you know what Grant's nickname for you is?' he said, with his other arm still around Grant.

'No, what?'

'Little Miss—'

Grant slapped Steve on the back of his head and Steve laughed.

'I'll tell you later sweetheart.'

Another bottle of champagne was popped just as there was a knock at the door. Eddie answered it to find Rosie, Tammy and Caroline looking as pretty as ever with yet more alcohol in their arms.

'Come in, ladies. Here, let me help you with some of those bottles.'

The girls said their hellos to everyone and each gave Steve a kiss on the cheek.

'So, how did you like your present?' said Caroline, pointing to the box of eggs on the table.

'Just what I've always wanted,' he replied with a grin.

'I wrapped it for you,' said Rosie with a big sexy smile across her face.

'Oh did you now?' Steve looked accusingly at his friends. 'Why doesn't that surprise me?'

Another knock at the door, this time it was Chris' girlfriend and her two giggling accomplices with even more alcohol.

'Fucking hell,' said Eddie, 'we've got more booze here than every bar in Davinchi's put together.'

'Not for long,' shouted Angus, sculling another beer.

Steve had brought a large ghetto-blaster with him which was continually being cranked up and would almost certainly attract noise complaints sooner or later. But what the hell, if that was the only trouble they were to find themselves in that evening they'd be doing well. Almost an hour later the party was in full flight, everyone was dancing and drinking on the balcony and around the room. Jason was dancing with Caroline, and admiring her filthy body. He was pleasantly drunk and pleasantly horny.

Before the night's through, I'm going to fuck her somewhere in the hotel, he thought.

Caroline leaned forwards and spoke into his ear.

'Jason, Tammy's got some Es which she's going to be taking with Rosie soon. I'm supposed to be dropping one as well but . . .' she paused, 'I know how you feel about them so if it really bothers you, I won't do it.'

Jason took a deep breath and sighed, he was actually quite touched that Caroline had asked him.

'Look,' he said softly, 'it's not that I'm a prude when it comes to drugs or anything, fuck, I've done it myself, on more than one occasion. I'm just concerned that you'll take a bad one and hurt yourself. I couldn't handle all that shit again.'

Caroline held him tightly.

'These are fine.'

'Are you sure?'

'Positive,' she replied.

Jason slapped her arse.

'Go on then, only one though.'

Caroline kissed him on the mouth and left him to refill his glass.

'Hey Jase,' said a half-pissed Steve, 'come with me, I've got something to show you.'

Steve led him into the fancy marble bathroom and locked the door. Sitting on the edge of the bath, the drunk State Body-building Champion took out his wallet.

'I know your feelings on that Ecstasy shit, but this is different.'

He pulled out a small, transparent bag a quarter full with a white chalk-like powder.

'You guys bought me twelve eggs and Jo bought me a gram and a half of the finest cocaine that money can buy.'

Jason smiled. 'Well that was very nice of her, how much does that stuff cost?'

'Haven't you ever had coke before?'

Jason shook his head.

'Well, it goes for about two hundred bucks a gram, but Jo gets it cheaper. Her brother's a bit of a dealer. I've only ever had it once before to tell you the truth, about a year ago. It's fucking great stuff.'

Steve took out a five-dollar note.

'Jason, my man, I know you're a total pussy when it comes to drugs, but just this once.' He smiled. 'Let's party.'

Jason looked at Steve and the bag in his hand.

'Are you sure this shit's OK?'

'Firstly,' said Steve, opening the bag, 'it's not shit, as far as coke goes this is the absolute dog's bollocks. Secondly, as far as being "OK" is concerned, you needn't worry,' he winked, 'I've already had some and believe me, it's fine.'

Jason pursed his lips.

'I still don't know.'

'Come on you big girl . . . for me.'

'You're a bad lad, Steve . . . oh what the fuck, let's do it.'

Back out in the bedroom, dance music was blaring and Angus was lying on his back while Grant held a cask of white wine over him and poured it into his open mouth. Once Angus had his fill, Mike immediately took his place as they tried not to spill any during the changeover. This, of course, was impossible and as they'd been playing this game for a while, the end of the bed and the floor below were soaked with wine.

Rosie, Tammy and Caroline had popped their Es and were dancing away on the balcony, waiting for the effects of the drug to kick in. They had several more tablets with them. Rosie was going to give one to Mike after he'd finished playing his silly boy games, and Tammy was probably going to offer one to Grant. As vicious and raw as she'd heard he was, Tammy couldn't help finding his boyish looks and mischievous manner very exciting, and more than a little attractive.

Chris and Eddie were out on the balcony with Lynda and her two friends, Julie and Susan. Eddie had just discovered that Julie and Susan were both barmaids from a club called the Metrodome which he used to work at down in Fremantle. So the conversation was mostly geared around who-knows-who and other facets of the club industry.

Steve tapped out a small amount of the white powder onto the toilet seat, put the bag back into his wallet and took out his Medicare card.

'Good to know they come in handy for something,' he said, and proceeded to use it to crush out any lumps in the cocaine.

'They call this stuff Charlie, don't they?' said Jason as he watched Steve divide the powder into equal halves.

'Yeah,' replied Steve, concentrating on the important task at hand.

'Why?'

'I don't know, shut the fuck up, I'm trying to do this.'

Steve was manoeuvring two piles of 'Charlie' into two thin lines with the Medicare card, each about two and a half inches long.

'Right. Now basically all you do is sniff it up your nose with a rolled-up fiver.'

'Well, you go first and I'll watch, Obi-Wan-Kenobi.'

Obi rolled the note into a tight tube as Jason watched the proceedings with morbid fascination. Leaning over one of the lines, Steve blocked off his left nostril with his left index finger and with his right hand placed one end of the tube just inside his right nostril and the other at the beginning of the powder. With one quick sniff he moved the note halfway up the neat line of coke as it disappeared into his nasal passage. He then swapped sides and repeated the procedure.

When the line was gone he stood up, tilted his head back slightly and gave two little sniffs to ensure that all the expensive dust was inside him.

Jason had been watching intently.

'So, do you feel anything?'

Steve laughed. 'No dickhead, it takes a while to kick in, about fifteen minutes as I recall.'

He handed Jason the note. 'Party time,' Steve said grinning.

Jason bent down to the toilet seat and put the rolled-up bill to his nose.

Jo and Simone were dancing by the bed, giggling and whispering as they drank champagne.

'So you don't mind doing it then?' said Jo.

'Mind! Are you kidding? He's a spunk, it will be a

pleasure. Besides, it won't be the first time we've done it.' The girls giggled.

'Well, if you thought your ex-boyfriend was good, you wait until Steve gets his hands on you.'

'Oh stop, this coke's making me horny enough as it is. To be quite honest,' continued Simone, 'I'm looking forward to fucking you again as well.'

The two girls moved closer together and began kissing as they danced.

'Both together!' exclaimed Jason as Steve handed him some chewing gum.

'Yeah, that's what they reckon. After you bastards have gone they're going to shag the shit out of me, and each other from what I can tell.'

'You lucky, dirty, lucky, lucky bastard. I hate you.'

'Come on,' said Steve laughing, the effects of the coke just beginning to hit. 'A man of your calibre, I'm sure you've had many a threesome.'

'No, never. I've always bloody wanted to, though. I've just never had the chance.'

Jason looked at the gum in his hand. 'Thanks mate, but I don't want one.'

'Keep it bro, you'll need it later.'

'Why?'

'You'll see.'

The two doormen rejoined the party in the darkened room.

'Never had cocaine and never had a threesome, eh?'

Steve said. 'Mate, you have never lived.'

Jason went for two beers just as a warm tingling sensation began to creep slowly over his entire body. He handed Steve his drink.

'Cheers Jase, how do you feel mate?'

Jason looked at Steve, his eyes wide open. 'Un-fucking-believable. It's amazing.'

As Jason spoke, the full effects of the drug swept through him, he felt euphoric, like a king. The warm tingling feeling intensified.

'It's as if I'm getting off on just talking.'

'I know, it's horny isn't it? In about an hour we'll do another line before it starts to wear off.'

Jason realised that he was chewing voraciously on his gum and made an effort to slow down. Caroline came bouncing up and put her arms around his waist, her breasts pushed into his back. He held her hands. It was amazing, all of his senses seemed to be magnified. He turned and held her in his arms. 'Fuck you're beautiful.' Tingles pulsed through his body as he spoke the words. The E that she had taken was working its dangerous magic too, and her eyes were locked into Jason's.

'I think I'm falling in love with you.'

Under normal circumstances those words would have made Jason run a mile. Mind you, under normal circumstances Caroline probably wouldn't have said them. Jason pulled her closer. 'Say that again.'

'I think I'm falling in love with you,' she repeated as she moved her face closer to his.

'Again,' he said softly.

'I think I'm falling—' before she could finish, their lips met and were crushed against each other as they locked into the most passionate, sensuous kiss that either one of them had ever experienced, albeit drug induced.

The party that was raging on in room eight hundred and nine would have looked quite outrageous if anyone not on drugs had walked in; girls kissing girls, big bastards lying on the bed covered in wine and Jason and Caroline semi-raping each other over the mini-bar.

Later on Steve and Jason disappeared briefly into the bathroom, only to reappear several minutes later with silly 'guess what we've just done' looks on their faces.

Steve was now in a corner of the room with two very affectionate girls teasing him with what was in store for him. Mike stood drunkenly up from the bed. 'HALLWAY RUN,' he yelled.

'Yes,' shouted Chris and Grant together. 'HALLWAY RUN.'

Jason tore himself away from Caroline's mouth.

'Oh no, we're doing a run,' he said with a grin.

'What the fuck is a hallway run?' said Eddie.

Steve answered. 'It's something we devised at last year's party. We all have to run from one end of the corridor, right round to the other end of the hotel . . . naked.'

'What?'

The other doormen had already began to remove their clothes amidst shrieks of excitement from the girls.

'Come on, Eddie, get your gear off,' said Angus, 'one goes, we all go. It's the rules.'

Eddie laughed and began unbuttoning his shirt.

'Whose stupid fucking rule was that?' shouted Jason as he took off his pants.

Steve looked up from removing his shoes. 'Yours.'

Within seconds of the run being announced, all seven doormen were stark naked, making their way to the door with hands over their genitals. The girls were laughing uncontrollably as they watched the group of big naked men prepare to leave the room.

'Right,' said Steve, 'as soon as we leave, we turn left, run down to the end of the hallway, touch the wall, then sprint to the far end of this floor, touch the wall there and leg it back here. Ready?'

'Ready,' they all shouted.

He opened the door and the magnificent seven dashed down the hallway while the girls crammed in the doorway trying not to spill their drinks as they watched their boys touch the wall, turn and run back towards them, totally naked on the eighth floor of the five-star hotel. Seven flopping penises slapped wildly against thighs and stomachs as they raced top speed past the hysterical girls who by now were crying with laughter.

'I don't believe what I'm seeing,' screamed Tammy in excitement.

As the seven nudists disappeared out of sight, Caroline looked mischievously at the other girls. 'I've got an idea.'

Steve touched the wall first closely followed by the others. Grant and Angus had already fallen over once as they'd tried to take each other out of the race. They were making such a shocking noise as they thundered down the corridor that they were half expecting to get busted.

Forty yards from their room, Jason could hear a lock being undone somewhere close by. 'Quick, back in the room,' he panted, 'someone's coming out.'

Steve arrived back first with Jason right behind him only to find that the door had been shut and locked.

'What the fuck!'

'Open the fucking door, someone's coming,' shouted Jason.

'Uh uh, what's the password?' came a voice from inside.

'I don't know,' shrieked Steve, as the others arrived. 'Hairy fucking dogs' bollocks for all I know.'

The third door down on their left began to open as the seven butt-naked bouncers hammered desperately against their door. Out from room eight hundred and six stepped a little old lady. The boys froze, and all heads turned towards her. The old lady squinted at them as she put her glasses on. Without flinching an inch, she looked at the somewhat unusual sight in front of her. Slowly, she looked down at the seven sets of genitals and then up to the faces of seven very embarrassed young men. At that precise moment the door opened in front of them, snapping them from their deadlock. The boys were so eager to get back inside that they all rushed in together, the front two tripped and fell heavily as the other five also fell and piled on top of each other.

As the large mess of arms, legs and bums moaned and began to get up, a flash went off as Rosie took a picture, and another, and another.

The little old lady smiled and giggled to herself as she returned to her room.

'I think the old girl fancies you, Grant,' said Mike.

'No mate, she was looking at you, I saw the glint in her eye as she was looking at your nob.'

They all laughed and continued to party.

Jason and Caroline sneaked off to the bathroom, to return twenty minutes later with guilty smiles on their flushed faces.

'And where have you two been?' giggled Rosie.

'Nowhere,' said Jason with a grin.

'You dirty bastards,' Steve said. 'You've been shagging in my bathroom haven't you?'

Jason was about to protest their innocence further when Caroline jumped in.

'Of course we have, we fucked each other stupid in the bathtub.'

Jason looked at her with his mouth open in amazement. 'I can't believe you just said that.'

'Don't play innocent with me,' she said with a wink. 'You love it. Now come and dance with me.'

She dragged him off and they danced and drank.

*

It was nearly three o'clock and Caroline, Mike and Rosie bid their goodbyes, soon to be followed by the rest of the revellers.

After saying his farewells, Steve sat down on the bed with half a glass of champagne. Simone was on his right and Jo went to the bathroom.

'I can't believe that we didn't get into any major trouble tonight, not even a complaint about the noise.'

'Or the nudity,' added Simone, raising her eyebrows.

Jo returned from the bathroom. The main light was out and the room was dimly lit by two lamps on either side of the bed. The music had been turned down to a reasonable level.

Jo sat down next to Steve and kissed him on the cheek and began nibbling his ear. Almost as if on cue, Simone did the same.

'Well, to the victor goes the spoils,' Jo said between nibbles, and Simone giggled.

'So spoil me,' replied Steve.

'We're all yours, what do you want us to do?' crooned Simone.

'I want to lie on the bed and watch you both together for a little while, and then . . . well, whatever goes.'

Jo and Simone stood up as Steve backed onto the bed with his drink. The girls began to kiss and touch, and then slowly started to take each other's tops off, licking and biting as they went. Simone sucked on Jo's large breasts as she undid the back of her short skirt. Steve watched, wide eyed with an almost painful hard-on. The girls were now down to their lacy underwear as they kissed passionately. Simone held Jo's right breast, while Jo had her hand inside Simone's knickers. They paused from their kissing and looked at Steve.

'So what do you think?' said Jo.

'Fucking amazing,' Steve said.

'Now,' said Simone, 'it's your turn.'

SNAP

Jason emerged from his bedroom just after midday and spent the next couple of hours on the phone chasing up prospective leads on Max's whereabouts.

After working for over a year in the nightclub industry, Jason had made some quite interesting and often dangerous contacts. The man he had just spoken to was a DJ from a neighbouring club who had contacts in the dogfighting circuit. The DJ had assured Jason that if his dog was to be used for a fight anywhere in WA then he would hear about it.

Jason also called the many vets and dog pounds he had phoned when Max first went missing, but unfortunately there was still no sign of him.

After making himself a coffee, he sat in front of the TV, looking blankly at the screen, not even aware that he was watching an SBS documentary on eighteenth-century Japanese carpentry. Jason's thoughts were with his missing friend, after a week of searching, he was almost out of ideas.

The phone rang, making him jump. It was Natalie, calling to confirm Wednesday's photo shoot at a quarry about an hour's drive from the city. She told him to bring along a selection of clothes and a towel.

He spent the rest of the day in front of the television, drinking coffee with the phone next to him.

Tuesday was spent much the same way.

He received several phone calls in answer to the ad he'd placed in the paper, but the dogs that the callers had described to him were obviously not Max.

The alarm sounded at 5 am, waking Jason from his restless sleep. Usually he would have just been going to bed at about this time, so his physical time-clock was not too impressed with what it was being put through.

He trudged to the bathroom and looked in the mirror.

'Fuck, I look like shit ... I still can't believe I'm doing this.'

He then showered, shovelled some muesli down his throat and left to meet Natalie.

'Good morning, superstar,' greeted Natalie.

'Hi, how are you?'

Jason looked around her studio. Having never been in one before, the whole set-up fascinated him. Everything seemed so white, the walls, the furniture, even the stereo in the corner was white.

A third of the studio was a lounge area littered with magazines and photos. The middle section was white all over with an enormous roll of paper hanging from the ceiling to the floor. A camera was set up on a tripod in front of it, flanked by what looked like two huge silver umbrellas on tall stands. As Jason was later to discover, these were actually lighting reflectors used to adjust brightness and shine during a photo shoot.

The third part of the studio was a darkroom. It didn't take much figuring out because it had a black and white sign above the door saying so.

Natalie was preparing her equipment for the morning's shoot and Jason was still looking around when the make-up artist arrived. She was introduced to him as Claire. Jason felt comfortable with her immediately. She was a friendly lady in her late thirties with a husband and two children.

'Right, well that's everything,' said Natalie, 'let's load up and we'll get going.'

'So, why do we have to do this so early?' asked Jason as they pulled up to a red light. It was just before six-thirty.

'The lighting is best for this type of work first thing in the morning. Believe me, I'd far rather have a midday start, myself.'

'Which agency are you with, Jason?' asked Claire.

'Agency?' he replied, a puzzled look on his face.

'Modelling agency, silly.'

'Oh . . . I'm not, I've never modelled before.'

'You're kidding,' she said.

Natalie smiled.

'Jason thinks that the modelling industry is a load of wank.'

Jason's eyes widened.

'I didn't mean . . . that . . . well, when I said . . .'

He spluttered for words but found none.

'That's OK,' Natalie said. 'Rosie said that you meant it in the nicest possible way.'

Jason pursed his lips.

'Yeah, well just wait until I see that girl again, I can't believe she told you I said that.'

Natalie and Claire laughed and they proceeded to chat and answer Jason's questions until they reached their destination.

'It looks more like a jungle than a quarry,' he said as they got out of the car.

'It does a bit,' replied Natalie. 'I've never actually been here before. A friend of mine recommended it to me.'

The three gathered up the equipment and made their way along a track which led into the quarry-cum-jungle. It reminded Jason of a Vietnam movie as they made their way through the dense green undergrowth.

Although it was the middle of spring, the mornings were still fairly chilly and this one was no exception. Combined with the fact that they were up in the hills the air had an even colder bite.

'It's bloody freezing,' protested Jason.

'No it's not, don't be such a wuss,' said Claire with a smile.

'It's all right for you, you don't have to get your gear off.'

'Well, if it makes you feel more comfortable, Claire and I will strip off as well for the shoot,' said Natalie.

Jason stopped for a second with a ponderous expression on his face.

'No,' he said seriously. 'I don't think that would be a good idea.'

Natalie looked at him.

'I was only joking.'

They carried on and reached a slow running stream with several pools and small waterfalls dotted around it.

'Oh wow, this is beautiful,' exclaimed Natalie.

'Perfect,' agreed Claire.

Jason was too busy thinking about undressing in the cold to notice the aesthetics of the landscape.

The two girls made camp in a small clearing near the stream. Claire produced a collapsible chair and motioned for Jason to take a seat.

'Now,' she said, 'seeing as you've never done this before, I'm assuming that you have never worn make-up, but then again in this day and age you never know.' Claire smiled cheekily.

Jason laughed.

'No, I'm quite happy to admit that I've never worn any before.'

She removed Jason's hairband and ruffled out his hair, then began to apply a greasy foundation to his face.

'Is it the same stuff that girls wear?'

'No, it's special modelling make-up. It's a lot thicker

than normal, to hide any blemishes. It also has to stop any facial shine.'

'What the hell is facial shine?'

Claire laughed as she began to highlight his eyebrows with what Jason thought looked like a miniature toilet brush.

'Skin is naturally quite reflective, so under some lighting conditions it shines and can come up white and quite glary on the photos.'

Claire finished the eyebrows and began applying a light powder over the top of the foundation.

'So is this stuff expensive?'

'Well, powders and foundation can cost up to eighty or ninety dollars.'

'What, for a box?'

'No,' she said giggling, 'for one of these little compacts.'

'Bullshit!' Jason looked down at her large make-up box, spilling over with compacts, lipsticks and all kinds of objects, completely foreign to the young doorman.

'There must be a small fortune in there.'

'Hmm, tell me about it. Still, I can claim it all on tax.'

She finished the powder and reached for a lipstick.

'You're kidding me, right?'

After Jason had his lipstick applied and eyedrops put in, he was feeling quite ridiculous but nevertheless ready for action.

Natalie had been examining camera angles and lighting throughout Jason's make-up procedures.

'Right,' she said, 'I think what we'll do is have you in jeans and an open shirt to start off with and just take it from there.'

He was already wearing jeans, so he replaced the T-shirt and jacket he had on with a sleeveless blue denim shirt and left it undone.

'Fuck it's cold,' he said stomping his feet and rubbing his hands together.

'Come on, Tarzan, up against the tree.'

'I feel more like bloody Jane with all this make-up on.'

Still protesting, Jason leaned against a tree near the water's edge.

'Lovely,' said Natalie, peering through her camera. 'Now, put your hands in your pockets and look straight into the camera without smiling.'

As Jason followed Natalie's requests, she began merrily snapping away, moving him around, smiling, straight faced, head to the left, right, up, down and so it went on.

'OK, that's got that one,' she said, fifteen minutes later. 'Let's get that shirt off and we'll change locations.'

Jason had no qualms about removing his shirt in front of the girls. After all, he had done it once or twice before, just not in front of a camera. Well not in front of a photographic one, anyway. Jason had a video camera at home that he had used several times before for . . . well almost certainly not what the inventor of the video camera had originally intended.

He was now sitting on a large rock by the stream

in a casual 'just hanging out' type pose. He was beginning to get used to having a lens in his face but he knew that the worst was yet to come.

After completing the shots on the rock, Natalie informed him that it was time to strip down to a pair of black bathers and wade out into the stream.

'What, in there? It's bloody freezing. My testicles have already disappeared.'

The photographer and the make-up artist laughed as Jason edged towards the water and took a step in.

'Oh shit . . . shit.'

'A bit cold is it Jason?' said Claire.

'I can't believe such a big, strong lad like you is afraid of a bit of water,' added Natalie.

Jason ignored them and made his way out until the water was almost up to his knees.

'Right,' he said with a shiver, 'what do you want me to do?'

'Well, you're not going to like me for this, but I want you to get on your hands and knees in the water and crawl towards me, looking into the camera with a sexy expression.'

Jason's face dropped even further than it already was as he looked down at the icy water.

'OK,' he said to himself, 'I can do this shit.' As Jason slowly descended to his knees, he felt the cold water biting into his legs.

'When you're ready,' shouted Natalie.

Taking a deep breath, Jason lowered himself into the stream and began to crawl towards the photographer, who he would have punched in the face when he reached dry land had it been a male.

'Good,' said Natalie, snapping away. 'Come on, sexier, there's a blonde with big boobs on the shore waiting for you . . . yes, good that's it.'

Jason came out of the water shivering.

'Right, once more, but this time I want your hair wet.'

Jason went to protest but decided to save his energy for the crawl back. Instead he muttered under his breath, 'Fucking hell, where's all the glamour? This is bullshit. Why can't we do this in a nice warm studio? Just wait until the weekend, I'm going to beat the shit out of someone for this.'

The girls couldn't quite hear what he was saying, but they got the general idea and were sitting on the bank giggling.

'My god,' said Claire softly, 'he's such a spunk. Where did you find him?'

'One of those friend of a friend things, you know. I think he's got a good chance of winning the Centrefold of the Year if these shots come out OK.'

Claire nodded in agreement just as Jason turned to repeat the longest ten yards in his life.

When he'd finished, Jason stood with a towel wrapped around himself while Natalie changed her film.

'OK kiddo, it's crunch time. Bathers off and up against the rock face, if you will.'

Jason nodded, and after removing his last remaining stitch of clothing, made his way across to the wall with his hands over his genitalia.

'Now listen,' continued Natalie, 'I know that the cold can affect a man's um . . . how can I put it, size.'

'Too bloody right it can.'

'Well there are several tricks of the trade that a lot of male centrefolds use to make themselves . . . respectable.'

Jason looked puzzled. 'Like what?'

'Well . . . you know, like touching yourself, or the windmill technique.'

Jason's eyebrows raised. 'What the hell is that?'

'The windmill technique, you take your willy in your hand and swing it around really quickly. Apparently it forces blood into it.'

For the first time in a long while, Jason blushed, although it was not noticeable under the make-up. As he reached the rock face, he couldn't help thinking, if the boys could see me now. He turned to face Natalie and Claire.

'OK you big spunk, hands away and lean back with your arms up.'

Jason took a deep breath and did as she asked. Natalie tried not to let her jaw physically drop as she looked down at his penis through the camera. Claire didn't care, hers had dropped.

'Bloody hell,' she said.

'What, what's wrong?' said Jason, following her stare down to his groin.

'Nothing,' Claire replied. 'All I can say is that you're

certainly not going to have any problems with the cold.'

Jason smiled and lay back as Natalie clicked away. Surprisingly enough, he felt quite at ease as he posed and flexed naked in front of the two girls. After finishing another roll of film at the rock it was time to hit the water again for some more of the same. By this time Jason was beginning to feel the effects of the cold on his manhood.

'Umm . . . excuse me but before we take these next shots I'm going to have to try that er . . . windmill thing.'

'Go for it,' said Natalie, not the least bit concerned.

Jason turned his back to the girls and took Mr Wriggly in his right hand and swung it around in circles. Blood began to rush into his semi-frozen member and Jason smiled to himself.

'Well I'll be fucked, it works.'

When Jason was happy with his 'appearance', the shoot continued and finished with several shots of him looking up at the morning sun, arms relaxed by his sides.

'Jason, that was one hell of a shoot,' said Natalie, genuinely pleased with the morning's work.

'And considering it's your first one,' added Claire, giving him the thumbs-up.

'Thanks,' Jason said putting on his pants. 'To be quite honest, I actually did enjoy it, even the nude bit wasn't too bad.'

The photographer, make-up artist and 'model' chatted while they packed up and made their way to the car for the drive home, during which Jason lay down in the back and fell asleep.

*

After saying goodbye to his new friends in the modelling industry, Jason set off into the city to buy something that he had always said he would never own—a mobile phone. Up until now he'd never needed one, but the knowledge that he could be missing calls regarding his dog was concerning him more and more. So a mobile it was.

Jason turned off the engine and rested the bike on its stand. As he walked into the showroom, a pretty young sales assistant approached him, leaving another one giggling and pretending to look busy.

'Can I help you, sir?' asked the blond assistant.

'Please, I can't handle all this sir stuff, Jason's fine.'

Following his experience that morning, Jason was in high spirits, after all he had just made two and a half grand.

'OK, how can I help you . . . Jason?'

'Right, I'm after a pair of black jeans, loose fitting, and maybe a belt to match,' he replied with a straight face. The assistant stared at him, unsure of whether he was serious or not.

'Er, this is a mobile phone shop, sir, I mean Jason. We don't sell pants.'

Jason broke out into a cheeky smile.

'Oh, so it is. All right, I'll take a phone then.' The assistant smiled back, realising she'd been had.

'You're a cheeky one. What sort of phone are you after?'

Jason looked around at the many display cabinets in the shop filled with hundreds of phones.

'Buggered if I know, it doesn't have to be a real flashy one. I'll probably lose it or drop it or something after a couple of weeks.'

'Well, what are you going to be using it for, business or social calls.'

'Er, that's a difficult one to answer, business I guess . . . sort of.'

The sales assistant showed Jason a few phones and after choosing one for him they sat down to fill out the paperwork. She took down his name, age and address and then asked Jason his occupation.

'Well I—'

'Let me guess, you're a model aren't you?'

Jason looked down at the table with a furrowed brow and then back to the sales assistant.

'I . . . I don't know.' The shocking realisation hit him that after this morning's photo shoot. Technically, he could now be referred to as a model. The girl gave him a puzzled look. Jason decided to go with it as model sounded decidedly better than bouncer.

'Yes, sorry, I do a few different things, but put down model, that's fine.'

She smiled and continued with the many forms and ID checks. Jason eventually left the shop with a new phone along with the shop assistant's name and number.

He returned home and promptly called everyone associated with finding Max and gave them his new mobile number.

'Fucking hell, a modelling photo shoot and a mobile phone, all in one day, what a total yuppie.'

Jason's home phone rang an hour later. It was Caroline.

'How's my gorgeous centrefold then?'

'Yeah, yeah, very funny.'

'What?'

'Just don't tell anyone about it, OK. I don't want the boys to find out.'

Caroline laughed.

'Jason, how long do you think you can keep it a secret? It's a national magazine, it'll be huge.'

'Oh my god,' he said slowly, 'I'll never hear the last of it. I'll have to leave Perth.'

'Don't be silly, everything will be fine. Look, I called to invite you to a party tomorrow night at a friend's house. It's a hot penthouse, overlooking the river, how about it?'

'Can I bring Mike and Steve?'

'Of course, bring whoever you want. I think Rosie's already invited Mike, anyway.'

Later that afternoon, the effects of the early morning start had begun to catch up with him and Jason was now half asleep in front of the TV when a loud trill made him jump.

'What the fuck . . .' It was his new mobile, ringing for the first time. It sounded again, loudly.

'Christ, there's no missing that,' he opened the flip and answered the phone.

'Hey you yuppie bastard, it's Steve. Any luck with Max yet?'

'No mate. You're actually the first person to call me on this thing. How the fuck did you get my number?'

'I just spoke to Mike.'

'Fair enough, so are you in for a party tomorrow night?'

'Mate, I'm still recovering from being bashed around the bedroom by two hormone-crazed nymphettes.'

'So what are you saying, you're not coming?'

'Don't be fucking silly, going to parties with you is what I'm going to write a book about one day, *Parties I Have Been to with a Bastard Called Jason* by Stephen Smith.'

Jason laughed. 'You wanker. Well listen, how are we going to get there, I don't want to take the bike and I'm sure you don't want to drive, and I know one hundred per cent that Mike won't want to either.'

'No worries, I'll get Jo to drop us off.'

'Won't she be pissed-off that you're going to a party without her?'

'Mate, after my performance on Saturday night she's my slave forever.'

'Hah, you wish. All right then, Studley, you get your Oscar-winning penis round here at about eight o'clock and we'll have a couple of beers before we go and check out the party.'

'Cool, see you tomorrow night.'

Thursday evening, Steve and Mike arrived at Jason's place within minutes of each other. The three boys sat around the kitchen table, each with a beer.

'Here you go,' said Mike, reaching in to his pocket, 'try one of these.'

'Cigars!' exclaimed Jason. 'Since when have you smoked cigars, James Bond?'

'I have the odd one, now and again, these are soaked in port, fucking delicious.'

Mike handed out the cigars and they lit them up.

'Do you inhale them like pot?' said Steve, an avid marijuana smoker.

'Yeah, of course you do,' said Mike winking at Jason.

Steve inhaled on the cigar and immediately lurched forwards coughing and choking as the other two roared with laughter.

'Oh fuck . . . shit, my lungs are on fire, you bastards.'

'Here mate, have another beer,' said Mike.

Steve took the beer and after coughing once more, punched Mike in the arm so hard he almost knocked him off his chair.

'Right, listen up,' announced Jason. 'Tonight, we don't get into any trouble whatsoever. Steve, no bashing up girls and Mike, well, everything you do is bad, so for god's sake, behave yourself.

'Fuck off, what about you, you're a trouble magnet.'

'All right, all right, let's just say that whenever we go out together something always goes wrong.'

'Or right,' said Steve. 'It just depends on how you look at it, really.'

'Whatever, but for tonight, let's try really, really hard to keep a low-profile—agreed?'

'Agreed,' repeated the two doormen.

Jo arrived at nine o'clock and found three half-drunk lunatics singing old Righteous Brothers' songs in a smoke-filled room.

They reached the soulful climax of 'You've Lost That Lovin' Feeling', each one of their voices sounding very much like a pig with its testicles caught in a barn door. When they could hold the note no longer, they rolled around in their seats laughing like schoolkids.

Jo broke out into thunderous applause and whistles, albeit with totally sarcastic intentions.

The boys thanked their screaming fan.

'Well, come on then you three, I'm tired and need to get some sleep, especially if you're expecting me to come and get you at some ridiculous time in the morning.'

The lads each grabbed an armful of beer and set off for the party in South Perth.

'Fuck me, how many Porsches are parked along this road?'

Jo pulled her Civic up alongside a white 911 Turbo and the Righteous Brothers piled out. Up and down the street were parked about a dozen expensive European sports cars. Mike whistled as he looked at a low black BMW.

'Whose fucking party is this, Rupert Murdoch's?'

'It's some hotshot stockbroker, an ex-boyfriend of Caroline's apparently,' Jason replied.

'Oh great,' said Mike, 'everyone else has probably brought two hundred-dollar bottles of Dom Perignon and we rock up with forty bucks worth of Toohey's Red.'

'Don't sweat it, brother, we can mix it with the best of them,' Jason said.

'Yeah, that's exactly what I'm worried about.'

As the three friends approached the penthouse, they found it pretty hard not to be impressed.

'Fuck me, look at this place,' said Steve, 'it's like something off "Miami Vice".'

Mike pushed the intercom button. 'This chick dumped him for you, she must be mad.'

Jason laughed. 'Fuck you both, anyway he's available now, so one of you fags can have him.'

The intercom was answered and the Righteous Brothers walked up to Don Johnson's three-level penthouse, attempting to trip each other up as they went. The door was opened by Caroline and Rosie with champagne in their hands.

'Hi boys,' said Caroline. 'Late again, well what a surprise, come on in.'

'See, I told you,' whispered Mike into Jason's ear as he nodded towards the champagne.

Caroline led them through a long, white corridor scattered with people drinking and talking. The kitchen was a hive of activity, as kitchens at parties always are, and standing next to the fridge was Caroline's ex-boyfriend, the stockbroker, and several of his friends.

'Andrew,' said Caroline, taking him by the arm, 'this is Jason, Steve and Mike.'

'Hi guys, Caroline's told me heaps about you.' Andrew shook hands with the three doormen.

'Uh oh,' said Mike, 'well don't believe all of what

you hear, Andrew, because most of it's probably true.'

Andrew laughed. 'Here, put your drinks in the fridge.' He motioned to one of two fridges that each looked as big as Mike's van.

'Yeah,' said Mike, 'the bastards at the bottle shop had run out of Dom so we had to settle for Chateau Tooheys instead.'

The vibes were pleasant and friendly and Andrew seemed to be a genuinely nice guy. He was about six foot tall with short fair hair and a pair of Clark Kent glasses.

The boys left Caroline in the kitchen socialising with Andrew and a shifty looking character in a pair of disgusting green jeans.

'I hate him,' Steve said as they walked into the multi-level lounge room.

'The mutherfucker's rich, good-looking and a really nice guy as well.'

'Yeah, too nice,' said Mike. 'It's guys like Andrew who get chewed up, spat out and walked all over by the kind of girls that we go out with.'

Jason stopped and turned to Mike, a philosophical look on his face. 'So you're saying that . . . being a cold, heartless mutherfucker who only cares about himself and his mates and will be unfaithful at the drop of a hat is . . . . a good thing to be,' Jason said.

'I couldn't have put it better myself.'

'Hmm, now that's an interesting concept.'

'Who's the dweeb in the puke green pants that Caroline was talking to?' Steve asked.

'Don't know, don't care,' Jason replied.

'He's a cop,' Mike said, 'I think he's a detective or something. I've seen him around, he's a real prick.'

'Yeah? A cop that's a prick, now there's a surprise.'

The three philosophers moved through the crowded room to a huge balcony and continued discussing the meaning of life with the spectacular view of the Perth skyline behind them.

The party crowd resembled a scene from 'Melrose Place'. Everyone was very well dressed, with not a hair out of place and had that unmistakable aura that indicated an abundance of money.

'Oh yes, check out those three.' Mike nodded towards a group of girls, obviously models, who were trying their hardest to ignore everyone else as they chatted amongst themselves, creating their own little world which no-one else was good-looking enough to be a part of.

'Fucking wankers,' said Jason. 'It's idiots like them who turn me right off the modelling industry.'

'Well, that's something you'll never have to worry about, you ugly twat. Anyway, how do you know they're not talking about jumping our bones.'

'OK, watch this.' Jason approached the girls.

'Excuse me, ladies.'

The three ladies finished their important discussion about what a pretentious bitch Jasmine was before they even acknowledged Jason's existence. They looked him up and down, stopping to stare disapprovingly at the beer in his hand but said nothing.

'I was wondering if you would like to come for a drink and a chat with my friends and me.'

The model nearest to him gave a condescending little chuckle and waved Jason off with a single 'no', then turned back to her friends and the three spent the next half an hour writing him off. Jason had just demonstrated to his mates a perfectly executed 'models' snub' and stood there picturing himself picking all three of them up together and dropping them off the balcony. He returned to his friends with a 'told you so' smile on his face.

'You just had to prove a point didn't you, you wanker,' said Mike.

Steve cut in. 'Hey that's not you-know-who, is it?'

The other two turned to see two guys in black jackets and ponytails, talking secretively to a slightly taller guy with short, light brown hair and horrid green jeans.

'No,' Mike said. 'It's two of his boys, though. I recognise them from the Leedervale.'

Caroline bounced over with Rosie and Tammy.

'And who are you boys perving at?'

'Nobody,' said Jason, smiling. 'Come here and give me a big sloppy tonguie.'

The party raged on and an hour later the boys and girls were up on the top floor in a large games room with a pool table and bar. Andrew and some of his many friends were with them, chatting and playing pool.

'Fucking hell,' said Mike. 'I think we have actually found a party where we're going to stay out of trouble.'

'I think you could be right, mate,' Steve said.

Jason and Mike had just let Andrew and his friend win another game of pool when Caroline slinked up to Jason, making sure he felt her breasts on his arm. He looked at her suspiciously. 'Oh yes, and what do you want?'

'How do you know I want anything, I could just be showing you affection.'

'Yes and that's very nice, now what do you want?'

'Look, you're probably going to spit the dummy, but the girls and I have been offered some Es for nothing.'

Jason looked at her in disbelief. 'Caroline, you did Es what, four fucking days ago, on Sunday.'

'Oh I know, but the guy who's got them is a cop so they'd be OK.'

'What! A cop pushing Es, it's that mutherfucker in the green jeans isn't it?'

'It doesn't matter, I won't do it.'

'Look,' said Jason, softening his tone, 'I'm no control freak. It's not up to me what you do, I just worry because . . . I care about you.'

'I know,' said Caroline as she kissed him softly on the mouth, 'and I love it.'

Caroline thanked the cop but politely declined his offer of free Es. However, he insisted and dropped them into her hand, telling her that she could take them another time.

'Well, just because you're playing the good housewife doesn't meant that we can't take them,' said Rosie when Caroline had explained what was going on.

'You bitch, you're not taking them without me, wait until next weekend and we'll do them together.'

'I agree,' said Tammy. 'It's no fun unless we're all in.'

Rose sighed. 'OK, you win, I'll wait. I just hope that Jason appreciates what you're doing for him. He'll have you dressed as a nun and singing in the choir next.'

Caroline laughed. 'Well, I don't know about the choir but the nun's costume has possibilities.'

A little later, spirits were high. The girls, having aborted their plans to drop an Ecstasy, had gone for the next best thing and were now happily drunk.

Jason and Steve were walking down the stairs to the bathroom when they came across the cop in the green jeans, shoving money into his pocket and handing a small packet of coke to a young man in a suit. Two other men were at the bottom of the stairs trying their hardest not to look like off-duty cops selling drugs, but failing miserably. Jason pushed roughly past the cop.

'Hey, watch what you're doing, mate,' he snapped.

'Fuck you, cop or not, I'll stick that shit so far up your arse you won't be able to walk for a month.'

The cop and his sidekicks below straightened up and looked at Jason aggressively, shocked at his remark.

'Whoa, sorry guys,' said Steve. 'He's afflicted,' he continued, pointing to Jason's head, 'a loony, just ignore him.' He bundled Jason off into the bathroom.

'What the fuck is wrong with you, have you taken too many hits to the head or something?'

'They're cops, selling shit to people, doesn't that bother you?'

'Of course it does, but mate, you can't wage a war

against everyone who sells drugs, especially the cops who do it. You'll just get yourself deeper in the shit than you usually are, and us with you because we'll have to back you up.'

'I know, mate, you're right.'

'Come on, let's have a piss and we'll go into the lounge and have a beer.'

Mike joined them while Caroline and Rosie remained upstairs playing pool. With another fresh beer each they joined in the dancing in the crowded lounge room. There were gorgeous girls everywhere and two very young ones began to dance and flirt with the three boys.

'So what do you do?' shouted a particularly stunning brunette to Jason.

'I'm a behavioural modification officer.'

'Oh wow, that sounds interesting. Is that like working with naughty children?'

Jason smiled. 'Yes, you could say that. How old are you?'

'Why?'

'Just curious.'

'Eighteen,' lied the sixteen year old. 'What about you?'

'Forty-two,' replied Jason.

The girl laughed. 'Bullshit!'

'I'm serious,' he said winking. 'There's a lot to be said for plastic surgery.'

The girl stared at him, unsure of whether to believe him or not. Jason continued to dance but the young girl stopped. She reached forwards and grabbed Jason's arms, digging her fingernails viciously into his flesh.

'Ow shit, what the hell are you doing?'

She stared blankly through him, with her eyes wide open and blazing. Jason could feel her swaying unsteadily as three of her fingernails snapped under the pressure on his arm.

'Christ, are you OK?'

The girl's mouth opened and a large stream of saliva ran out down her chin and onto the floor just as she began to shake uncontrollably.

'Kristy, what's wrong?' her friend cried out.

She sank to her knees, unable to answer. If Jason hadn't been holding onto her shoulders she would have fallen down altogether.

'Oh my god,' yelled her friend. 'Kristy.'

The girl was shaking with frightening intensity.

'Lay her down,' said Mike. 'It looks like she's having a fit or something.'

Amidst the screams in the background, Jason called for someone to ring an ambulance. Kristy, unfortunately, wasn't having a fit. She was suffering from a massive chemical reaction caused by one of the many toxic ingredients in the Ecstasy tablet she had taken not half an hour earlier. As she lay convulsing on the floor in front of a room full of horrified partygoers, she went into the later stages of a total neurological shutdown. Her brain was, in effect, frying itself.

Jason was on his knees next to Kristy as her movements began to slow down. Caroline and Rosie arrived just as she stopped moving altogether.

'Caroline,' yelled Jason, over the still thumping music, 'you know first aid, what the fuck's wrong with her?'

Caroline felt for Kristy's pulse rate. There was none. She then put her ear to the young girl's chest but could hear no heartbeat. Tilting her head back in textbook CPR, Caroline began administering several short breaths into the girl's saliva-covered mouth, followed by several compressions to her chest.

'Has she taken anything?' she screamed. The girl's head slumped to one side. 'Hold her head back, Jason.'

'She had an E that's all, just one,' blurted Kristy's friend.

Through her tears, Caroline proceeded to administer CPR for nearly ten minutes while Jason held Kristy's head. Completely exhausted, Caroline fell back onto her heels and began to cry freely. Jason looked at her, and then down at the white face of the young, dead girl whose head he still held in his hands.

Whispers surged around the room and several girls sat and wept over the distressing scene they had just witnessed. Kristy's friend erupted in a fit of rage as she flung herself at a man standing at the back of the crowd.

'You bastard, you fucking bastard, it's your fault.'

Another guy grabbed her and held her tightly. 'It's OK, Belinda, it's OK.'

With his jaw clenched tightly and his eyes swelling, Jason slowly looked up to see a pair of green jeans behind several other people. The cop stood, staring down at him, flanked by his two cop mates. Jason carefully placed Kristy's head on the floor and rose to his feet, not taking his eyes from the cop's. He stepped towards them, followed closely by Mike and Steve.

'Listen arsehole,' said the one in the green pants, his voice shaking, 'we're police officers, back off.'

Jason continued towards the retreating officer until the man's back hit the wall.

'I'm warning you, mate, you touch me, and you'll be in big fucking trouble.'

Jason looked into his eyes with a coldness that made the cop swallow hard.

'I'm always in big fucking trouble,' said Jason, and drove his head into the cop's nose, sandwiching his head against the wall with such force that the cop's skull cracked slightly and his legs buckled. Jason grabbed his shirt, not allowing him to fall down. The other cops made a grab for Jason but were intercepted by Mike and Steve.

The cop's nose had split open almost an inch, with the bone momentarily visible before blood engorged the area. Dazed and bleeding, he raised his hands to his face, leaving his mid-section open. Jason planted his right fist into the cop's ribs, doubling him over, then Jason promptly pushed him back up against the wall and punched again, feeling at least two of the ribs snap beneath his fist.

The other two cops fought with Mike and Steve, but weren't faring much better than their counterpart who was now trying desperately to cover up from Jason's numerous blows. Finally, Jason took the cop by the hair, allowing him to sink to his knees, but he kept his head up.

'Swallow this, mutherfucker.'

The police officer was too dazed to see the knee raise swiftly up towards his unprotected jaw and smash it sharply to the right. His head whiplashed violently, knocking him out instantly. Jason let go of his hair and watched him fall to the ground. He then stood, panting heavily over the cop's motionless form.

'I think it's time we left, amigo,' said Mike.

Jason looked back at Caroline sitting on the floor next to the lifeless body that, not twenty minutes ago, had been a young happy girl dancing with him at a party.

'But what about—'

Mike cut him off. 'Mate, there's nothing we can do. Come on, no matter what happens now we've just fucked up three cops, it's time to leave.'

Mike and Steve ushered Jason towards the door. They left the apartment in silence. The music had been turned off during the brawl and now the front room was a macabre spectacle of many motionless people not knowing what to say, do or even think as they stood around staring at each other, the beaten cops, and the poor girl lying in front of them . . . dead.

The three doormen hailed a cab, and as they drove off, an ambulance pulled up outside the apartment building.

SLAMMER

Jason had spent the whole of Friday staring blankly at the TV screen, half expecting a knock at the door from the police, but it never came. Just before eight o'clock Mike called.

'How are you doing, mate?'

'Oh you know, still a bit freaked out about the whole thing. I can't believe we haven't heard from the cops.'

'Yeah well, I wouldn't count our blessings just yet, it's still early days. The fuckers are probably just biding their time. I can't imagine they'll let us get away with hammering the shit out of three of them, even under the circumstances.'

'You never know, they might want to keep it quiet.'

'Who knows.'

The two friends talked some more, then finished when Caroline arrived. She had brought around some pizza and soft drink which they had in front of the TV. Caroline told Jason that the ambulance crew had taken

Kristy away, leaving one of them behind to tend to the injured cops. Soon after that, the penthouse had been descended upon by an army of police who took statements from everybody. Apparently when the question had been raised about the cops' attackers, no-one had given an accurate description of the three boys, let alone named them. Several of the partygoers had stated that the cops deserved it, after all they were the ones who were selling the drugs in the first place.

'Mind you,' said Jason, 'no-one there knew us, anyway.'

'You'd be surprised. I had several people comment to me that you were the bouncers from Davinchi's. You just did what everyone else wanted to do, so I don't think that anyone is going to dob you in.'

'Hmm, we'll see.'

That night, spirits were low but the three doormen were glad to be in the bustling club environment where they could lose their thoughts in amongst the crowds. Mike and Steve, although greatly saddened by the death of the teenager, weren't affected as deeply as Jason who had held the girl in his arms right up until the moment she died. He now roamed the upstairs bar, not bothering to stop and chat to the regulars as he usually did, nor did he notice the two brunettes who were trying to flirt with him as he passed by. At the end of the night, Mike and Steve stayed behind for a staff beer but Jason returned home for some much needed sleep.

*

Just before midday on Sunday, he was woken by his mobile with another call about his lost bull-terrier.

'Yeah he's pretty big, mate, with a black eye patch,' said the informant, in a broad Australian accent.

'But I mean big, Max is massive and really clumsy,' Jason said.

'Aren't they all?' the man laughed. 'But listen, I think this dog could be yours, fair go he's a big bastard all right, come round and take a gander.'

Jason hurriedly took down the caller's name and address and flew out of the house. He had a feeling that unfortunately this wasn't Max, however it was the most encouraging lead so far. Jason had received all kinds of crack-pot phone calls from people claiming that they had his dog. He'd even had one call from an old lady who had found a white cat with black markings, but the old dear didn't know that a bull-terrier was a dog. So the fact that he was on his way to meet some dude called Darren in a suburb not ten minutes away to see a big white bully was at least a step in the right direction.

When Jason arrived at Darren's place, he was greeted with a strong Aussie handshake and a 'G'day mate'. But Darren and his girlfriend Tanya's friendliness could hardly make up for the disappointment of seeing a dog that was definitely not Max chewing on a bone in their backyard.

'So that's not him, eh mate?' said Darren.

'No, I wish it was but . . . no, Max is another seven or eight kilos heavier than this one.'

'Struth, that is big. Well, would you like a beer or something while you're here?'

'No thanks, Darren, I'll be off, mate, thanks anyway.'

Jason said his goodbyes trying not to show his true feelings which were bordering on despair.

After waving farewell to the amiable couple, he roared off up the road at a dangerously fast speed.

Several other people called that afternoon in response to his ad but to no avail. Caroline also rang to see how he was faring and they talked for almost half an hour. Jason appreciated the call and her genuine compassion touched him. They agreed to meet for a drink later that night at the Leedervale Hotel.

Now, to set the scene of the Leedervale Hotel on a Sunday night is a difficult task, several words spring to mind—mayhem, packed, chaotic, and very, very loud, to name but a few. Also, the Leedervale is huge. As its popularity grew, dance floors, podiums and extra bars were built to cope with the ever-increasing number of people. Now, the place hardly resembled a hotel at all, but a vast maze of bars all packed shoulder to shoulder with off-duty nightclub workers, models, local Perth identities and the odd scattering of gangsters here and there. The gangsters were impossible to miss with their black clothes, ponytails and suspicious eyes, glancing around darkly at everyone near them.

Three go-go dancers were cutting sick on the roof of the bar—one lean black dude and two young girls wearing bike pants, bras and not much else.

'Fuck me, this place gets more and more like a rave party every week,' shouted Mike.

'No shit,' yelled Grant, 'but there's more dirty women here than you can poke your todger at.'

The boys moved further into the hotel-cum-rave, acknowledging several of the doormen who worked there, most of whom they knew from one club or another.

Just hoping to bump into someone at the Leedervale was an impossibility. So the three doormen had arranged to meet their friends at a bar in the courtyard. As they approached it, with Grant leading, as people always made an attempt to get out of his way, Jason saw a familiar flash of black hair and tanned, athletic flesh. A double take confirmed that they belonged to the vision that he'd dribbled over at the Brookside Bar, the gangster's girlfriend.

'Mike, Mike.'

'What?'

'That girl's here.'

'Which girl?'

'That girl from the Brookside.'

'Yeah and so is Macey, I saw him over at the front bar with his army. Do us all a favour and keep the fuck away from her.'

'Well, you're no fun.'

The boys finally emerged from the throng of people and arrived at the bar, where they were greeted by Steve and Jo. Caroline, Rosie and Tammy were also there, being chatted up by a couple of hopeful young lads.

Once Caroline saw the boys, however, the young hopefuls were swiftly dismissed and the group of friends ordered drinks and settled in for a good session of drinking and chatting.

Occasionally a friend of someone in the group would come and say hello and have a quick drink before cruising off into the impossibly busy courtyard.

'Still no luck with Max?' yelled Caroline.

Jason had just begun to feel the numbing effects of the alcohol relax his aching body, but the mention of his missing dog bit into him and made him stiffen slightly.

'No, but I'll find him,' he replied dismissively.

Caroline sensed his unwillingness to talk about it and changed the subject to that of another drink. Jason readily agreed and more beers were consumed. The events of the past couple of weeks had begun to weigh heavily on the young doorman: the brawl at the casino, Max's disappearance, his approaching centrefold and of course the death of the young girl only several days ago. On his seventh beer now, Jason was as relaxed as he could be under the circumstances. The pleasant feeling of being nicely drunk and amongst good friends was exactly what he needed at this point in time.

The four girls were chatting amongst themselves and the boys were doing the same. Grant was sipping on a bottle of water as he was still on his course of antibiotics, although the yearning for a beer with his mates was growing ever stronger.

Just as another 'war story' was about to unfold, Steve, Mike and Grant simultaneously looked past Jason at someone behind him, then he felt a tap on his shoulder. If there had been a guy behind about to clock him, the boys would have done something by now, so Jason figured it was OK to turn around slowly, rather than spin quickly with a hand drawn back in a fist ready to hammer the person tapping on his shoulder. He turned, and was pleasantly surprised to be greeted by the 'cover of *Vogue* smile' he had seen a couple of weeks ago at the Brookside Bar. He felt his heartbeat quicken.

'Hi, I'm Jane, I wanted to come and say hello properly.'

'I'm glad you did,' replied Jason with his trademark smile, 'my name's Jason and these are my fellow church-going friends, Michael, Grant and Stephen.'

The three 'Christians' introduced themselves very politely to Jane and her scantily clad friend Kim.

'So, you all met at church did you? That's very sweet,' said Jane with a look that said, 'What a load of bullshit, but let's hear it anyway.'

'Well, my father is actually a priest, which I'm a little bit embarrassed to admit. Michael and Stephen are altar boys and Grant here is in the choir.'

'Oh right, a bit of a singer is he?' said Jane, standing close to Jason to hear him over the music.

He felt her hot breath as her lips brushed against his ear-lobe, and a chill went down his back.

'Definitely,' he replied, looking into her dark brown eyes. 'This boy could sing the birds out of the trees.'

'And I bet you could charm them out,' she said.

Behind them, the girls had noticed Jane and Kim talking to the four boys. As much as she tried, Caroline couldn't help stealing occasional glances at Jason and the girl he was talking to. Admittedly she was very attractive. Too bloody attractive, thought Caroline as pangs of jealousy and a little sadness dug into her. She ordered another drink.

Jason kept up with the bullshit for a little while longer then the conversation turned to work, hobbies, taste in music, etc. It turned out that Jane kept herself busy designing furniture, interior decorating and a healthy modelling career. As much as he was enjoying talking to her, and as much as the alcohol was giving him that 'don't give a fuck attitude', Jason couldn't chase the nagging thought from his mind that he was chatting up the girlfriend of WA's nastiest criminal.

After talking for over twenty minutes, Jane told him that she had to get back to her friends.

'OK, where are you going to be? I'll come and find you later on.'

'Probably not a good idea, where are you going after this place shuts?'

'Wherever,' Jason said. 'We're just going with the flow.'

'Well, this place shuts at nine and I've got to take Kim home, can you meet me back here in the carpark at, say, ten?'

Jason smiled and was just about to reply when all shit broke loose not five yards away from where they were standing. Five or six lads had begun brawling over a spilt drink and were now intent on killing each other. Grant, the large choirboy, took a step towards the fighting, but Mike and Jason each put a hand on his shoulders.

'Whoa big guy, we're off duty, let their boys handle it,' shouted Jason.

Grant stopped.

'Those fuckers are pretty much going for it, let's bash them just for the hell of it.'

'If their boys are in any difficulties it will be my pleasure to jump in, but for now, let's just chill out.'

The Leedervale's adequate security arrived quickly and after a scrappy round of grabbing, dragging and the odd punch in the mouth here and there, they managed to get all six of them into the carpark. Outside, the six lads continued pushing and shoving until they gave up and left to have more beers somewhere else.

Jason turned back to Jane to agree to her suggestion but she and Kim had disappeared into the crowd.

Caroline hadn't been the only one watching Jason and Jane as they'd chatted and flirted. A heavy-set guy with a ponytail and a black leather jacket had also watched with interest and was now finishing his report into the ear of his employer at the front bar. James Macey leaned against the bar, he wore a full-length black coat over a black T-shirt, black pants, and, of course, black shoes, along with his trademark ponytail. This man was someone not to fuck with. Standing next to him was another sinister looking character, Greco.

Greco was Macey's live-in, right-hand man and very rarely left his side. The two gangsters looked as if they had come from the same mould, although Greco was slightly bigger and seemed to wear a permanent frown on his face. He had served several short jail terms for the odd violent crime (as had most of Macey's boys) and was rumoured to have carried out a number of hits over East in which five people had died. It had actually been only two, but Greco was quite happy to let the rumours bump up his numbers.

'OK,' Macey said in his husky, monotone voice, 'find out who he is and watch Jane until she goes home, then call me.'

The sidekick nodded and slunk away. Macey drained his whisky and it was quickly replaced with another.

'Everything OK?' said Greco.

'Just some cocksucker talking to Jane, apparently he's a bouncer from Davinchi's.'

Greco smiled. He liked bashing bouncers, they were always good sport.

'Having a good night?' said Jane as she approached Macey.

'Always,' he replied, and smiled at her. 'A white wine,' he said to the barmaid, without looking at her.

When he smiled, the corners of his mouth were only slightly raised and never developed into a full 'lips apart' type grin. Whether Macey was greeting an old family friend or watching one of his employees sink a knife into a victim's guts, his smile always remained the same. Jane's wine arrived and Macey handed it to her.

'Thanks.'

'My pleasure.' Macey raised his glass, 'A toast.'

'What are we toasting?'

'Us,' he replied.

As they clinked glasses, Macey winked at Jane, and another ponytailed sidekick walked up and whispered into his ear.

Jason leaned up against an old, white F-100 truck. It was quarter past ten.

When the hotel had closed, his group had gone on to the Sunset Club, then, after making the excuse of being tired, he had left for a coffee to kill some time until ten.

He'd been waiting for almost half an hour now and his conscience was working overtime.

'You dirty, cheating, lying bastard. What about Caroline?'

'Oh leave me alone, she's not my girlfriend . . . not officially, anyway.'

'Well, that's not the impression you've given her, is it? She thinks that you're being faithful to her, the poor misguided child.'

'Oh fuck off, I'm only meeting Jane for a chat.'

'For what? You lying piece of shit, why are you hiding in a darkened carpark then and why did you bullshit to your friends?'

'I'm not hiding, you tosser.'

'Wanker.'

'Prick.'

'Fuck it,' he said under his breath, 'she's not going to show.'

Just as Jason was checking his watch for the fifth 'last time', a car pulled in and drove slowly towards him, stopping next to the truck. The window of the blue sedan buzzed down and Jane looked up at him.

'Sorry I'm late.'

'Not a problem, I only just got here myself.'

Jane got out from the car, she was wearing a silver miniskirt with a black aerobics top and black knee-high boots. For the first time, Jason noticed a small ring in her navel glinting in the darkness.

'I would just like to say,' said Jason, 'and you'll have to excuse my language, but you are fucking gorgeous.'

Jane smiled. 'Well, my friend thinks that you're pretty hot yourself.'

She stood in front of him.

'Is that right, and what do you think?'

Jane moved closer, her face only inches from his. He put his hands on her hips.

'I think . . . that "hot" doesn't do you justice,' she said slowly, moving even closer.

Their eyes closed at the same time, and as their lips met, Jason could feel his heart pounding against his T-shirt. Jane held onto his arms as they explored each other's mouths. She kissed well, Jason thought, very fucking well. In fact, as far as kissing went, he couldn't fault her. Jane had much the same impression and as their kissing became more passionate, Jason pulled her tightly into him. She responded with a moan as she felt his hard cock push against her. Jason ran his hands over her tight little arse as she held his face and pushed her tongue deep inside his mouth. Driven by lust he picked her up and placed her gently on the bonnet of the truck. With a gasp, Jane opened her mouth as if to say something but stopped herself. Jason looked into her eyes, she was one of the most exciting girls he had ever seen.

Fucking hell, I want this girl so badly I'm shaking, he thought to himself.

Sitting up on the truck's bonnet, her knees were the height of Jason's chin. He followed Jane's brown legs with his eyes, then up her skirt to the clearly visible, white underwear, then back into her eyes. He began kissing her thighs. Jane reached behind his head and slid the band from his hair, allowing it to fall down the sides of his face and brush against her legs. Jason reached up with his right hand and guided Jane down onto her back. As he kissed his way up the inside of her thighs, Jane opened her legs slightly and Jason slid his arms under her knees and held onto her arse, raising it up.

'I want to taste you,' he said, as he licked around the edges of her underwear.

'Fuck, yes,' she said breathing heavily. She reached down and pulled her lacy G-string over to one side of her pussy, Jason pushed his tongue as deep inside her as he possibly could and started making circles.

'Oh my god,' moaned Jane, as she began to slowly fuck Jason's mouth.

By the time she reached her first orgasm, Jane was scratching at the truck and had inadvertently bent one of the windscreen wipers almost completely off.

Waiting until he was sure that Jane had finished coming, Jason pulled her off the truck. As soon as her feet touched the ground she kissed him with a loud moan.

'Fuck, you are hot.'

'Turn around, bend over and stick that little arse out for me.'

'You're a dominant bastard, aren't you,' she said as she slowly turned around.

'Does that worry you?' he asked, opening a condom packet.

Jane put her hands against the truck and as requested stuck out her perfect little arse for him. 'What do you think?'

Jason fitted the condom and lifted Jane's skirt up over her waist to reveal her lacy G-string. With one hand he kept it pulled over to one side and with the other guided his cock into her hot, wet pussy. Jane threw back her head as Jason filled her body, he placed his other hand on her back and he began to pump himself inside her.

'You feel un-fucking-believable.'

Jane couldn't answer as another orgasm had just begun rippling through her body leaving her speechless. In the dark carpark of the Leedervale, up against a white truck, they fucked. Jason finally came inside her with such a force that his legs almost gave way. Panting and trembling he leaned against Jane with his cock still inside her. She reached back and held his head while they spent a few moments recovering.

A cigarette fell to the ground and was extinguished with a black boot. The figure in the shadows of the carpark blew out the last lungful of smoke, turned and walked away from the scene he had just watched by the white Ford. He pulled out a mobile phone from his black jacket and punched in the number of his employer.

Detective Peter Hampton dialled the number again.

Fuck, this bastard's hard to track down, he thought. The detective had already been around to the unit twice over the weekend with two uniformed cops but it had been empty.

'If this arsehole's a bouncer, he's probably still in bed. Come on you prick, wake up.'

Jason stumbled to the kitchen, the only reason he went to answer the phone at such an ungodly hour was in the hope that it was a call about Max.

'Hello,' he said croakily.

'Hello, is this Jason Slater?'

'Yeah, who's this?'

'This is Detective Peter Hampton from Perth CIB, I'm calling with regard to an incident that occurred at a party that you were at last Thursday.'

Jason tensed. 'Oh right, what's up?'

'Well, the whole thing is a bit messy at the moment.

There's a bunch of people who left the party before the police arrived, so now we have to get them in to give statements.'

The detective's tone was very matter-of-fact, even bordering on friendly.

'Is it possible for you to come into the station to see me and tell me what happened? It's purely routine.'

'Yeah, no worries, when's good for you?'

'Well ASAP really, how are you fixed at about one today?'

'Not a problem,' said Jason, relaxing slightly.

'Good, I'll see you at one o'clock then.'

Jason put the phone down and shuffled back to bed, muttering as he went, 'Ten o'clock in the fucking morning, how rude.'

Detective Hampton put down the phone and smiled. 'Got him,' he said to himself, and went for a coffee.

Jason thought about his conversation with the detective as he rode towards the station. The cop had sounded pretty friendly and hadn't mentioned anything about the fight, so hopefully it was just going to be a case of rattling off a quick statement about what he'd seen and leaving out the part about the brawl.

Jason arrived at ten to one, he had arranged to meet Steve at Hardie's at two, so all being well, he would be in and out of the station within an hour.

After waiting in the lobby for several minutes, Jason

was greeted by Detective Hampton with a smile and a handshake.

'Jason, thanks for coming in at such short notice. We'll just go upstairs to one of the interview rooms.'

Hampton seemed to be a pleasant enough guy, he was about thirty-two or three and a couple of inches shorter than Jason, but a bit stockier. He opened the door and smiled as Jason went in.

'Take a seat, would you like some coffee?'

'That would be great, white with one, thanks.'

'No worries, I'll be right back.'

Jason placed his helmet on the floor and unzipped his leather jacket. As he stretched he wondered if this was the station that Eddie's brother worked from. Jason began to think about the party, the poor girl, and that mutherfucker of a cop. Jason was only too happy to help if it meant that the cop was charged and thrown out of the force. Hampton returned with the coffee and another detective.

'This is Detective Wesley, he is keen to listen to your story, if that's OK.'

'Yeah, no problem.'

Jason took his coffee and the two officers sat down opposite him in the small room.

'Now,' Hampton said, 'tell us exactly what happened on Thursday night.'

'From when?'

'From when you arrived at the party.'

Jason proceeded to recount the events of the night in question, including the first time he saw the cops selling the drugs, the exchange of words they'd had and then the horrific nature of the girl's death.

Throughout Jason's story, the detective took notes without interrupting. When Jason had finished Hampton looked at him.

'What about the brawl?'

Jason looked at him. 'What brawl?'

'Come on, Jason, we know a scuffle broke out afterwards which you were involved in. You're not in any trouble, but we need to know everything that happened that night so that we can take the appropriate action.'

Jason sighed. 'OK, when I realised that the girl was dead and that it was their fault I lost my temper.'

'And who wouldn't, right?' said Hampton. 'So then what happened?'

Jason gave a brief account of the brawl but made sure not to mention Steve or Mike.

Hampton took more notes while Jason had finished his additional statement. The detective then looked at his partner and back at Jason.

'So, you hit the police officer first?' Hampton asked.

'Well . . . yes. I mean a girl had just died in front of me and he was responsible so I hit the bastard, I'd bloody hit him again if I had the chance.'

'Well listen Jason, we've got a bit of a problem here because I've got several witnesses, including three police officers, whose statements are very different from yours.' Hampton's tone had become noticeably less friendly.

Wesley, who had remained silent until now, looked at Jason with steely eyes.

'Let me put it this way, you lying piece of shit,' he said, 'we know you're the one who was selling the drugs and then you and your thug mates assaulted the police officers when they tried to stop you, isn't that what really happened?'

'No!' exclaimed Jason, a look of disbelief on his face. 'What the fuck's going on here, I came in to help you, what's all this shit?'

'Shut your fucking mouth, boy,' spat Wesley, rising from his seat.

Hampton raised his hand to stop his partner.

'Listen Jason, you've already admitted to assaulting the police officer, so you might as well admit to the drugs as well. To be quite honest, you're fucked. I mean look, you're a bouncer, and you're going to stand up in court and accuse three respected police officers of dealing drugs . . . I don't think so.'

Jason couldn't believe what was happening, where were the handshakes, the coffee and the smiles.

'Look, I've got witnesses who saw exactly what happened.'

'So you are calling the police officers liars?' said Wesley, with hate in his voice.

'Yes, I fucking well am.'

Wesley lunged across the table and aimed a slap at Jason's face, but Jason jumped to his feet and easily blocked the overweight detective's blow.

'Come on then, you little fucker,' snarled Wesley, frustrated at having his blow blocked.

'Wesley, go and get a uniform and send him in here,'

Hampton said. 'Jason, just take a seat and calm down.'

Detective Wesley scowled at Jason as he left the interview room. Jason sat down.

'You'll have to excuse my partner, Jason, we've got nothing against you personally, but I do have several statements pointing the finger at you. So obviously we have to look into it,' Hampton said, playing the good cop.

'So what happens now?' Jason asked.

'Well, we have to take you to East Perth lock-up, where you'll be fingerprinted and charged.'

'What!' Jason snapped. 'What do you mean charged, does this mean I'm under arrest?'

'Yes it does.'

The door opened and a young uniformed officer came in and stood in the corner of the room.

'You'll have to wait here, I'll be back in five minutes,' Hampton said.

The detective left the room with his notes, leaving Jason with his elbows on the table and his head in his hands.

'So what do you think?' said Wesley out in the corridor. 'Can we get him on both?'

'No,' replied Hampton. 'We can definitely nail him on the assault charge, but there were too many witnesses there to pin the drugs on him as well, but by the time we've convicted him of hitting Scottie he'll be hopeless as a witness and there'll be so much confusion surrounding the case, we'll easily get it dismissed as misadventure or something, the boys will be fine.'

'OK, well let's get the little cocksucker down the nick and charge him before he can get himself a lawyer.'

The drive to East Perth seemed to take forever, although in reality it was just over five minutes. No-one spoke. Jason had expected to be handcuffed but to his surprise this was not the case. His mind was almost blank with incomprehension. He had never been arrested before, although that was more through luck than anything else.

Shit, Jason thought, I can remember half a dozen times when I probably deserved an assault charge but this . . . this is bullshit.

Upon arrival at the lock-up he was escorted to the front desk to check in. A tall, thin officer was there to handle the proceedings.

'So who have we got here then, another bad guy?' the officer said.

Jason looked up at the cop behind his little 'king-shit' desk.

'My name is Jason.'

'Oh, the bad guy's got a name, and what's your surname, Mr Jason?'

Jason gave the cop his surname and was informed that he had to leave his helmet, phone, jacket, belt, shoes, ring and even his hairband at the counter, all the while being referred to as 'the bad guy' and generally patronised. He was then taken through to a cell in his socks, jeans and T-shirt, trying hard not to feel humiliated, which under the circumstances was almost impossible. He was handed over to a uniformed officer who opened the heavy metal door to the cell. As Jason walked inside, a stench hit him squarely in the nostrils. Smelly feet, vomit, urine and other body odours made for a cocktail of the most repugnant smell that Jason had ever experienced.

Fucking hell, he thought, it's worse than one of Max's farts.

The door was closed behind him with an ominous metallic clang, leaving him facing four very dirty looking specimens sitting on a bench against the wall. The cell was horribly small, with a revolting steel toilet in the corner which he could barely bring himself to look at, let alone contemplate using. He stood in front of the door with his hands in his pockets, not wanting to touch anything through fear of infection.

As soon as he had walked in, three of the scumbags had begun pointing and sniggering at the 'pretty boy' who was to share their cell.

'What are you in here for, eh?' drawled scumbag number one. 'You look a bit too pretty to be in here.'

The scumbag's friends sniggered like hyenas.

Jason stared directly at him. 'And you look way too fucking ugly to be in here.'

The three hyenas stopped laughing and looked at each other, number two and three waited to see how their leader wanted to handle the newcomer's insult. Number one looked at the six foot, muscular guy standing in front of him. Jason's eyes were cold and menacing, betraying any 'pretty boy' image that he had first observed.

The man gave an uneasy smile. 'I like this guy, pretty boy's got balls.'

The scumbag tried to maintain his sarcastic tone in

order to camouflage the fact that he was backing down from a confrontation.

'Seriously, what are you in for mate?'

'Assault,' Jason said.

'Smack some fucker did you?'

'A cop . . . well three actually.'

'All right!' exclaimed number one. 'What a legend.'

The other two also voiced their pleasure at Jason's crimes and began chatting about their own dealings with the law. The fourth person in the cell remained quiet, with his hands clasped together and his head down. He was older than the others with a big bushy moustache, and was dressed in a white singlet and blue footy shorts. Throughout the four hours that Jason spent in the cell, the guy with the moustache said nothing, and for that, Jason liked him.

One by one, the five cell-mates were taken away to be fingerprinted and photographed. The three scumbags talked constantly about their failed car insurance fraud and used the word 'cunt' two or three times in every sentence, causing Jason's jaw to tense whenever he heard it. Jason toyed with the idea of beating them senseless just to pass the time, but under the circumstances it probably wasn't a good idea.

Finally, the door opened. 'Jason Slater, this way,' said the cop.

The look on the cop's face suggested that he was pissed off with just about everything that life had to offer. Jason considered making a wisecrack about 'Constable Care' but thought that he'd probably get a fat lip for his trouble. The officer ushered him into a processing room where a harmless, goofy looking cop took over the festivities, while the other one stood guard at the door.

'Have you ever had your prints taken before?' inquired Goofy.

'No.'

He took Jason's right hand and rolled his fingers in the black ink and printed them onto a white card, then he took a palm print and repeated the process with the other hand. After finger painting with his new-found friend, it was time for Jason's photograph to be taken.

If his situation hadn't been so serious, it could have been quite an amusing experience. The cop motioned to Jason to take a seat and he was handed a placard with his name and other details on it.

Two photo shoots in one week, he thought.

Goofy positioned himself behind the camera.

'Excuse me,' said Jason politely, 'don't I get a make-up artist or anything, what about facial shine?'

The cop looked up momentarily from the camera, then back down again, totally unimpressed with the prisoner's comments. Jason had a smile on his face for the first time that day. Oh well, he thought, it cheered me up anyway.

The photo shoot completed, Jason was taken to some dude called a Justice of the Peace who laid the charge and set bail. Jason was charged with 'assault occasioning bodily harm' and had bail set at one thousand dollars which he had to sign for. The JP then informed Jason that he was to appear in court in a week's time to enter a plea. Finally, he was escorted to a back office to collect his belongings. Organising this was the first female cop Jason had seen at the lock-up. He got the feeling that although she was working on her best impression of a hard-nosed bitch, she was really quite a nice person under all that official cop bullshit. Jason put on his belt and shoes and everything else that had been taken from him. As his helmet and jacket were passed over to him, he felt like pieces of his identity were being returned and he was a human being once more, instead of scum in a prison cell.

'Sign here,' said the cop.

Jason signed and then looked at her with a cheeky smile. 'Thanks.'

The cop felt her knees go weak and she accidentally bit her lip. His smile developed into a grin, he couldn't resist it. He then turned and walked out of the building.

Fresh air had never tasted so good and Jason had never felt as much freedom as he did right now as he sped through various Perth suburbs on his motorbike. Arriving home, he walked into his apartment to the sound of the phone ringing.

'Hello.'

'Jason, it's Grant.'

'Hey, Grant, you'll never guess what—'

'I know where Max is.'

Jason froze. 'What?'

'I said, I know where Max is.'

KNUCKLEDUSTERS

'So where is he?' said Jason, barely able to control his excitement.

'Well, there's good news and there's bad news.'

'Don't fuck with me, Grant, where's Max?'

'Well I don't know where he's being kept at the moment, but he'll be on a large farm down in Mandurah on Wednesday night, he's being used for dogfighting.'

'And that's the bad news.'

'No, the bad news is who's got him.'

Jason wasn't quite sure whether he wanted to know the answer to his next question, but he asked anyway.

'Who?'

'The Jackals.'

'Oh fuck.'

'Exactly, how do you want to handle it?'

Jason paused. 'Seven o'clock tonight, here at my place. You call the lads from the Sunset and I'll call the rest of the boys. It's time we had a "staff meeting".'

Jason finished his conversation with Grant and

immediately called the other doormen as well as two more from the Leedervale Hotel, Lucas and Shane.

The last time such a staff meeting had been called was almost a year ago when Angus had been stabbed by a street gang member outside the movies. An appropriate plan of action had been decided upon in a meeting, and the resulting carnage had made news headlines around the country. The gang never did re-form.

Around Jason's kitchen table sat nine of the most experienced and feared bouncers that Western Australia had to offer, Steve, Mike, Chris, Angus, Eddie, Grant, Shane and Lucas. Shane was a Welsh carbon copy of Chris, and Lucas was a six foot five, 132 kilo monster who by day was a very successful computer programmer.

Jason delivered the last of the coffees to the table and remained standing.

'Gentlemen, thank you for coming.'

No-one made any smart remarks. They didn't know what they had been summoned for, but they all understood that a staff meeting meant only one thing—trouble.

'You all know that Max, my dog, was stolen nearly two weeks ago. I don't know who originally took him but he's now in the hands of the Jackals.'

The doormen exchanged glances but said nothing.

'On Wednesday night, they're fighting him at a farm down in Mandurah, and I'm going to get him.' Jason stopped to take a sip of coffee. 'As far as I'm concerned, if you're all willing to come with me, great, god knows I need the help, but if, for any reason, any of you don't want to be in on it, there's no problem, no hard feelings. It's not going to be the same as with the street gang, these guys aren't just young idiots with flick-knives, they're big, mean mutherfuckers who, I must admit, are the last people I want to fuck with. So, it's up to you.'

Jason sat down and the doormen once again exchanged glances.

Angus rose from his seat. 'I can't speak for the other boys, but you all came to help me last year, so as far as I'm concerned . . . I'm in.'

'Me too,' said Chris.

Lucas and Shane nodded in agreement.

'Well, I have to come along,' said Eddie. 'Someone's got to be the sensible one.'

Grant just sat there smiling. Jason looked at the two remaining doormen, Mike and Steve.

Mike opened his hands. 'Do you even have to ask us?'

Jason smiled. 'No brother, I don't.'

'So,' said Eddie, 'before all this male bonding makes me puke, what's the plan?'

'Right,' said Jason, standing again. 'The last thing I need right now is a war with a fucking bikie gang. So I suggest that we sneak up on the ugly bastards, swipe Max and get the hell out of there before they realise what's happened.'

'And just how are we going to do that?' said Mike. 'It's going to be like a bikie social club get-together, there'll be loads of the cunts.'

'True, but if you have a look at this . . .' Jason took a piece of paper from his pocket and unfolded it. 'I think there's a way we can do it.'

'What's that?' asked Lucas.

'A present from our informant. It's a rough map of the farm, apparently he's been there before.'

'Are you sure that this isn't a set-up for us to get hammered?' said Eddie.

'Yes, I'm sure,' said Grant, 'the informant is my cousin.'

Eddie nodded. 'Fair enough.'

The map showed a farm house on the left and a large barn to the right where the fights were to take place. Built onto the back of the barn was an extension.

'According to Grant's cousin this is where the dogs are kept in cages,' Jason said, pointing to the extension. 'It's like a store room or something. There are two doors, one that separates the shed from the barn, here in the left-hand corner, and a side door here on the right that leads outside. There would probably only be one guy looking after the dogs, two at the most. What I suggest is that two of us go to the holding room via the side door, take out whoever's in there, grab Max and fuck off before the rest of them sus out what's going on.'

'What about everyone else?' asked Steve.

'You'll all be sitting in a couple of cars with baseball bats, in case we get busted and the shit hits the fan.'

'How will we know if the shit does hit the fan?' Steve said.

'Headphones,' answered Shane.

'Exactly, can you get hold of a set from the Leedervale by Wednesday?' Jason asked.

'No problem.'

'Fuck all this sneaking around,' snapped Grant. 'Let's just get some more of the boys together, gatecrash the party and kick some fucking arse.'

'Grant, no-one would like to see those fuckers put in hospital more than me, but mate, a few of us would almost certainly end up there as well. Who knows, one of them might even pull a gun and start shooting. Why risk it when we don't need to? Think of it as a military operation.'

Grant sighed. Unfortunately what Jason was saying, did make sense.

'All right, but I want to be the one who comes in with you and clobbers at least one of them.'

Jason smiled. 'I don't have a problem with that.'

The war party went over a few details of their planned raid. They were to take Mike's van, which at least five of the assassins could fit into. Shane had an old Kingswood which would fit the rest. Both vehicles were dark in colour so with the headlights turned off they would be almost invisible as they approached the farm. As with the previous street gang 'incident', they agreed that as far as weapons were concerned, guns and knives were out, but otherwise, almost anything goes. Shane was to organise a set of interlinked headphones which they used at the Leedervale to notify each other of any trouble. One set was to be worn by Jason as he attempted to find Max, and the other by one of the boys waiting inside the van. So the plan for Wednesday night was to drive down to Mandurah, leaving at eleven, to arrive just after midnight when the fights were scheduled to begin. Then it was a case of raiding the farm, snatching the dog and bailing, hopefully without getting caught. If they did . . . well, they'd handle that if and when it happened.

Jason spent the whole of Tuesday brooding over who had his dog and what they'd put him through. The Jackals were one of three bikie gangs in WA and they were the biggest and, at times, most vicious of all.

Jason was at the gym, pounding away some of his frustrations on a large punch-bag in a corner of the room. Two hard left hooks, followed by a straight right, shook the metal beam that the bag was chained to.

'Fuck,' he growled, leaning against the bag. Sweat ran freely down his face and back. He had learned through Grant's cousin that Max had been put in two fights already. The first was with an Alsatian that Max had killed and the second with a large, undefeated pit-bull, owned by another gang. The second fight had gone on for well over half an hour, which was almost unheard of in dogfighting circles, the average fight being around ten minutes. The pit-bull had survived, although it was now in retirement after Max had torn its right front leg completely off in the final stages of the bloodbath. The eye-witness had reported that Max had suffered some horrific cuts and had lost half an ear, but on the whole he was OK. Tomorrow night, however, Max was to be matched against not one but two prize-fighting Staffordshire bull-terriers in the main bout of the evening. 'Not if I can help it.'

Jason took a step back from the bag and let fly with a right hook that would have broken a gorilla's jaw. He continued to hammer the bag like a man possessed, as several gym users tried not to stare. One younger body builder quietly voiced everyone's thoughts to his workout partner.

'Fuck me, I wouldn't like to be on the receiving end of that.' The partner nodded slowly in agreement.

'So we go and fuck him up tonight, yeah?' Greco said as he cleaned out the barrel of a gun silencer.

'Greco, you have no patience, haven't you learned the importance of timing yet?'

'But what's there to wait for? The sooner his head is separated from his shoulders the better.'

Macey looked out of his lounge-room window at the panoramic views of the city and river.

'It'll happen soon,' he said coldly. 'Very soon.'

The next twenty-four hours passed by painfully slowly. Jason had told Mike, Steve and Caroline about his arrest and the fun and games he'd had down at the lock-up with the boys in blue.

Caroline received the news with frustration and anger and had insisted that they should do something, maybe even to press charges against the cop himself. But as Jason pointed out, our fine, upstanding Police Force is prone to the occasional bout of corruption, and he had a sneaky feeling that the cops he was up against would more than likely tell the odd, teensy weensy little fibs in court to get themselves out of trouble.

Mike was not surprised but he was concerned about the possibility of his own arrest. Jason was quite shocked at this paranoia. Although the thought of being arrested and charged for assault wasn't a pleasant one, he knew that his pommy mate from the cess pits of inner-city Manchester had been through much worse. Jason got the impression that there was something that Mike wasn't telling him, but he decided not to pry.

He made them promise not to tell anyone else about his court appearance, after all, it's not the kind of thing you want to broadcast.

By seven o'clock on Wednesday night, Jason had just finished a large bowl of pasta and was watching TV. On the table in front of him were his brass knuckledusters, a metal rounders bat (about half the size of a baseball bat) and a steel, telescopic baton. When compacted, the baton could just about fit into a pocket, and to use it you only had to flick it out firmly and, hey presto, a foot and a half long baton extended out from its heavy base, ready to bash an assailant senseless. Jason had christened it on the kneecap of a knife-wielding gang member and it had proved itself to be devastatingly effective.

Steve and Mike arrived together at seven-thirty,

gradually followed by everyone else over the next hour. Jason's front room was a hive of testosterone-charged activity. The boys were comparing weaponry—baseball bats, police batons, nunchakus, knuckledusters and a wide variety of other nasty looking instruments of pain. Angus reached carefully into his gym bag and slowly began to pull out his pride and joy.

'Check this out, boys.'

The room fell silent. Jason looked disbelievingly at Angus.

'What the fuck is that?'

In his hand he held a length of heavy-duty chain, about three feet long. On both sides of each link was a razor blade, meticulously welded into place. Angus looked at the stunned faces of his mates.

'What? What's wrong?'

'You have got to be kidding,' said Chris.

'Don't you like my new toy?'

Jason stared at the evil-looking chain hanging from Angus' hand.

'Forget it. There is no fucking way you're taking that.'

'I agree,' said Mike. 'One of us will probably end up wearing it.'

'But—'

'No,' said Jason.

After several minutes of protesting, Angus put away his toy, obviously unimpressed that no-one approved of his invention. He sat in silence with a grumpy expression on his face, like a spoilt child sulking after being told off.

*

The time approached ten-thirty and the boys had just finished a second cup of coffee.

'OK,' said Jason, 'let's get loaded up.'

The many tools of that evening's trade were gathered up and loaded into the two vehicles. Jason double-checked that Angus hadn't sneaked his razor-studded chain along, and the nine doormen set off on the hour-long drive to Mandurah.

The trip down was a sombre affair. It wasn't like the ride to intercept the gang a year ago when they'd played loud psych-up music and had arrived pumped up and ready to party. This time they all realised that a confrontation had to be avoided if at all possible. Jason sat next to Mike in the van adjusting the headphones, both sets had brand new batteries. They drove steadily down the long, dark coastal road.

'Mike, pull up alongside Shane and sound the horn.'

He moved out into the right-hand lane and accelerated until he was level with the dark Kingswood. Jason wound down his window.

'What?' shouted Shane.

'Give this to Steve for a soundcheck.'

Shane pulled the car over to within inches of the van, took the headset, and passed it back to Steve. Jason wound up the window and Mike dropped in behind the Kingswood.

'Good timing,' said Mike, as a semitrailer screamed passed them.

Jason put on the headset and pulled the mouthpiece to his lips.

'Steve can you hear me? Steve, answer me, dickhead.' The line crackled.

'I heard that, mutherfucker.'

'Good, I'm glad you did. I hope you hear me when I'm yelling for back-up.'

Steve laughed. 'So what's the signal if you need help?'

'How about, help, help they're beating the shit out of me?'

'Yeah, that should do it.'

'Ask Shane what the range is on these things.'

'OK.'

There was a brief pause.

'Half a kilometre, he says they can hear each other over the noise of the Leedervale clearly enough, so they'll be perfect for this.'

'Cool.'

The road map led them through a series of country laneways. They pulled over just under a kilometre from where the farm was marked on the map. As arranged, the vehicles' lights were turned off but the engines were kept running. Even the bulbs from the courtesy lights had been removed so that when doors were opened no light was emitted. Jason jumped down from the van and walked over to the Kingswood.

'OK lads, just as we planned. Grant are you set?'

Grant flashed an iron bar which could separate in the middle to become a lethal set of nunchakus. 'Ready.'

'Steve?'

Steve tapped his headset. 'Ready.'

Jason returned to the van and the two vehicles slowly made their way along the road that led to the farm in almost total darkness. There was just enough light coming from a weak half-moon to make the drive possible.

'There it is,' said Mike, quietly.

Through the trees, they caught glimpses of the lights from the farm.

'Right, keep your eyes peeled for the barn.'

As they drew nearer, the lights of the large house made it easy to see the layout. Just as the informant's map had shown, the house was situated in the left corner of the complex. To the right was the huge barn that was usually home for an industrial harvester which was now parked outside to make room for the night's entertainment.

The boys stopped at the beginning of a private laneway which led about a hundred yards into the centre of the farm.

Jason shoved a small pair of bolt-cutters into his jacket, winked at Mike and left the van.

Grant was waiting for him, and with a slap on the back the two Ninja warriors walked stealthily up either side of the dark lane. Wearing black jeans and dark jackets and caps, they were well camouflaged in the shadows. They reached the end of the lane and crouched behind a tree, the area in front of the barn was littered with dozens of bikes.

Fuck me, Jason thought, there must be over a hundred bikes here.

Lined up in front of the bikes was a handful of trucks and old bombs. The boys could hear voices and the occasional bark of an excited dog coming from behind the closed doors of the barn in front of them. Not a soul was about, everyone seemed to be in the barn.

'Steve, can you hear me?'

'Yes, mate.'

'We're at the top of the lane, the compound's empty, we're going over to the barn.'

Just as the two boys began to run across the semi-lit yard, roars and cheering erupted from within, startling them momentarily. They reached the right-hand side of the building and hid in the shadows of the harvester. In between the cheering, the fighting dogs could clearly be heard, snapping and snarling as they tried to rip flesh from each other's bones; the noise was hideous. Further down the side of the barn, Grant found a small gap through which they could watch the gruesome spectacle within. Crammed inside were close to one hundred and fifty bikies and their friends, all shouting excitedly around a cordoned-off circle about fifteen feet in diameter. In the circle were two bull-terrier crosses, half crazed with blood lust as they clambered all over each other, gouging and tearing with horrific results. Jason motioned for Grant to follow him down to the back of the barn where, all being well, they would find the dogs. Jackpot, round the back was the large shed extending from the main building. Jason could hear the clanking of chains and the whining of several dogs.

'This is it,' he whispered.

'Steve.'

'Yes mate.'

'We've found the shed. We're just about to go in, stay sharp.'

They reached the side door, and Jason put his ear up against it, inside he could hear two voices.

'So, how d'you reckon the big feller'll go?'

'I don't know, mate, he's a fair fighter all right, but he's up against two of Jacko's staffies, it could go either way.'

'Well my money's on the big daft bugger, shit, all he has to do is headbutt one of them with that thick skull of his and that'll even up the odds straight away.'

The two bikies laughed.

'Listen, are you OK here? I want to go and watch the rest of this fight.'

'Yeah mate, no worries, just bring back another six-pack with you.'

Jason heard the noise of the crowd increase as the bikie opened the door to the barn and then quieten slightly as he shut it.

The boys looked at each other and nodded. Grant stayed in the shadows while Jason pushed the side door open and staggered inside, performing his best impression of a totally pissed-up drunk. The bikie looked up from his beer as Jason staggered to the left.

'Is this the shithouse, mate?' he drawled.

'No mate, it's not, you blokes aren't allowed back here, go outside and piss.'

Jason leaned unsteadily against a stack of hay bales.

'I don't need a piss, mate, I'm going to throw up.'

The bikie got to his feet. 'No you're not, not in here, fuck off outside and do it.'

'It's too late, I'm gonna chuck.'

'No you bloody don't.'

The bikie grabbed Jason, spun him around and marched him back towards the open door, giving him a solid shove as they got there.

'Go on, spill your guts outsi—'

Grant's iron bar fell on the bikie's head with such force that he dropped immediately to the floor, where he remained.

'Shit, I think I killed him.'

'Fuck him, wait here and if he moves, whack him again.'

Jason stepped briskly back into the shed where there were about a dozen large cages. All but two of them contained heavily muscled fighting dogs going berserk as they tried to get at each other. Jason scanned the room.

'Where are you, ugly?'

Over the noise he could hear Max's familiar bark and his heart raced. He took several steps forwards and down on the right he found what he'd come for. Max went crazy when he saw his master. Jason retrieved the cutters from his jacket and took the padlock in his trembling hands.

'Hey dumb-fuck, how are you?' Max licked his hand as he lined up the lock in the jaws of the bolt-cutters.

'Hurry up, arsehole, I think the fight's almost over,' called Grant.

Jason didn't need to be told. With one powerful movement, the cutters sliced through the lock, and Max crashed his way out of the cage with his head, just as the door leading to the barn was kicked open and in came three very large bikies, laughing and carrying a stack of beer.

Jason stood up, and their laughter ceased. He gave them a friendly smile.

'Hi.'

'What the fuck do you think you're doing?'

'Umm . . . I just wanted to take a closer look at this fine dog,' he said, taking a step backwards.

'With fucking bolt-cutters?'

Jason took another step back. Max wagged his tail.

'Oh shit.'

'What's up . . . what's going on?' said Chris urgently.

Steve motioned for them to keep quiet. 'Trouble.'

The doormen began scrambling out of the car.

'No, not yet . . . wait.'

The three bikies advanced slowly towards Jason as two more came through the door. The one in front pulled out a long bowie knife from his leather jacket.

'Stealing one of our dogs, eh? I'm gonna cut your balls off and shove 'em down your throat.'

Jason continued to retreat to the open side door as Max began growling at another dog in a cage nearby.

'There's really no need for that, gentlemen, I can explain everything.' Jason started to raise the bolt-cutters. 'Well actually . . . I can't,' and he threw the heavy tool as hard as he could at the approaching lynch mob. He then turned and ran straight over the still unconscious bikie in the doorway.

'Fucking run,' shouted Jason, as he passed Grant, with Max right behind him.

'I'll be right with you,' he hissed.

As soon as the first bikie reached the door, Grant swung the steel bar with all his strength into the man's face, knocking him clean off his feet. The bikie landed on top of the other one, momentarily blocking the doorway as the others piled into him. The large blond doorman then turned, and for the first time in his life, ran, as the other bikies clambered over their fallen mates, followed closely by a dozen others who had been notified of the intruders.

Jason and Grant sprinted, top speed, along the side of the barn towards the front yard, Max stopped to pee against the harvester in front of Grant.

In full flight, Grant kicked the bull-terrier square up the backside. 'Move it, you dumb cunt.'

Steve's voice crackled over the headset, 'Jason, what the fuck's going on . . . Jason?'

'Start the cars . . . start the fucking cars now, we're getting the hell out of here . . . now.'

Steve ordered both the vehicles to start up. 'Have you got the dog?'

'Yes, and half the fucking Jackals as well, start driving, we'll dive in.'

The two boys reached the laneway and looked back to see a large group of very upset bikies chasing after them. Luckily, none of them were what you would call athletic. The two doormen had managed to pull away from them, but not far enough as far as Jason was concerned. He could still hear the words 'cunt' and 'kill' being spat out after him, along with further references to the removal of his genitals.

Jason, Grant and Max reached the road and saw the welcome sight of their two vehicles driving away slowly with the back doors of the van open for them. Panting heavily, they put their heads down and ran towards the doors. Max was the first to arrive and leapt straight into the van and promptly began to assault the boys' faces with his tongue.

The bikies reached the road just as Grant and Jason were being dragged up into the van and the doors were closed behind them.

'Hit it,' yelled Lucas.

Mike floored the pedal and sounded the horn to signal Shane to do likewise.

By the time the breathless bikies had returned to the barn to raise the alarm and get their bikes, the two vehicles, containing nine very pumped doormen, were gone.

Jason and Grant lay on their backs gasping for air amidst cheers and laughter from their mates. Max was licking Jason's mouth as he tried weakly to push the dog away. Finally, he sat up and looked at his long-lost friend. Even in the darkness, Jason could see several deep cuts on Max's face that were going to scar quite badly and he had indeed lost half of his right ear.

Jason smiled. 'Fuck, you look more gorgeous than ever,' then he grabbed his dog in a bearhug. Max wagged his tail and dribbled on Jason's sleeve.

When the boys arrived back at Jason's place, they pulled out two cartons of beer that they had bought earlier to either commiserate or celebrate their daring adventure, depending on how it turned out. Now, the nine desperadoes were sitting around the lounge room drinking and affectionately slapping Max who had gone totally loopy with the excitement of being reunited with his master and his mates.

'You should have seen the look on Jason's face as he ran out of the shed, it was fucking hilarious,' laughed Grant.

'Fuck you, you lanky twat.'

'Well, you both missed the sight that we saw from the back of the van as you ran after us being chased by a bikie gang, now that was funny,' Eddie said.

The doormen were by now half pissed and laughing uncontrollably. Almost in tears, Grant attempted to talk.

'Halfway through the compound, Max decided to take a piss.' Grant held his stomach, he was laughing so much it hurt, 'so I kicked him up the arse. I swear to god, he flew three feet.'

Jason was laughing so hard, he slipped off the end of the couch and spilt beer all over himself and the floor. Max bounded over and began to lick it up. The boys

..brated their victory into the small hours of the morning.

They finally agreed to meet the following afternoon at Hardie's Cafe and left for their respective homes. Jason retired to his bedroom and fell into a deep sleep with Max next to him, salivating on the pillow and snoring heavily.

He awoke the next day to the unmistakable aroma of a bull-terrier's fart.

'Oh my god, you smelly fuck, I'm giving you back to the bikies.'

He turned over and buried his face in the pillow just as Max farted again, loudly.

'Right, that's it, you win, I give up.'

Jason climbed from his bed and made his way to the kitchen.

'Bastard . . . Jesus, my eyes are burning.'

He made a cup of tea and collapsed in front of the TV.

Half an hour later, Jason's stomach informed him that it needed food. Upon opening the fridge he was confronted with five shelves of virtually nothing except for two cheese singles, a half empty can of flat Diet Coke and something in the bottom drawer that looked like it may have been a vegetable once upon a time.

'It's not my day today.'

He went back to his highly toxic bedroom and pulled on some tracksuit pants and a T-shirt. Then he walked up to the local deli in search of some eggs and bread, rubbing the sleep from his eyes as he went. In the deli, he grabbed an armful of groceries and placed them on the counter, then went to the magazine stand for a newspaper.

As he reached down for the paper he froze, his mouth slowly fell open. Immediately in front of him was a stack of the latest *Australian Centrefold Magazine*, each with a full-size head and shoulders picture of him, smiling on the cover.

'Oh . . . my . . . god,' Jason stood up.

'Are you all right, mate?' said the deli attendant.

Jason looked blankly at him.

'Hey, is that you on the cover of—'

'No,' Jason snapped, gathering up his groceries. 'Here's twenty bucks, keep the change.'

Without waiting for a bag, he half walked, half ran home, desperately trying not to drop his armful of shopping on the way. Dumping the food on the kitchen table, he grabbed his mobile and punched in Natalie's number. It was engaged.

'Fuck.' Jason slammed the flip shut. 'Fuck, fuck, fuck.'

As much as he had mentally prepared himself for the release of his centrefold, he'd had no idea that he was actually going to be on the cover.

Max plodded into the kitchen and stretched.

'Max, pack your bags, we're leaving the country.'

Jason sat down as his mobile rang. He looked at it, wondering whether he should answer it or not. Maybe he'd just let it ring out. The ringing continued and he finally gave in.

'Hello,' he said sheepishly.

'Jason, you big fucking poof.' It was Grant. 'I've just seen a picture of your—'

Jason slammed the phone shut and lowered his head and began to bang it repeatedly against the table.

'No' . . . bang . . . 'No' . . . bang . . . 'No' . . .

The phone rang again.

THE CONTRACT

By eight o'clock on Thursday evening, Jason had received calls from almost every single person that he knew in Perth, and a few he didn't. The calls had ranged from derogatory name-calling followed by hysterical laughter from his mates, to one marriage proposal from some lunatic he'd never heard of before called Deborah.

Jason now sat in front of the TV, pissed as a fart after he'd cracked under the pressure and raided what remained of the previous night's beer supply. He burped loudly.

There was a knock on the door.

'Come in, it's open.'

It was Caroline, she'd dropped in to check on her 'little centrefold'. She entered the lounge room with a smile on her face and a copy of the magazine in her hand. Her eyes narrowed when she saw Jason on the couch.

'You're drunk, aren't you?'

'Yep,' he replied, bleary eyed.

'Well, I don't know what you're so upset about, the

pictures are fantastic, all the girls at work were speechless.'

Jason attempted to say, 'Yes, speechless would be a good description of today's events,' but thanks to the nine beers that he'd consumed it came out as unintelligible drivel.

'What?' said Caroline.

'Nothing.'

'Have you even seen the photos yet?' she said, raising the magazine.

'Shit no, the cover was enough for me.'

Caroline stayed with Jason for the rest of the evening and after taking a couple more calls, she helped him to his room and put him to bed, where she sat by his side, running her hand over his head until he passed out. Max appeared at the door.

'You poor thing, you've been through so much haven't you?'

Max wagged his tail.

'Well, at least he's got you back now.'

Caroline kissed Jason on the forehead and left him to sleep.

The big news of Max's return had been overshadowed by the release of Jason's glamorous photos, which everyone had seen by now. However, the following two nights at work weren't half as bad as he had been expecting. The worst part was when he arrived at the club to be greeted with thunderous applause from the entire staff of Davinchi's.

After that, their amusement had turned to fascination and Jason was swamped with questions and more than a few 'I've seen your penis' type looks from the several barmaids who hadn't already seen it in real life.

On Saturday night, over a dozen girls had approached him and complimented him on a job well done. When he returned home he had to empty his bulging pockets which had been stuffed full of phone numbers.

'Fucking hell, this isn't so bad,' he said to himself as he dumped them on the table.

Over the next few days he was continually recognised in the street and one of the waitresses at Hardie's Cafe presented him with a copy of his magazine to sign. That freaked him out.

'Unbelievable,' he said to Mike. 'Last weekend I had some slut call me a shit-bag and try to kick me in the bollocks, now I'm signing autographs. This is too weird for me.'

Mike laughed. 'Fuck off, you love it.' The two mates ordered more lattes from the gushing waitress.

Jason eventually fell out of bed when the phone, ringing for the millionth time, finally became too much to bear.

'Hello.'

'Hi, is this Jason?'

'Guilty.'

The chirpy voice on the end of the line giggled. 'It's Lesley Dale from *Australian Centrefold Magazine* in Sydney, how do you like your photos?'

'Oh hi, er . . . still speechless, actually.'

'That's great, now Jason I've got a huge favour I have to ask you.'

Jason closed his eyes, what more could they possibly want from him. 'And what's that, Lesley?'

'I need you to hop on a plane tomorrow and come and see us in Sydney.'

Jason's eyes opened. 'Sorry, can you run that by me again?'

'Well, we're currently deciding on our new Centrefold of the Year and you're hot on our list of finalists. So we would really like to meet you in person.'

Jason's head was spinning, primarily from the alcohol binge that he and Mike had gone on the previous evening, but also from trying to comprehend what he was hearing over the phone.

'Well, yeah I'd love to. Tomorrow you reckon?'

'Yes, I'm sorry it's such short notice, is that OK?'

'Yes, that's fine, it's all just happening so quickly.'

Lesley filled him in on some necessary details and promised to reveal more when he arrived in Sydney. He was to collect his ticket at the airport at five-thirty in the morning for the 6 am flight. The two-hour time difference meant that he would arrive at midday, Sydney time. He would be collected at the airport and taken to the hotel where he would receive a full itinerary for the afternoon and evening's appointments. His return flight to Perth was booked for early on Saturday morning.

Jason sat down on the beanbag with Max, trying to figure out what to do first. He had to get one of the boys to look after Max, that wouldn't be a problem. He didn't have to worry about getting a lift to the airport either, as Lesley was having some Cab-Charge vouchers, whatever the fuck they were, couriered over to him that afternoon. The only thing that concerned him was that he would have to leave work at four in the morning, go home, get his shit together and go straight to the airport.

Christ, I'll be knackered, Jason thought to himself. Fuck it, I'll see if I can get the night off. He called Eddie and after a brief period of negotiations that turned into pure begging, Eddie finally agreed but only after making it quite clear that Jason owed him favours for the rest of his natural life.

Jason put the phone down. 'Yes.'

Next he called Mike, Steve and Caroline to tell them about his little trip to Sydney. He instructed them to tell the others that he was going to the Gold Coast to visit his sick grandmother. At six-thirty Steve arrived to take Max to his place and left, after a coffee, with the dog plodding happily after him.

Jason couldn't remember the last time he'd gone to bed at ten o'clock on a Thursday night. It was a strange feeling to be lying there, knowing that usually he would be with the boys partying or out and about with a girlfriend, but after a while he drifted off to sleep with his alarm set for 4.30 am.

It was still dark when the cab pulled up in front of the domestic airport. Jason had got six hours sleep but considering that his average was about nine, it wasn't surprising that he had dozed off in the back of the cab.

'That's eighteen-fifty, thanks mate.'

'Eh what, oh right I've got one of these Cab-Charge things.'

Jason signed the white docket and handed it to the driver. He walked into the brightly lit airport where only a few people were dotted here and there.

'Hi, I've got a ticket reserved for me, Jason Slater,' he said to the cute ticketing clerk.

'There you are, Mr Slater, have a good flight.'

She gave Jason a sexy look as she handed him the ticket.

'Thank you,' he replied, forcing out a half-hearted smile, it was far too early in the morning to flirt. Jason looked at his ticket as he made his way over to the check-in desk.

'Oh shit, first class . . . nice one.'

Upon entering the aircraft with his fellow first-class travellers, he was greeted by the several beaming hostesses and shown to his seat.

'There you go, Mr Slater, have a pleasant trip.'

'Thank you.'

Mr Slater took a seat in a large, plush, blue armchair by the window. The seat next to him was empty which was a worry. Jason thought of his last flight, and the one before it, and every other one before that. He was convinced that the bastards in charge of seating allocation had it in for him, he was always put next to a screaming shithead kid, or some smelly git with a body odour problem. He could even remember one time when he was put next to a nun who must have been at least ninety, that was a laugh a minute. What cruel surprise did the seating people have in store for him this time, Quasimodo's mother-in-law perhaps?

Business and economy class piled in. 'Hah, peasants,' scoffed Jason, stretching out in his armchair, and there was still no sign of passenger 3B. He was just beginning to think that he'd got lucky and he'd have an empty seat next to him when a huge form appeared at the entrance of the plane.

'Oh . . . my . . . god.'

The form moved slowly over to his aisle and began to walk towards him.

'Jesus Christ,' said Jason, into his hand. 'This chick must be four hundred pounds.'

As the planet-sized person approached, Jason lowered his head, closed his eyes and crossed his fingers, repeating in his head, 'Please god, no, please.'

There was a moment's pause, then Jason heard the locker above seat 3B being opened and closed. He then sensed someone sitting down next to him

'Well, thanks a lot god.' Jason slowly opened his eyes and turned towards Jupiter to do the polite thing and introduce himself. A frown covered his face as he looked upon someone who was definitely not the person he'd watched approaching him. Jason opened his mouth and raised his finger but stopped himself just before he was about to say something really stupid.

'Hi,' said the girl who was going to be sitting next

to him for the following four hours, 'I'm Petina, pleased to meet you.'

Jason closed his mouth, realising how ridiculous he must have looked and shook Petina's hand. She was a stunning Italian girl with long black hair, deep brown eyes and a body that Jason realised was obviously awesome, even though he had managed not to blatantly perv on her yet. He had wanted to say, 'Hi Petina, I'm Jason and you are fucking gorgeous,' but decided to keep it down to the formalities.

'You look a little surprised to see me, were you expecting someone else?'

'No . . . no um . . .' Jason was still in shock. 'So, what are you going to Sydney for?'

'I'm in a show on a boat that cruises the harbour, I'm a contortionist.'

Jason's adam's apple bobbed up and down as he swallowed. Thank you god, he thought. Thank you.

During take-off, Jason managed to steal a few glimpses of her. She wore a short black skirt, high heels and a white, loose fitting blouse which failed gloriously to hide her quite magnificent breasts.

As soon as the plane levelled out, Jason found himself being waited on hand and foot by the larger-than-life hostesses. He told Petina that he was going to Sydney to meet with some people from a magazine to negotiate a modelling contract, which he rationalised to himself later as being 'sort of true'.

'It's funny,' she said, 'but I'm used to people freaking out when I tell them what I do, or I get guys making lurid comments, but you just took it in your stride, I like that.'

Jason smiled, as soon as Petina had told him that she was a contortionist, he had pictured her bent over backwards, almost in two, as he ate her pussy and she took his cock into her mouth in some bizarre, sexual, gymnastic position.

'Yeah, I bet you get that a lot, some people can be so rude and immature.'

'I must admit though,' she said with a wicked smile, 'being as flexible as I am certainly does make sex a far more interesting concept.'

Jason felt Mr Wriggly move in his underpants. 'Hello,' said the mad wriggler, 'did someone mention sex?'

'Well, do tell,' said Jason.

After almost an hour of Petina talking quite openly about her sexual capabilities, Jason had a hard-on that he honestly thought was going to tear a muscle.

'Petina,' he said, just as she was going into the details of yet another position in which she was capable of having sex, 'I have to go to the bathroom.'

She looked cheekily at him.

'And yes,' he continued quietly, 'if you think that I'm going in there to play with myself, then you're absolutely right.'

Petina giggled. Jason decided to push his luck a little further, he released his seatbelt and leaned over to whisper in her ear.

'I'm going to take my cock in my hand and wank

myself stupid while I think about fucking you.'

Petina looked at him, breathing quite heavily. 'We definitely have to meet up in Sydney.'

Jason stood up and edged passed her, out into the aisle.

'Fuck yeah.'

He returned from the toilet cubicle fifteen minutes later and took his seat next to the gorgeous Petina.

She smiled. 'Feel better now?'

'Much,' said Jason. 'It's a pity you didn't join me.'

'I almost did but . . . well I figured I'd save it for when we meet up again.'

Jason winked. 'Good idea.'

In between bouts of sexually orientated conversation, Jason spent the rest of the trip dozing off and daydreaming about his life. Apart from being overjoyed to have his dog back, he was a touch concerned that the bikies might plot some sort of revenge attack on him. However, Grant's informant had told him that Max had passed through several hands before ending up with the Jackals, and they had no idea where he'd come from in the first place. Still, if Jason had learned one thing, it was that you can never be too careful, so Steve was going to keep the dog for a week or so until things had died down a bit. Even with all the precautions that he'd taken, the fact still remained that there was a large, vicious bikie gang out there that wanted a certain person's testicles on a plate, and although they supposedly didn't know who that person was, he did, and it wasn't the most comfortable feeling in the world. Jason began to think of his court appearance later in the week at which he would enter a plea of not guilty, but then he chased it from his mind.

Fuck it, one thing at a time, he thought.

He was going to leave all his worries in WA, have a damn good time in Sydney, and then deal with everything else when he got back.

Jason slept for the rest of the flight. The plane landed gently at Sydney Airport a couple of minutes after midday. Petina gave him a contact address and her mobile phone number which he was happy to accept. Jason made sure that Petina went first as they filed off the plane so he could perv unashamedly at her phenomenally trim backside which she wiggled happily for his benefit.

Fuck me, this place is a mad-house, Jason thought as he entered the terminal.

Lesley had told him that he would be picked up at the airport, and to look for someone carrying a sign with his name on it. As impossible as this task seemed in amongst the sea of faces and cards, he saw his card being held up just as he reached the bottom of the escalators. He jostled his way towards it and found a meticulously groomed, middle-aged man wearing a spotless, grey chauffeur's uniform.

'Hi,' said Jason, a little unsure of whether or not he was the right Slater. 'I'm Jason Slater.'

'Mr Slater, welcome to Sydney, my name's Albert, I'm your chauffeur. Is that your only bag, sir?'

'Yeah mate.'

'Allow me, sir.' Albert attempted to take Jason's bag.

'No, that's OK, I've got it.'

'Certainly, this way, sir.'

Jason followed him through the crowd out to the frenzied pick-up and drop-off zone. Albert walked matter-of-factly over to the longest, whitest stretch limousine that Jason had ever seen in his life.

'Holy fucking shit.'

'Excuse me, sir?'

'Oh nothing . . . nice car.'

'Thank you, sir.' Albert walked around to the passenger door.

'Al, I can't handle all this sir shit, call me Jason.'

Albert laughed. 'OK . . . Jason.'

Sir Jason tentatively stepped inside his first limo. As the door was closed behind him, he sat down on the back seat and looked around.

'Mutherfucker, this thing's even got a TV . . . and a bar.'

Albert got in the front and eased the car smoothly away. The window separating the driver from the limo's cabin buzzed down.

'Is this your first time in Sydney, Jason?'

'Yeah it is, I can't believe how many people there are here. It's packed.'

As they drove, Albert gave Jason the full guided tour, pointing out famous landmarks and other popular attractions. Jason spent most of the trip pinned against the darkened glass, drinking in everything he possibly could.

The limo pulled into the driveway of the Southern Star Hotel at quarter to one. It reminded Jason of the

Burswood Casino Hotel and then some. He reached for the door handle but was beaten to it by the hotel's doorman who looked like something from a Hollywood movie, as did the entire facade of the hotel.

'Welcome to the Southern Star, sir.'

'Thanks, mate,' said Jason as he hopped out of the limo with a silly smile on his face.

Albert retrieved his bag and handed it to one of the hotel's porters.

'Well, Jason, I believe I'm picking you up again in an hour, so I'll see you then.'

'Oh OK, cool.'

Albert left, and Jason followed the porter into the marble hotel foyer. It was dripping with chandeliers, paintings and all manner of expensive ornamentation. Once more, Jason failed miserably at the fine art of pretending to be unimpressed.

'F . . . u . . . c . . . k m . . . e.'

'Pardon me, sir?' said the porter as they reached the front desk.

'Nothing . . . listen, are you guys sure you've got the right bloke, Slater, Jason Slater?'

The porter just smiled and returned to his duties.

Jason turned to face a tall, thin male receptionist who was looking at him quite strangely.

'Hi,' said Jason.

'Mr Slater, so nice to meet you.'

Jason frowned, the receptionist was talking with such an effeminate voice, it was almost comical.

'If you can just sign here, I'll give you a key and

have someone show you up to your room.'

At first, Jason thought that the twit behind the desk was taking the piss out of him, and was seriously considering dragging him over the counter and breaking his nose when another male porter walked over to collect his bag with a swagger that he'd only seen before in the movie *Priscilla, Queen of the Desert.* The porter picked up his bag, making the receptionist look like Sylvester Stallone. Jason signed the book and with an awkward smile, followed Priscilla to the lift.

As he entered the suite on the twenty-sixth floor, Jason made a determined effort not to be impressed. On the right was a double bed the size of his lounge room and at the far end was a huge window overlooking the Sydney Harbour Bridge on one side and the Opera House on the other. The porter put Jason's bag down and left him gawping at the view. He finally tore himself away from the window and turned to check out the rest of the room. On his bed was a folder headed '*Australian Centrefold Magazine*—Attention Jason Slater'. Inside it was a welcome note from Lesley telling him to use the hotel's room service and they would pick up the tab, and a schedule of his appointments for the rest of the day. He had an hour to himself before he was due to be picked up by Albert at two-fifteen and taken to a meeting at a restaurant with the head honchos from the magazine. Jason stripped off and jumped into the shower in the most lavish bathroom he had ever seen. Afterwards, he called room service and ordered some coffee and a sandwich which he had in front of a huge TV with in-house movies.

Needless to say, he chose one from the adult viewing section.

His mobile rang just as a very well-endowed young man, wearing a crotchless Spiderman costume, was about to finish an impressive performance with two blonde things. Jason turned down the volume as he didn't want whoever it was on the other end of the line to hear 'Yes, yes, fuck me, Spiderman, you dirty bastard.'

'Hello.'

'Hey, you ugly twat, how's Sydney?' It was Mike.

'Yo, mate, you wouldn't believe this place, I was picked up at the airport by a dude called Albert in a big fuck-off limousine. Now I'm in a hotel room that I reckon Kerry Packer would cream his pants over.'

Jason excitedly told Mike about the room and the cast from *Priscilla* downstairs.

'Well, watch yer bum over there mate, I've heard all kinds of things about Sydney, and you being a pretty boy and all.'

'Fuck off, you pommy git.'

The two mates chatted briefly, exchanging a few more racist insults and then finished with promises of a beer when he got back.

Within minutes of finishing the call, his room phone beeped. It was Stallone on the front desk informing him that Albert was downstairs, waiting to drive him to the meeting.

This is ridiculous, he thought, strapping his bum-bag around his waist. Not two weeks ago, I was arrested and thrown into a smelly cell, now I'm being picked up by a fucking limo.

He stuffed his phone into the bum-bag and left the suite. As he walked past the front desk Sly gave him a very friendly look.

'Have a lovely afternoon, Mr Slater.'

Jason smiled, 'Thanks, mate.'

Mike's words resounded in his ears. 'Watch yer bum, watch yer bum . . .'

Jason left the hotel with the receptionist and porter staring after him.

'Oh my god, what a spunk,' said the porter.

'Hands off, I saw him first.'

'Well, I think he's straight, anyway,' the porter said, making a face.

'Hmm, aren't they all when they're sober.'

The twenty minute cruise to the restaurant seemed to take a matter of seconds.

When the limo stopped outside, Jason could feel butterflies partying on down to his stomach, after all he was about to meet with some very powerful people to discuss what could turn out to be a whole new career for him. Albert opened the door.

'I'll wait for you here, sir.'

Jason looked at the chauffeur.

'Sorry, I mean Jason.'

Jason slapped him on the back and walked into the French restaurant with a name that he wasn't even going to attempt to pronounce. Inside, he was greeted by a stunning French maître d.

'Hi, my name's Jason Slater. I'm here to meet some people from *Australian Centrefold Magazine*.'

'Ah oui, *Monsieur* Slater, they 'ave been expecting you.'

Jason looked at her and smiled.

God's potatoes, he thought, I could blow just by listening to her talk.

'This way, plees.'

Jason followed the wiggling French *derrière* into the main restaurant area, which was about half full with late-lunchers and full-time socialites. By the time they reached the table Jason had three quarters of an erection and had almost forgotten what he was there for.

'Jason.'

He snapped out of his bum-induced trance and looked up as the maître d trotted off with a slight giggle.

'Hi,' said Jason, wide eyed and trying, hopelessly, not to look as if he'd been busted perving. 'Nice to meet you.'

Three ladies were sitting around a painstakingly well set table, drinking red wine. The lady to his left was the first to speak.

'Take a seat, Jason. I'm Lesley, I spoke to you on the phone yesterday.'

The ladies introduced themselves. Lesley was the head of marketing and promotions, she was about thirty, with a big friendly face. In the middle was Karen Beechwood, the editor of the magazine. Karen was a very attractive lady in her late twenties, she had masses of dark brown hair and wore a pair of glasses which gave her that raunchy, 'being shagged over a desk from behind', kind of secretary look. The lady on his right introduced herself as Fiona Kingsley, the owner of the publishing company that ran the magazine along with several others. Jason thought that he should bow or curtsy or something but instead he reverted back to the golden rule of 'If in doubt, smile'. He sat down feeling very much at the mercy of the three businesswomen in front of him.

'So, how was your trip over, and the hotel, OK?' asked the boss.

A vision of Petina on her hands and knees while he rogered her from behind in a superhero's outfit flashed through his mind.

'Yes, fine thank you, the room, the limo, everything is just . . . unbelievable. I feel like I've won Lotto or something.'

Fiona smiled, she had a fairly good idea that the young man in front of her wasn't used to the kind of treatment currently being bestowed upon him. She found his genuine gratitude and enthusiasm pleasantly refreshing. The boss continued.

'I hear you're a security officer in Perth, exactly what kind of security are you involved in?'

At this point in time Jason had two choices: one, to out and out lie his arse off, or two, tell the truth. Seeing that they probably already knew and were testing his honesty, he thought that number two was the way to go.

'It's actually nightclub security,' Jason said humbly. 'When people ask what I do I say security officer, it sounds a lot better than bouncer.'

The three ladies smiled. 'It must be quite dangerous, do you ever get hurt?' Karen asked, keen to hear some gory details.

Jason figured that playing down his occupational role at this juncture would be a good idea.

'No, not really, it depends on what sort of club you work at. The one I'm at is a very up-market venue, we never get any real trouble there.' He thought back to his last victim at Davinchi's when he'd had to carry him out, bleeding and unconscious after a vicious clothesline.

'Well that's good to know,' Karen said, sipping at her third glass of wine.

Jason looked at her momentarily and gave her a non-flirtatious smile. Under different circumstances he would have given her a full-bore, cheeky, 'have I got something for you' type grin, which he knew was one of his best assets. However, Mr Wriggly was just going to have to take a back seat and behave himself.

A polished waiter arrived and delivered four leather-bound menus. The polite chit-chat continued until they'd made their choice and had their order taken. All the while, Karen had been running her finger slowly around the rim of her glass and throwing Jason some seriously steamy looks. He could almost hear Mr Wriggly talking to him, 'Jason . . . hello . . . is it time to come out and play yet?'

'No, fuck off you bastard.'

'Oh come on, she's filthy isn't she, come on, get me out so I can take a closer look.'

'No . . . no get down, you always get me into trouble, piss off.'

It was too late, by the time the entree had arrived, Jason had a hard-on that he could have beaten a whale to death with. Worse still, a pubic hair that had been harmlessly wrapped around the end of his dormant plonker had caught itself in the fold of his foreskin and was now being pulled at painfully by his relentless erection, causing major discomfort.

'Right, now,' said Fiona, in between mouthfuls of garlic snails, 'it's time we filled you in on exactly what's happening.'

Good, thought Jason. Down to business, maybe now I can get rid of this bloody hard-on.

'We've brought you over here for the main purpose of simply meeting, and getting to know a little more about you. First, if you did win the Centrefold of the Year would you be willing to move to Sydney?'

Jason opened his mouth to answer when he felt a de-shoed foot touch his shin. He closed his mouth, not daring to look over at Karen whose foot he figured it must be, and cleared his throat.

'Er . . . yes . . . certainly, if I did win, I'd love to move out here.'

Karen's foot moved up to his knee as she innocently picked at her prawn cocktail. Fiona continued.

'The Centrefold of the Year is expected to do another photo shoot for a special issue, would that be a problem?'

Jason flashed a quick glance at Karen to beg for mercy just as her warm foot rubbed against his inner thigh. She looked straight into his eyes with no intention whatsoever of mercy.

'Um . . . no, not at all. I think a second one would be a lot easier than the first.'

Fiona fired more questions at Jason who by now was in serious pain caused by the game of tug of war currently being played between his penis and the pube down in his underpants. As he swallowed the last mouthful of food, Karen's toes reached his crotch and began tickling at his balls. Mr Wriggly was beside himself and hardened more than Jason thought was possible. The pube stretched, and Jason raised his hand to his forehead in pain.

Snap.

The hair was plucked from the follicle that it had grown from causing Jason to let out a barely audible squeal.

'Are you OK?' asked Lesley.

Jason looked up, his eyes had begun to water.

'Yeah . . . I'm fine, I've just got a bit of a headache, probably all the excitement, could you excuse me while I go to the bathroom.'

'Certainly.'

Jason faked an 'I'm OK' kind of smile and walked as normally as he could to the bathroom. As he disappeared, the three ladies laughed.

'What a cool customer,' Lesley said.

'I know,' replied Karen. 'He hardly even flinched when I reached the top. Do you remember last year when one of the boys spat his beer out all over the table?'

'Well, put your shoe on again and give him a break when he comes back,' Fiona said, still smiling.

'Oh fuck . . . shit . . . you bastard.'

Jason was doubled up in one of the cubicles, as he desperately loosened his belt and pulled down his zip. He took his rapidly softening organ from his underwear and held it comfortingly in his hands.

'Oh . . . my . . . god,' he said in relief.

After over a minute, he removed one hand and tore off some toilet paper to wipe the tears from his eyes. He then sat down on the toilet seat, still with one hand over his goolies. Looking at his groin, he reached down and picked out a lone hair, obviously the offending culprit. He held it up.

'You bastard.'

Jason returned to the table after ensuring that not a single pube was anywhere near being wrapped around his nob.

'How's the headache?' said Karen, in a friendly, almost sympathetic tone.

'Fine thanks.'

Jason sat down, but made sure that his seat wasn't as close to the table as before. The ladies smiled as he took a sip from his glass of wine. Jason spent a total of two hours with Karen, Lesley and the boss, during which he was asked about everything from his religious beliefs to whether he had a criminal record or not. To the latter question he'd tentatively answered no, and in all honesty he wasn't telling a lie, but the voice of his conscience was saying, 'You lying bastard, you bashed a cop, you're going to jail, you bloody criminal, and you'll probably end up being shagged up the bottom by a five hundred pound psychopath with a foot-long willy.'

He took another sip of wine in an attempt to nullify his conscience, it worked.

After saying his farewells, he left the restaurant more than a little pissed. Albert was waiting for him out the front with a bottle of champagne chilling inside the limo.

'So what do you think?' asked Fiona.

'Perfect,' said Karen.

Lesley nodded in agreement.

'Well,' said the boss, raising her glass, 'here's to the new Centrefold of the Year.'

They clinked their glasses and drank a toast to the young man who was currently pouring himself a glass of champagne, completely oblivious to the fact that a decision had just been made which would change his life forever.

Albert pulled up outside the hotel just on five o'clock. Jason had two and a half hours before he was due at a cocktail party being held by the publishing company. He spent the time chilling out in his room, watching dirty movies and thinking about his meeting with the three ladies. Thankfully, Karen had ceased torturing poor Mr Wriggly which had left him free for the remainder of the meeting to try to charm the pants off Fiona. In fact, Karen's whole demeanour had changed quite drastically after he'd returned from the bathroom. She had asked him some very hardline questions as well as some quite tricky 'what ifs'.

Jason had tried to weasel out as much information as possible but the trio had remained fairly tight lipped. The only vague clue he'd got was when he asked them just how short the short list was. Fiona gave a wry smile and answered, 'Very short' with what he was sure was a quick wink across the table at Lesley.

Just after seven o'clock, Jason called Steve to check on Max.

'Fucking smelly bastard. Get back here and take this psychotic muther—' Jason put down the phone before Steve could finish his sentence. Max, at least, was doing fine. The effects of the champagne and the red wine had left Jason sleepy and he was just beginning to doze off when the phone rang. It was his mate on the front desk informing him that Albert was waiting. He slipped on a mustard coloured sports coat over a tight, blue T-shirt. He wore black jeans and shoes and tied his hair back. He checked his reflection on his way out.

'Not bad.'

Jason left his key at reception and walked out into the noisy Sydney night where the limo was waiting majestically for him. Albert opened the door. Inside were Lesley and Karen, each with a glass of something bubbly.

'Hi, ladies,' said Jason, somewhat surprised to see them in 'his' limo.

Lesley poured him a drink and they set off to the cocktail party.

'So whose party is it?' he said.

'It's our female Centrefold of the Year's twenty-first birthday, so we're putting on a bit of a get-together for her,' Karen replied. 'It's going to be a publicity nightmare, but I'm sure you'll enjoy it,' she said with a sexy smile. 'All the girls will be there.'

Jason's brain tried not to go into meltdown as the realisation of what Karen was saying sank in.

Party, he thought, twenty-first, girls, centrefolds ... girl centrefolds ... oh my god. He took a large sip from his drink and tried to think of how to address a female centrefold model.

Fuck, what do you say to them, 'Hi I saw you in January's mag, great tits,' no, that probably wouldn't go down too well, he thought. How about, 'Hi, I just wanted to say that I actually prefer silicone to the real thing.' No I'll probably get a smack in the mouth for that one. Oh well, I'll just take it as it comes.

The car pulled over on a busy street outside a packed, split-level bar. At the front door were two bouncers in tuxedos and a cute doorgirl, checking people off the guest list. She smiled when she saw the ladies approach and she greeted them with a kiss on the cheek.

'And you must be Jason, hi I'm Jessica.'

'Hi, nice to meet you,' he replied, using every ounce of willpower in his body not to look down her very low-cut top. He followed Karen and Lesley who walked into the bar with an air that said, 'Ho-hum, another celebrity filled cocktail party, how many have we been to this month?' Jason, however, felt like he was walking into

Aladdin's cave. It was incredible, everywhere he looked were suits, gorgeous waitresses, celebrities he'd seen on TV, and breasts, acres and acres of plump, tanned, shiny breasts, pushed up unashamedly to the very top of the short dresses that had the near impossible task of restraining them.

'Fuck . . . ing . . . hell.'

'Well Jason, this is it, a typical Sydney party, what do you think?'

'Unbelievable.'

Just in front of them was a photographer taking a shot of a very glamorous girl. She was quite short, with a petite figure and beautiful, long blond hair. Jason touched Lesley's arm.

'Isn't that—'

'Yes, she's from that soapie, oh what's it called, I can't remember, anyway there's lots of them here, I'll introduce you to her later, here, grab a drink.'

Lesley stopped a waiter and relieved him of some of his load. As they walked up the stairs Jason had to stop his jaw from dropping. Dotted around the party were about a dozen photographers, snapping away at sports stars, TV personalities and the obligatory gathering of 'the girls'. One of the girls had just walked past him and flashed a smile that left nothing to the imagination, and neither did her dress.

'Jesus Christ, they must have cost a fortune.'

Lesley and Karen took Jason around the party and introduced him to almost all the girls, and a good quantity of the celebrities. After two hours, he had exchanged phone numbers with four of the hottest women he had ever seen, along with one number given to him by a very friendly male designer which he discreetly 'lost' afterwards. Jason had just finished a conversation with an unfeasibly tall model when he turned to find the little soapie star beaming up at him.

'Hi,' she said, oozing cuteness, 'Karen said to come and introduce myself.'

'Hi, I'm Jason, pleasure to meet you,' he replied holding out his hand.

She took it, and Jason shook hands with his first, real-life soapie starlet. They chatted away. Unless he was badly mistaken, he was sure that he could sense that chemistry thing happening. He wasn't mistaken.

'So, where are you going after this party?' she asked.

'I don't know, I'm kind of under the control of Lesley and Karen, so it depends on what they've got in store for me. I've got to be on a plane in a few hours, anyway.'

'Well listen, I'm going to a club with a girlfriend so if you can get a leave pass, come with us.'

'Cool.'

Just then a photographer interrupted them. 'Can I get a shot please?'

'Sure,' the soapie star chirped, and draped herself over Jason.

After several shots she left him with a wink and, 'I'll be back.'

'What's your name, mate?' asked the photographer.

'Jason Slater,' interjected Lesley. 'One of Australia's hottest centrefolds.'

'Thanks,' said the photographer, and left to find another photo opportunity.

'Hey, Lesley,' said Jason, 'are we staying here or are we going somewhere else?'

Lesley narrowed her eyes. 'Why?'

'I've been invited to a club afterwards.'

She exaggerated her shock. 'What, with—'

Jason nodded.

'Well, you don't waste any time do you?' she said with a smile. 'Of course, go for it. Just make sure that you don't miss your flight, here I'll give you some more Cab-Charges.'

Lesley fished out several more of the dockets and winked at him. 'Behave yourself now.'

He smiled. 'Of course.'

Just after two o'clock the little starlet appeared from nowhere, linked arms with him and escorted him down the steps towards the front door. Several cameras flashed as they passed by.

A cab dropped the three partygoers at their destination, a hard-core dance club on Oxford Street. They were waved past the queue and made their way upstairs where the two girls received a warm welcome from a guy wearing short, pink bike pants and a singlet. He was introduced to Jason as Rico, the manager. Rico led them through the ridiculously crowded club to one of the bars and instructed another lycra-clad young man behind the bar to look after them with drinks. After an hour of bar-tab abuse the soapie star leaned over to Jason.

'Do you like to dance?'

'Shit yeah.'

With that she took his hand and led him to the dance floor while her friend chatted with Rico. The dance floor was a mad spectacle. In fact, the whole club was a bit of an eye-opener for a small-town Perth boy. The dress code was minimalist, to say the least—girls in skirts so short that their underwear was clearly visible as they danced. Some danced only in their bras and skirts. The guys went a step further with dozens of them parading around in just their shorts. Jason thought of Davinchi's where shirts weren't even allowed to be untucked, let alone taken off.

John Travolta and Olivia Newton-John hit the dance floor in grand style. By all accounts, Jason wasn't a bad dancer and could even throw in a few spins here and there without falling over. His partner, however, was going off, running her hands through her hair and over her breasts, the full works.

'You're hot,' Jason said to her.

'What?' she said, moving closer.

'You . . . are . . . hot,' he yelled.

Without replying she put her hands on his hips and began to rub herself up against him. Jason ran his fingers through her long hair. She closed her eyes.

Within seconds their mouths were locked together with an urgent passion. Soon after that they found an almost pitch-black corner of the darkened nightclub. Jason had his right hand on one of her petite breasts, squeezing it gently. His other hand was clasped around one of her butt-cheeks, he could feel the outline of her tiny G-string under the satin material of her short, red dress. She was rubbing herself up and down his erection.

'Fuck,' he said into her ear, 'you make me so hard . . . touch me.'

Without hesitation she moved her hand down to his crotch and moaned when she felt his hard cock beneath his jeans.

'I bet you're wet, aren't you?'

'Yes,' she gasped.

Jason ran his hand down over her stomach and up under her dress, she looked into his eyes as he slipped his finger up inside her G-string and ran it up and down the length of her soaking wet pussy. Panting heavily, she pulled down Jason's zip and removed his throbbing cock from his pants. It was so dark and crowded in the club that it would have been almost impossible to tell what the couple in the corner was doing, not that anyone would have cared anyway. She expertly wanked at Jason's shaft as he eased his wet fingers from her, moving them up to his mouth. He looked into her eyes as he licked the moisture from his fingers.

She watched his every move. 'Fuck you're dirty.'

He smiled. 'Turn around.'

Complying with his wishes she turned around and pushed her little arse against his naked cock. Jason rubbed himself in between the cheeks of her arse.

'Just imagine I'm fucking you.'

'Oh yes.'

'I want to come over your arse, would you like that?'

'Yes . . . come all over me.'

Jason took his cock in his hand and began wanking himself against her. 'Lift up your dress for me.'

She reached round and raised her dress. Although he couldn't quite see it, he could certainly feel her peachy arse as he brushed against her soft, warm flesh.

'I'm going to come.'

'Yes, all over my arse.'

Jason held her waist tightly with his left hand while his right held his cock and his come shot out all over her, hitting her G-string and dress. She pressed her hips against him.

Jason spun her around and kissed her deeply.

'Christ, you are amazing,' he said.

She reached behind, and rubbed her hand into the come on her arse.

'Ooh, I can feel your come. It's so sticky.'

They kissed and touched for another twenty minutes.

'Come home with me.'

'I would love to but I've got to be on a plane pretty soon, I have to leave like . . . now to pick up my stuff from the hotel and get my shit together.'

'No,' she moaned, 'come and make love to me.'

Jason shook his head in frustration. 'You wouldn't believe how much I'd love to, but I've got to go.'

'Well, when will you be back in Sydney?'

Jason laughed. 'All being well, very soon.'

The two nightclub-facility abusers exchanged numbers and, after promising almost a dozen times to call her when he got back to Perth, Jason battled his way out of the club and jumped in a cab. When he arrived back at the hotel he made a mad dash to pack his few belongings. He almost threw the key at Sly at reception as he ran out of the hotel and into the nearest cab.

By the time the taxi pulled up at the airport, his name had already been called twice over the PA while a plane-load of disgruntled travellers were waiting. He just made the flight and ignored several tuts and impatient comments as he took his seat. When the plane finally took off, Jason looked out the window with a silly grin on his face.

'Just wait until I tell the boys about this.'

BUSTED

Jason's flight landed in Perth almost five hours later. He made his way out of the airport to look for a cab in the crisp, morning air. He had managed to steal a couple of hours sleep on the way back from Sydney but he was still feeling incredibly tired.

There was hardly anyone else around as he waited at the taxi rank, and he thought of the vast contrast between Perth and Sydney airports.

A cab slowly pulled up next to him and an overweight driver hauled himself out of his seat to help his fare put the bag in the boot, although it ended up that Jason had to help the cabbie. After what seemed to be a never-ending journey, as the cabbie's driving was as slow as his physical demeanour, Jason arrived home at around 7 am, dumped his gear and promptly went to bed and stayed there for the next eight hours.

The mobile phone woke him in the afternoon.

'One of these days I'm going to throw this fucking thing out of the window . . . Hello.'

'Hey Jase, you filthy porno merchant, can I bring this lunatic dog of yours back yet or what?'

'Hi Steve, yeah mate, bring him over.'

'Thank fuck for that, were you asleep?'

'Yeah.'

'You lazy mutherfucker.'

'Fuck you.'

Jason put the phone down and turned over to grab at least another hour's sleep when there was a knock at the door.

'Oh big, hairy, lesbian bollocks, what now?'

He looked at the bedside clock, it was five-thirty. Jason vaguely remembered inviting Caroline over for a pizza and a video that evening before he went to work. He begrudgingly climbed out of the bed and opened the door, forcing out a sleepy smile.

'Hi gorgeous, how was Sydney?' she said, planting a big, soft kiss on his mouth. 'I want to hear all about it.'

Jason might have been half asleep but his conscience wasn't.

'Yeah, go on Jason, tell her all about it, you two-timing bastard, tell her what you did with that soapie star in the nightclub, you bloody pervert, go on.'

'I'll make us a coffee first, what video did you get?'

A cheeky smile spread across her beautiful face as she reached into a plastic bag and pulled out a video that was obviously a porno, judging by its cover.

'It's from my brother's extensive collection, I thought we'd have some fun tonight before you go to work.'

Jason looked at the video in her hand, then at her

mouth, then at her cleavage pouting over her top, then he slowly looked down at her slim waist and long legs wrapped in a short, black skirt. His cock flexed and hardened under his blue trackie pants, then he looked back up into her eyes.

'Damn, I'm a lucky man.'

He pictured himself wiping everything off the kitchen table and taking her on top of it then and there. He stepped towards her in order to turn his thoughts into reality when a big, white form appeared at the door and headbutted the bottom glass panel, cracking it badly. Max stepped back, wagging his tail profusely, and prepared to charge the door again when Steve grabbed the dog by the collar.

As soon as Jason opened the door, Max barged through and proceeded to affectionately assault his master.

'Hey porky,' said Jason, slapping Max in the head. 'Hey porkier,' he said to Steve.

'Very funny, Mr Skinny. Looks like another pane of glass is fucked.'

Jason glanced at the cracked window and shrugged. He turned his attention back to Max.

'How's my boy?' Max licked his face.

Caroline stood with her arms folded, shaking her head.

'Honestly, the dog gets more of a welcome than I do.'

Jason stood up.

'Oh sorry, sweetheart.'

He grabbed Caroline's shoulders and began licking her face.

'Oh yuck, get off, yuck, you're disgusting,' she shrieked.

After Caroline managed to fight him off, Jason made coffee and they went into the lounge room where Jason gave a heavily censored account of his activities over East. Throughout the story, Steve had a look on his face as if to say, 'Yeah right, and what really happened?'

'Well,' said Caroline, 'it certainly sounds as if they took good care of you over there, but you still don't know whether you've won or not?'

'No, I've just got to keep my fingers crossed and hope for a phone call.'

Caroline went to the kitchen to make more coffee and Steve leaned closer to Jason and whispered, 'You're full of shit, you can't tell me that you never got any pussy out there.'

Jason motioned for him to keep his voice down.

'Listen mate, I've got a couple of stories that'll make your fucking nose bleed but I can't tell you now, we'll have a bit of a get-together with all the boys during the week, sink a few beers and I'll tell you the unedited version, OK?'

Steve reluctantly agreed to wait for the juicy gossip, although it was torture for him.

'After this coffee,' continued Jason, 'sling your bloody hook.' He nodded towards the kitchen. 'Mr Wriggly needs feeding.'

'Oh charming,' said Steve loudly as Caroline returned with a tray of coffee.

'What is?'

'He's telling me to piss off because he wants to be alone with you,' Steve said smugly.

Jason lowered his head and covered his eyes in embarrassment.

Caroline smiled. 'Well only if you don't mind, Steve, you see I've brought a dirty video over and I want to watch it while Jason fucks me.'

Steve's eyebrows raised and his mouth opened in astonishment as he looked over at Jason, whose features were much the same as he in turn looked disbelievingly up at Caroline. She smiled sweetly and placed the coffees on the table and trotted off back into the kitchen with the tray.

As ordered, Steve left after the coffee with an embarrassed smile and wave.

'Well . . . have fun,' he said on the way out.

'Fun' was probably an understatement. They fucked each other stupid as the 'actors' in the film did the same, ending with Jason withdrawing his cock from Caroline's pussy, placing it in her eager mouth and finally shooting his come all over her breasts at exactly the same time as it happened in the movie.

He would have liked nothing more than to remain cuddled up on the couch for the rest of the evening with Caroline and her pillow-like breasts, but work was work and dollars needed to be earnt, especially as he'd already missed out on Friday's pay. Caroline protested and attempted to use her more than adequate feminine charms to persuade him to take the night off. However, realising that she was fighting a losing battle, she ended her argument by calling him a 'stubborn bastard'.

It seemed that everyone at Davinchi's knew about Jason's supposedly sick grandmother on the Gold Coast and was keen to express their concern. Even several patrons who he barely knew, asked after her.

'Fucking hell,' he shouted into Mike's ear, 'it's getting embarrassing, it reminds me of that movie, *Ferris what's his tit's Day Off*.'

'What?' shouted Mike.

'Never mind, I'm going to fuck off to the front door, I'll send Grant in.'

Mike gave him the thumbs-up. 'No worries.'

By 2 am the shift had passed by fairly uneventfully. They'd had one fight upstairs but the brawlers had been ejected quite easily and had moved away from the club.

At two o'clock, Chris arrived from the Sunset Club and Jason had to assure him that his grandmother was OK.

'Hey, guess what I did today?'

'I don't know, finally got a root.'

Chris ignored Jason's wisecrack.

'I bought that Jag.'

'You didn't . . . you flashy mutherfucker.'

'Yep, traded in the Statesman and drove it home this afternoon. It's round the back.'

'So when do I get a ride?'

'Well, I've promised to meet a couple of friends at

the Roundabout Club and then I'll come back and take you for a spin after work.'

'Cool.'

Promising to return, Chris left Jason and Eddie at the front door and walked around to his new car.

The jag wasn't exactly new, in fact it was an old 1973 Series 1 XJ6, but after a full rebuild, a burgundy paint-job, massive mag wheels and a dark tint, the fifteen thousand dollar car looked like it was worth a million. Well, it did to Chris anyway.

The alarm bipped twice as he pressed the de-arm button, then he climbed into the pristine leather and walnut interior and turned the key in the ignition. It started first time, of course, and purred like only a Jaguar can. With a smile of satisfaction on his face, Chris reversed out of the carpark bay and cruised down to the Roundabout Club.

The Roundabout was only a short distance away and Chris' new pride and joy delivered him there in a matter of minutes. He found a suitable space in the carpark, plenty of light, not too far from the club but then again not too close and, of course, empty spaces on either side.

The alarm blipped once and he made his way inside the club, acknowledging his brothers in arms on the front door. He was supposed to have been there at two, but it was now almost three-thirty and the crowd had begun to thin out.

Circling the club, Chris could see no sign of his friends. He wouldn't have bothered going down there in the first place but one of the girls in the group was an absolute stunner and had enthusiastically requested the pleasure of his company.

'Fuck it,' he said, scanning the club. 'Oh well, maybe next time.'

He chatted briefly with Luke, the manager, then left.

As Chris approached the Jag, he stopped and stared at what was happening in front of him, half expecting it to be a hallucination and disappear.

Standing beside the car, with one hand on the polished paintwork, was a tall man in his mid-thirties wearing a suit, pissed as a fart and urinating on the ground right next to the Jaguar.

Chris' jaw clenched as he continued walking through the carpark. As far as he was concerned, the mere fact that this guy had his hand on the car was a crime punishable by death. He took a deep breath.

'Just relax,' he said to himself. 'You've managed to keep clear of any assault charges so far, let's just keep it that way.'

Chris pressed the de-arm button and the car's lights flashed as the alarm blipped. The offending urinator unsteadily looked up at the approaching figure, trying not to lose his balance as he did so. If the man's eyesight had not been so badly affected by a shocking excess of alcohol, he would have been able to see just how big and angry the young man actually was. Instead, all he saw was a black and white blur, seemingly swaying from side to side. Then the blur spoke.

'Make sure you don't piss on my car, mate,' said

Chris, trying to hide his rage behind clenched teeth as he unlocked the door.

'Yeah, yeah, yeah,' drawled the drunk in the suit. 'I won't piss on your fucking car.'

'You'd better not!'

Chris got into the car and took another deep breath. 'OK, just start the car, he'll get out of the way and I can fuck off.'

The key was turned, the Jag started and Chris put it into reverse. Looking in the rear-view mirror he couldn't believe it, the bastard was still there, still with his hand on the boot, and still urinating.

The window buzzed down and Chris sounded the horn.

'Get out of the way, arsehole.'

'Oh get fucked, or I'll piss on your car.'

Chris looked over his left shoulder in time to see the suit stagger round to face the car and urinate all over the gleaming, burgundy duco.

The veins in Chris' thick neck gorged with blood and pumped it into his head, turning it an angry red colour, several veins stood out on his forehead. Before he even realised what he was doing, Chris had got out of the car and was striding, blind with fury, towards the suit.

The punch came from way, way back. Chris was almost facing away from the recipient when he let it fly. The drunken suit, still urinating, looked up just in time to see, what he figured out later at the emergency ward, was a large fist crashing into the side of his jaw.

The suit's feet lifted several inches off the ground as his head whiplashed sharply to the right. Chris pulled his arm back, ready to hammer his victim again, but it wasn't necessary.

He had landed heavily on the ground and remained there, unconscious, with his cock still in his hands as the last remaining stream of urine left his body and soaked into his pants.

Chris stood above him, fists clenched. A vision of jumping high into the air and stamping on his head with both feet, smashing it into the ground like a watermelon, entered his mind. Fortunately, reality returned to the furious young doorman.

Several people who were standing around the entrance to the club had watched the fun and games in the carpark. Two of the bouncers were applauding Chris' efforts while a group of girls were ranting and raving, claiming that the unconscious form on the ground was a friend of theirs and the doormen should do their job and apprehend the hooligan responsible. The boys continued clapping.

Chris glanced over at the pandemonium at the doorway and then back down at the prostrate form beneath him.

'Time I fucked off, I think.'

He quickly dragged the suit out from behind the car and jumped into the still running Jag. He reversed out of the carpark and made good his escape just as several of Mr Soggy Pants' friends arrived on the messy scene.

Chris reached Davinchi's and turned off the engine.

He looked at his hands, still shaking from the adrenalin rush.

'Jesus Christ, I'm getting just as bad as Jason.'

A smile spread across his face and turned into a grin as he thought about what had just happened, then he began to laugh. By the time Chris reached Eddie and Jason at the front door, tears were rolling freely down his cheeks and he was laughing so hard that he could barely walk in a straight line.

'What the fuck is wrong with you?' Jason said.

'Are you pissed or something?' added Eddie.

The club had just closed, and Chris motioned for them to go inside where he could tell them his bizarre story over a beer. Eddie locked the doors and they sat down to listen to Chris as he relived his encounter in the carpark at The Roundabout Club.

Sunday came and went as Sundays do and now, at nine-thirty on Monday morning, Jason was on his way to the Perth District Law Courts to enter a plea and have a trial date set. Caroline had wanted to go with him for moral support, which had touched him, but Jason just wanted to get in and out on his own without any fuss.

The last few days had left him feeling drained, in fact the last couple of months would have been enough to give a Wall Street stockbroker an ulcer. So, under the circumstances he was handling things extremely well. Jason had to admit that he was almost looking forward to his first, but hopefully last, court appearance. He was keen to check out, first hand, the judges in their wigs, the jury and all that kind of shit, and who knows, there might even be a glamorous girly taking notes, just like in that episode of 'Married with Children', who he could flirt with.

Much to to his disappointment, however, there were no wigs, no jury and definitely no glamorous girls, shit, there wasn't even a judge. After waiting his turn amongst dozens of others, all he was required to do was stand up in front of a packed courtroom of two people and enter his plea of not guilty. He had wanted to say, 'Not guilty, you fascist Nazi bastard' and then moon the dude in the court hearing the pleas, but thought better of it. His trial date was set for six months' time.

Jason had spent a total of an hour and a half at the law chambers, bored shitless, mostly waiting around for something to happen. The highlight of the whole experience was when a fully gowned judge had tripped over in the corridor on his way to a courtroom and spilt his coffee all over the back of a uniformed cop in front of him.

Fuck me, that was a laugh a minute, Jason thought, climbing onto his bike. Oh well, I'll see you shitbags in six months.

Back home, Jason collapsed on the couch with a coffee and a 'Gladiators' video. His phone rang.

'Hello.'

'Thanks for the phone call, arsehole.' It was the soapie star.

'I'm so sorry, but there is a reason.'

Jason searched his mind for a good enough excuse why he'd completely forgotten to call her.

'I was mugged outside the airport and spent a large part of Saturday in hospital, unconscious.'

'Are you serious?'

'Unfortunately, yes.'

'Oh you poor sweetheart.'

Jason extracted a good half an hour's worth of sympathy from his incredibly unbelievable story and then they talked of their shared nightclub experience. Their conversation ended in agreement that one way or another they had to get together again as soon as possible.

Soon after his call to Sydney had finished, Mike rang.

'Hey, Jase, you Aussie twat, are you still on for tonight?'

'Yeah mate, you bring the beers and I'll supply the stories.'

'OK, dude, they'd better be good.'

'Mate, have I ever let you down?'

Steve, Mike, Angus, Grant and Chris sat in the front room, slack jawed as Jason finished his story.

'. . . and then I arrived back in Perth.'

'A contortionist!' exclaimed Chris.

'She played footsie with your nuts under the table!' said Steve.

'A fucking soapie star . . . in a nightclub . . . over her arse . . . you're full of shit,' added Mike.

'Lads, you can believe what you want, but every word I've told you is the truth, I swear to god.'

'So what's the story, when do you find out if you've won or not?' Grant said.

'I've just got to wait for a phone call I guess, even if I don't win I'm thinking about giving Sydney a go anyway.'

'Well, I can't say I blame you after what happened over the weekend,' said Steve, still shaking his head. 'Christ, I'll come with you.'

The doormen laughed and drank until the early hours of Tuesday morning.

When the storyteller finally scrambled from the bedroom it was well after midday. He made his way out to the mailbox with a head a touch sore from the previous evening's alcohol abuse, and retrieved his mail, an electricity bill, a bank statement and a letter addressed to him in scruffy, almost childlike writing.

'What the fuck is this?'

Back inside, he threw the two boring letters on the table and opened the third. It contained four pages of the same childlike writing along with several photos and . . . 'A wedding ring!' exclaimed Jason.

He quickly scanned through the letter, it was from Deborah, the wacko that had called him last week. She was pledging undying love for her new found centrefold hero. The letter went on to give some lurid details of just exactly what she was going to do to him on their honeymoon, her language along with her spelling was atrocious. Jason had to stop reading when he reached the part which informed him of her passion for anal sex with a variety of garden vegetables.

The photos were of her, her small child and her ex-husband. Jason grimaced as if he was sucking on a bitter lemon when he looked at one of the shots of Deborah, a short, overweight woman in her late twenties with short, tight, black curly hair.

'Fuck me, you're ugly.'

He threw the letter and its contents on the table and ran his hands despairingly through his hair.

'Great, I've got cops and a bikie gang after me. Now I've got a short, fat psychopath who wants me to marry her and shag her up the backside with a zucchini, just what I need. How the fuck did she get my address?'

Jason spent the rest of the day trying to forget about the letter. Caroline called him and they agreed to meet later at Hardie's Cafe.

At five-thirty, Jason was in the shower when his mobile rang again. Dripping wet, he wrapped a towel around his waist and answered it.

'Hi Jason, it's Lesley from *Australian Centrefold Magazine*.'

'Hi Lesley, how are you?'

'Good, listen we want to bring you out for the award show next week, it's on Wednesday night so we'd be looking to put you on a flight on Tuesday.'

Jason's pulse raced.

'Does this mean—'

'I really can't tell you anything more at this point, I'm really sorry.'

'Well, I know that it's got to be kept a secret and everything, but I need to know whether or not to pack up all my stuff and move out. I've got a dog that I'd have to arrange to bring out with me as well as a few other loose ends to tie up.'

'I know it's awkward but at the moment that's just the way it has to be. Look, I'll give you another call at the end of the week and maybe I can shed a bit more light on what's going on then. I'll send your tickets off tomorrow so you'll get them by Friday.'

'OK, thanks Lesley.'

Oh well, Jason thought. If nothing else, it means I get another trip to Sydney.

His eyes widened. 'Yes.' He reached for the phone and called his Sydney starlet.

Jason had arranged to be at Hardie's at seven, so to arrive at twenty past was still not what he technically consider to be late. Fortunately, Caroline was well aware of his time-keeping techniques and had only just arrived there herself.

'Hey gorgeous,' he said planting a heavy kiss on her cheek.

'Hi, how has your day been?'

'Unreal, I've got a new girlfriend. Do you want to see a picture of her?'

Jason laid out the contents of the letter including the ring as Caroline gave him an uncertain frown. She read the letter and her frown changed to a grin.

'Oh my god . . . what a lunatic.'

'Tell me about it, my first pyscho fan, cool huh?'

'Well, it's kind of funny, but you really should report this to the police, this is some pretty sick stuff.'

'The cops, are you serious?'

Caroline read the rest of the letter, grimacing as she struggled through the worst of it. Jason ordered coffees as he watched in amusement at her reactions.

'Well,' she said, bravely finishing the letter, 'there's never a dull moment with you, is there?'

They drank their lattes and Jason told her about the call from Lesley and his next trip to Sydney.

Caroline told him that the funeral for the girl who had died at the party was held on the Friday that he was away. She had gone along with Rosie and Tammy.

They finished their first drink and ordered a second. While Caroline went to the bathroom, Jason reached over to a neighbouring table to pick up a newspaper that had been abandoned. He flicked through it to check out some belated footy results. Halfway through the paper he stopped and back-tracked a couple of pages to where he hoped to god his eyes were playing tricks on him.

'Oh . . . shit.'

Slap bang in the middle of the social pages was a good sized picture of him, descending the stairs of the Sydney party, arm in arm with you know who. The caption below blatantly flaunted the fact they they had left together and were later seen 'canoodling' at a popular Sydney nightspot.

'Oh my god . . . I'm dead.'

Caroline made her way back to the table, Jason slapped the paper closed and placed it on the seat next to him.

'What's wrong with you?' she said, looking at his hopelessly guilt-ridden face.

'Nothing . . . I . . . nothing.'

Jason's phone rang, he could have kissed it. He fumbled with the flip.

'Hello.'

'Jase, it's Mike, where are you?' he sounded serious.

'At Hardie's, mate, what's up?'

'Perfect, listen, I'm in Rosie's car about five minutes away and we're being followed by a car full of fucking idiots, they're shouting all kinds of shit and throwing stuff at us, I've got a bit of a situation here.'

Jason rose from the table.

'Mate, hang in there, I'll meet you somewhere, how about the fountain at Trenton Park next to Steve's place.'

'Yeah, no worries, just get there quickly, these fuckers are crazy.'

Jason closed the phone and grabbed his helmet.

'What's wrong?' Caroline asked.

'Sweetheart, I've got to go, Mike's in trouble, hopefully it won't take long, I'll come straight back here.'

Jason ran out of the cafe, dialling Steve's number as he went.

'Steve, it's Jason, listen up, Mike's in trouble, meet me at the Trenton Park fountain now.'

Without waiting for an answer, Jason shoved the

phone into his pocket and jumped on his bike. The park was five minutes away, he would be there in two.

Steve scrambled from his comfy sofa and, after grabbing a baseball bat from the kitchen, sprinted out towards the park which was just over the road.

The trouble for Mike and Rosie had begun when an old bomb full of noisy idiots had pulled up next to them at a set of traffic lights. Mike had casually looked over at them, as you would, and had been greeted with pleasantries such as, 'What are you looking at, arsehole?' and 'Hey, I want to fuck your girlfriend.'

Mike had replied with a smile and a finger as they pulled away from the lights. This sent the five animals in the old Gemini into an aggressive frenzy. They began throwing cans and bottles at Rosie's car as they chased them around the outskirts of the city, one bottle had already connected with the back of her late model Toyota and smashed a tail-light.

The old Gemini bumped the back of Rosie's car, and Rosie by now was terrified. They were still two streets away from the park.

'Mutherfuckers,' Mike said, as the car jolted. 'As soon as we get to the fountain stay in the car and lock the doors.'

'What are you going to do?' said Rosie fighting back her tears.

Mike took his knuckledusters from his jacket. 'Just a little social work.'

Steve arrived at the fountain, panting. Jason screamed around the corner a matter of seconds later. There was a carpark fifteen yards from the fountain. He slammed on the rear brake and skidded along almost sideways for the last five yards. Steve ran over to him.

'What the fuck is going on?'

'Mike's being followed by some cockheads, he's coming here now, we're the welcoming committee.' He looked around the carpark. 'We'll wait behind this van.'

The area was well lit and there were four or five cars as well as the van dotted around the edge of the carpark.

They didn't have to wait long. With tyres screeching, Rosie's Toyota turned into the laneway leading to the park, very closely followed by the car full of human refuse. Even though Mike couldn't actually see Jason, he was relieved to see his bike and had a fairly good idea of what was going down. Rosie slammed on the brakes and skidded to a halt. The driver of the Gemini did the same and came to a stop a matter of inches behind them. Five drunken hooligans piled out of the car, two of them had shaven heads and the other three had long, greasy hair. They all wore the obligatory chequered flannelette shirts over tight, black jeans. The youngest was about eighteen and the oldest was maybe twenty-two or three. Mike got out of Rosie's car, his dusters on his right hand.

The five bogans advanced on him, a couple of them were a little taken aback with the size of the guy in front of them, but fuck it, he was on his own.

'So you think you're a smart cunt, do you, eh?' one of them sneered. 'Well, you're going to get your fucking head punched in, how do you like that?'

'Excuse me, gentlemen,' said Jason politely as he and Steve appeared from behind the van. The five scrawny bogans turned to see him spinning a set of dusters around his finger and Steve with a baseball bat looking frighteningly massive. With the odds drastically reduced, the five scumbags began to display typical bully characteristics.

'Look, just fuck off OK, this has got nothing to do with you.'

The sneer had vanished and his tone of voice had only half the venom it had thirty seconds ago.

'Hey,' said Mike.

Just as the bogan that had done the talking turned, Mike planted his metal-clad fist into his left eye, sending him sprawling on his back with three large lumps of flesh gouged out from above his eye by the brass points of the knuckleduster.

Another one made a half-hearted lunge towards Mike and was met with a backhander that reshaped the contours of his nose.

Steve and Jason moved towards the other three.

One raised his open hands. 'We were only messin' around, honest, we don't—'

A thump in the mouth from Jason stopped the bogan from talking . . . for quite a while. Even without the lump of metal covering his knuckles, Jason would still have knocked a couple of teeth out. With it, however, the result was a bloody, torn mess of a mouth with six teeth completely smashed. Three of the bogans now lay moaning and bleeding on the ground.

Steve reached one of the two remaining brave warriors.

'Please, please don't hit me with the baseball bat.'

Steve smiled. 'OK' and promptly headbutted him squarely in the face, which had much the same effect as the bat, anyway. The one Mike had back-handed began to get up, so Mike kicked his legs from beneath him and slapped him hard in the face.

'Stay there, arsehole.'

One last bogan remained intact. Jason grabbed him by the shirt and slammed him up against the car.

'You're just a bunch of spineless little cocksuckers, aren't you?'

'We were just having a bit of fun,' he said with a trembling voice. 'We weren't going to—'

'Shut the fuck up.'

Jason shoved him down over the bonnet of the car and pinned him there.

'Stephen, the baseball bat please. Michael, I think the honour should be yours.'

Jason leaned closer to the terrified bogan's ear. 'Are you having fun yet, mutherfucker?'

Mike took the bat and stood over the pathetic specimen pinned to the bonnet. He lined up the bat with his head.

'Just make sure you hit his head and not my hand.'

'Don't worry, you won't even get any brain matter on you.'

The bogan screamed as Mike raised the bat high above his head.

'Goodbye, arsehole.'

Mike brought the bat down with all his force towards the scumbag's head but at the last minute shifted his weight and sent it smashing through the windscreen of the car.

The teary bogan whimpered. A foul stench wafted up from his trousers.

'Oh my god, you smelly little bastard.'

Jason pushed Smelly Pants down onto the ground next to Mike's victims, and Steve frogmarched the other two over to join them.

'Now,' said Jason, 'whose piece of shit car is this anyway?'

None of them answered.

'Oh, well, no matter, it won't even look like a car in about three minutes.' Jason adopted a poncy English accent. 'Tally-ho Michael, in your own time, old boy.'

Mike saluted Jason and Steve as they stood guard over their prisoners and then went to work on the Gemini with the baseball bat. Rosie watched in amazement from the safety of her car. As Jason had promised, three minutes later the car was a wreck. Mike walked triumphantly over to his audience quite breathless.

'Bravo, Michael, now all we have to do is solve the problem of getting this vehicle out of the way so that you and your girly can leave. I know,' Jason said in an overly enthusiastic tone, 'you look after your mates here and allow Stephen and me to take care of it for you.'

'Too kind,' replied Mike. 'Far too kind.'

As Steve and Jason approached the wrecked car,

one of the battered bullies dared to speak through blood and broken teeth. 'You can't keep us here like this.'

'Shut up, idiot,' came the reply along with a heavy whack on the back of his head.

They remained silent. Jason and Steve put their backs against the side of the car and squatted down, gripping the base of the chassis.

'On three, OK,' said Jason. 'One, two, three.'

The two doormen strained against the weight of the car and lifted it almost three feet off the ground.

'How the fuck are we going to push it all the way over?' said Steve laughing.

'I know, you hold it there while I turn around.'

'What?'

'Don't be a pussy, you're a strong lad.'

Steve held the car up while Jason spun around to face the car, Steve then did the same while Jason held it.

'Right . . . push the fucker.'

Between them they managed to push the car up onto its side and then it was just a matter of tipping it over onto its roof.

The weakened supports gave way as the car landed, causing the roof to collapse in on itself.

Dusting off their hands and smiling, they returned to where Mike was applauding their efforts.

'Thank you,' said Jason holding his hands up in fake modesty. 'Thank you. Now,' he said looking down at the pile of bodies in blood spattered flannelette shirts. 'I hope that this will prove to be a valuable lesson for you boys, because next time you decide to terrorise someone, they might not turn out to be as nice and reasonable as we have been.' Jason winked. 'See you kids.'

Steve and Mike got into Rosie's car and Jason went to his bike after agreeing to meet back at Steve's place for a well-deserved coffee. They left the carpark with the old Gemini on its flattened roof in a sea of glass with the five bogans staggering to their feet and one of them in desperate need of a clean pair of AC/DC underpants.

Jason detoured via Hardie's Cafe to ask Caroline to follow him back to Steve's place. She had gone, and on the table was the newspaper, open at the social pages on which he was featured. He looked down at it.

'Shit.'

MACEY

Jason spent a good part of Wednesday and Thursday trying to contact Caroline, but all in vain. She refused to take his calls. He had thought about telling her that the photo in the newspaper was one of those bastard paparazzi things but decided against it. She wasn't stupid, and no matter how much of an expert bullshitter he was, the evidence against him was overwhelming.

He was now down on the beach with Max.

'Bloody hell,' he said, kicking at some sand. 'I've been busted before but never like this, a picture in the fucking paper, how am I supposed to get out of that one?' Usually, being busted wouldn't have bothered him at all, he would have put up his hands and admitted guilt, no worries. Unfortunately, the problem he now faced due to his overactive loins was that he had just lost a girl who he did actually have some feelings for, as much as he hated to admit it. Max ran past him with his snout covered in wet sand and a dead seagull in his mouth. Jason was just about to shout at him to drop it when his phone rang. He could only just hear it above the noise of the wind.

'Hello,' he said, turning away from the wind and covering one ear; the line was shocking.

'Hi Jas . . . it's Le . . . ley from *Aust . . . entrefold Maga . . .*'

'Hi Lesley, you'll have to speak up, the line's terrible.'

He angled the aerial inland and the reception improved slightly.

'Jason what I'm g . . . ng to tell . . . is conf . . . ial, you c . . . n't tell any . . . ne.'

He could just about decipher the broken sentence.

'Yeah, OK.'

'You've won . . .' the line crackled badly.

'Say again, I can't hear you.'

'You . . . ve won . . . entrefold . . . the Year, pack your suitcase.'

Jason received enough information through the bad reception to understand what Lesley was telling him. She said that more information would be couriered over to him the following day, well at least that's what he thought she had said. The call finished.

Jason sat down heavily on the sand, the realisation of what that phone call had meant began to sink in as he stared out over the rough ocean. He had got what he wanted, what he needed. A new start in a new city and a way out of all the mounting trouble that he found himself in, that was the good part. Then there was the flipside, he was leaving his beloved Perth and his best mates, friends that he had spilt blood with as they'd fought together side by side. He had never felt such an intense bond with anyone since his family had fallen apart. The boys, Steve, Mike, Chris, Angus, Eddie and Grant had become his family, and now he had to leave them . . . all over again. It began to rain, Jason hardly even noticed, he remained on the beach, deep in his thoughts for over an hour.

The next day the package arrived as Lesley said it would. He signed for it and excitedly tore it open. Weighing up all the pros and cons of yesterday's news, Jason had come to the conclusion that what was happening was not only for the best but was going to be one hell of an adventure as well. Inside was a letter of congratulations along with a twelve-month contract and a one-way air-ticket, first class, of course. The letter emphasised the fact that he was to tell no-one about the contract until it was made public the following week at a big glitzy party in Sydney. Lesley had agreed over a further phone call that he could tell his family the news, however Jason's idea of 'family' was probably not the same as hers.

He flicked through the twelve-page contract which listed some of his commitments as the new Centrefold of the Year. These included guest appearances and promotional work around the country, for which he would be paid well. Jason shook his head.

'Let me get this straight, they're going to pay me to travel around the country, drinking beer, having my photo taken and shagging lots of dirty women,' a broad smile spread across his face. 'YES, now that's what I call work. Max,' he shouted. The dog plodded lazily out of the lounge and over to Jason who patted him roughly around the head.

'Pack your bags, you ugly, seagull-eating, poo-faced git. We're going to Sydney.'

Jason spent the rest of the afternoon floating around the house on a high that he had never experienced before. He had so much to do, so much to organise. His bike, Max, both of which he would have sent out to him as soon as he found a place to live. Rent, work, packing, all of a sudden the list seemed endless and everything had to be done before he left on Tuesday afternoon.

By ten o'clock that evening, Jason was still hyperactive and after getting ready for work, he jumped on his bike and left for Davinchi's for the last time.

He decided he would invite his 'family' around for a piss-up barbeque on Sunday afternoon and tell them about the move to Sydney over a beer and a sausage.

'Yo Jason,' said Eddie jovially as he reached the front door of the club. 'I hear you and the boys had a problem with some bogans earlier this week.'

'No, you heard wrong, mate. It was them that had the problem, not us.'

'Well it sounds like one of them needs a new car now, anyway.'

'Yeah,' Jason said. 'And another one needs some new underwear.'

Eddie laughed. 'Well listen, Rambo, dump your stuff in the cloakroom then join me out here.'

Jason saluted. 'Yes sir,' and went inside.

By twelve o'clock, the doormen were positioned

around Davinchi's, ready for whatever the night was going to throw at them, and of course, as usual, it didn't take long.

Mike had just grabbed a guy by the arm and was pulling him out of the females' toilets.

'Get your fucking hands off me, arsehole.'

'Mate, you can't go in there.'

'Yes I fucking can, my ex-girlfriend's in there and she owes me money.'

The guy tried to break free of Mike's grip.

'Listen, chill the fuck out, I don't want to have to throw you out but if you don't stop being an idiot I will.'

'You couldn't throw me out. I know martial arts, I'd kill—'

Before Bruce Lee could finish his sentence, Mike had spun him round and grabbed him from behind in a headlock. He then proceeded to drag him backwards through the crowd towards the door.

'Excuse me . . . coming through . . . excuse me.'

Once he reached the front door, Mike gave Mr Lee a goodnight shove out of the club.

'What did he do?' Eddie asked casually.

'Bad attitude.' Mike winked. 'But be careful, he knows martial arts.' He smiled and was just about to return inside when a group of people walking up the street caused him to stop and stare. Now there was nothing unusual about a group of people walking up Lake Street on a Friday night but this particular group was different. One was dressed as Mickey Mouse, one as Daffy Duck, Goofy, Snow White, Father Christmas . . . the list went on.

'Am I seeing things?' said Mike.

Eddie and Jason followed his stare.

'Oh my god,' said Jason, 'it looks like a Disney movie just came to life.'

Eddie smiled. 'Not quite, it's a fancy-dress party. They're guests of one of the owners.'

'You mean they're coming in here?' Mike said. 'Dressed like that?'

Eddie nodded. Mike raised his eyebrows and disappeared back inside shaking his head.

'Hey, mate,' came a drunken male voice from inside a Darth Vader costume. 'We should be on the doorlist, we're from T.J.'s fancy-dress *hic* party.'

Eddie looked at the pissed Darth Vader and his twenty or so accomplices.

'You don't say.'

They were allowed to jump the queue amidst laughter and a few wisecracks from bystanders.

Jason looked at Eddie. 'I don't know, but I've got a bad feeling about this.'

Eddie slapped him on the back. 'Don't stress mate, where's your sense of adventure?'

Jason gave a sarcastic smile. 'Very funny.'

The streets were packed and inside the club it was mayhem.

'Fuck it's hot in here,' Grant shouted to Steve, almost an hour later. 'The airconditioning in here is fucked.'

'No, they just don't turn it on, the hotter it is, the more people drink, it's all dollars mate.'

An announcement by the DJ cut short their conversation. 'Security to upstairs bar, security to upstairs bar.'

Mike, Steve and Grant bounded up the stairs. Mike was almost certain that the DJ, Russell, had been laughing as he'd made the announcement, and he wasn't wrong. Russell had watched a brawl erupt when someone in a gorilla suit had inadvertently knocked several drinks over a table of people next to him. The group of drunken males hadn't taken their drenching too well, and an exchange of words had sparked what had now turned into quite a large bar brawl between the guys wearing the beer and what seemed to be the entire cast of *Who Framed Roger Rabbit*.

The three doormen arrived upstairs to see the gorilla holding someone over the bar by the throat with one hand and punching him in the face with the other. One of the other beer-drenched guys had grabbed Goofy in a headlock and was laying punches into his face, but the long rubber snout was proving to be excellent protection.

Mike stopped in his tracks, 'What the fuck?'

Grant and Steve looked at the sight in front of them, then at each other.

'So who do we throw out?' said Steve.

Grant shrugged. 'Everyone I guess,' and he moved into the brawl.

Mike was dragging one guy off Father Christmas who had a nasty blood nose that was running down into his white beard. Santa promptly hit his attacker in the face as Mike held him.

'Oi, pack it in,' Mike yelled, but it was no good, Santa was out for blood.

Grant was trying desperately not to laugh as he restrained Darth Vader from fighting with some other guy. Steve, meanwhile, was struggling with another two.

Eddie and Jason were talking to a couple of girls at the front door when Mike came bundling through with a battered and bleeding Father Christmas in a headlock.

Eddie stood aghast.

'What the fuck is—'

'No time to explain,' Mike gasped as he let Santa go. 'It's going off up there,' and he disappeared back inside.

Eddie shook his head. 'I don't believe this is happening, Jason go up and give them a hand.'

Jason didn't think that Eddie would appreciate him saying 'I told you so', so he just gave a nod and went inside. Halfway up the stairs he stepped to one side as Grant, who by now was laughing hysterically with tears in his eyes as he dragged two guys down the stairs, one of them being Mr Vader, as they continued to fight.

Jason reached the top of the stairs to see the mad spectacle still raging on around the bar. Russell was laughing so hard he thought he was going to be sick.

The gorilla had successfully bashed one guy but then had turned to cop a kick in the nuts and was now doubled up on the floor. Poor old Daffy Duck hadn't fared much better and had taken a heavy blow on his . . . er . . . beak and was now unconscious.

The boys had to work overtime to drag, push and

carry all the brawlers out of the club. They now stood out the front of Davinchi's, panting and sweating as the arguing continued.

'It was the fucking gorilla that started it,' claimed one of the brawlers.

Several minutes of bickering passed until a police van pulled up and Eddie's brother got out with a bemused look on his face. He glanced over at Eddie who just shrugged and shook his head. The two police officers began taking statements as they were swamped with claims of assault by both normally dressed people and bleeding cartoon characters alike.

Dominic had emerged from his office and was chastising Eddie in front of Jason and Steve.

'You knew they were friends of T.J.'s, how could you let your animals throw them out?'

'Well it—' Dominic cut him off.

'I don't want to hear it, I'll be talking to your boss about this.'

'Dominic,' Jason said, 'it's not Eddie's fault, they were—'

'Who fucking asked you, Goldilocks?' spat Dominic. 'You just keep your mouth shut and look pretty like you're paid to.'

Dominic turned smugly to return to his office after having shown his staff who was boss when he was grabbed by the front of his jacket and slammed up against the wall, winding him. Jason's face was only inches away from his.

'Listen, you smart-arsed little mutherfucker,' Jason

said in a quiet voice so that only Dominic could hear, 'one day I'm going to get you on your own, with no-one else around, and I'm going to beat you to within an inch of your fucking life.'

Jason held him so tightly that his feet were almost off the ground.

'Oh and by the way . . . I quit.'

Jason released his grip and Dominic almost fell down. Eddie had made no attempt at restraining Jason.

'Sorry, Eddie.'

'No worries.'

'I'd better get my gear and fuck off, can you tell the boys . . . actually don't worry, I'll call them tomorrow.'

Jason retrieved his gear from the cloakroom, and after a slap on the back from Steve and a handshake from Eddie, Jason left the club that he had worked at for the past twelve months.

It had been threatening to rain all evening and as Jason walked through the carpark, it began, not a torrential downpour but certainly harder than normal. He reached the bike and was just about to put his crash helmet on when a movement in one of the wing-mirrors caught his eye. Rapidly approaching him from behind were two dark figures, obviously not autograph hunters.

Jason spun around to face them and lashed out with his crash helmet using all his strength. He caught the one nearest to him full in the face, snapping his nose to one side and knocking him flat on his back. The other one began to reach inside his jacket. Whatever it was he was going for, Jason didn't want to find out and, using the momentum from the previous strike, he uncoiled like a spring and again lashed out with the helmet, smashing the man in the side of the head, jerking it violently to the left. Jason then swung the helmet high over his head and brought it crashing down on top of his attacker's skull, sinking him to his knees.

As the two men attempted to regain their composure, Jason placed what had been a very effective weapon on his head, jumped on the bike, turned the key in the ignition and kicked the gear arm into first. With a spinning rear wheel and sliding almost sideways, Jason disappeared into the streets of Northbridge, leaving his dazed attackers dragging themselves over to a black Mercedes in a darkened corner of the carpark.

'Mutherfuckers,' shouted Jason as he accelerated out of a corner.

Even in the darkness he had clearly seen the slick, black hair and the ponytails of the two men.

'Fucking Macey's boys . . . shit.'

As he hammered for home, Jason's mind was racing with a dozen different things.

Macey's after me, Jason thought, fuck, that must mean . . . Jane. What's my next move? What was that fucker reaching for? No, I don't want to know, I'll grab Max and some of my shit and bail out, I'll hide at one of the boys' places until Tuesday. It was a gun, it fucking must have been, shit, I wonder if they've been to my place already . . . oh no . . . Max!

Jason accelerated even more and, after coming dangerously close to stacking it twice, he arrived home.

He jumped off the bike and with his trusty crash helmet in one hand and dusters on the other, ran up the pathway to his unit.

He slowed to a walk when he neared the end of a high, wooden fence that obscured his front door. His senses were on edge, any movement whatsoever would be greeted with almost five kilos of fibreglass in the face.

He stopped and listened, from behind the fence he could hear something, it was crying . . . a girl crying.

What the fuck is going on? he thought.

Jason warily peered round the end of the fence. Sitting on the ground outside his front door was Kim, Jane's friend and flatmate, and next to her was Max, nuzzling into her with a pile of broken glass next to him.

Jason scanned the immediate area to see if anyone else was around before he spoke.

'Kim.'

She jumped with fright.

'Oh my god . . . Jason, thank god you're here.'

She raced over to him, grabbed him in a hug and sobbed into his chest.

'They've got Jane, I'm sure they have. I got home from my girlfriend's house and our apartment was trashed, Jane was gone and there was blood on the sofa and carpet. Jason, I'm scared, I didn't know what to do so I got your address from Jane's diary and came here.'

'It's OK.' Jason stroked her hair. 'It's OK . . . did you call the cops?'

'No I can't, he'd kill me if I called the cops on him,

he does business with half of them anyway.' Her crying intensified. 'What are we going to do?'

Jason looked uneasily around.

'Do you have a car?'

'Yes.'

'Right, the first thing we're going to do is get the fuck out of here.'

He led her by the hand into his house and they gathered up as many of his things as they could and stuffed them into a suitcase. They loaded up her car within a matter of minutes and headed off to Mike's place as Jason knew where he hid the spare key. Jason led the way on his bike.

As they had been packing, Jason had briefly told her of his close call in the carpark. Kim said that Macey had given no indication that he knew about Jane and Jason's 'encounter' in the Leedervale carpark, which of course Jane had told her all about, but obviously he had known all along.

They arrived at Mike's place and as Jason retrieved the key, Kim gave him directions to Macey's house. It turned out that it was only a couple of hundred yards along from where the now infamous party had been held where the young girl had died. Once Kim had safely locked herself and Max in Mike's place, Jason jumped back on the bike and sped off for South Perth.

He was there in minutes.

On the way, he had thought about calling the cops, but firstly, if he told them that he suspected Macey, the gangster, of kidnapping his own girlfriend they would have probably laughed and told him to 'piss off', and secondly, well . . . they're fucking hopeless anyway.

Jason parked his bike and left the key in the ignition. He then snuck around the back of the large house that belonged to the dangerous gangster, notorious for his passion for guns, armed with a knuckleduster, his mind and not much else.

That's it, I'm fucked, he thought, peering through a heavy iron gate. If I go in there he's probably going to shoot me . . . if I'm lucky.

Up on the second floor, through a slight opening in a curtain, Jason could see a ponytailed figure which he guessed must be Macey, pacing up and down the room, yelling and waving his hands around, he did not look happy.

Jason looked up at the twelve foot wall surrounding the house.

Oh well, if there is a god, now's the time to show your face, he thought. As he backed up for a run at the wall, the possibility of video surveillance crossed his mind. However, he was up and over it before the thought had enough time to sink in.

Luckily for Jason, Macey didn't feel the need to have video cameras to protect his property, after all the thought of anyone breaking into his house was totally inconceivable. In fact, apart from the high wall enclosing the house, security was pretty non-existent.

Jason ran across the lawn and hid behind a tree

next to the house, he could just about hear what was being said above him.

'I take you out, huh? Buy you clothes, coke, Es, anything you fucking want and this is how you repay me, you fucking whore.'

A slapping noise followed.

'. . . and stop crying, you fucking slut, just wait until the boys return with your boyfriend, then I'll give you both something to cry about.'

Greco was standing in a corner of the room, watching contentedly as his boss vented his anger on Jane, he never liked her anyway.

Well, thought Jason, I don't think there's any doubt that I've come to the right place.

He tried a back door but it was locked, as was another that led into some kind of conservatory.

A little further on, he came across a window open about four inches. He placed his hands under it and pushed, it lifted easily, his pulse quickened and he climbed in as quietly as he could. The room was in darkness and Jason could vaguely make out two large desks, each with computers on them.

Upstairs, Macey had renewed his verbal, and probably physical, assault on Jane.

Jason reached for the doorknob in the darkness and turned it very slowly. Beams of soft light shone through as the door opened.

Jason slipped the dusters over his right hand, not much use against a gun but fuck it, if he was going to go, he was going to go swinging.

As he made his way out into the dimly lit hallway, he heard another slap followed by a whimper and more crying. He passed a large kitchen on the left and peered inside. On the workbench was a chopping board with the remains of a tomato, some cheese and breadcrumbs on it. Next to the board was a medium sized kitchen knife. Jason quietly stepped inside and took the knife, he held it in his left hand with the blade facing upwards, hidden behind his forearm. From the hallway he reached a spacious lobby, with a large, white stairway to his right.

'So where the fuck are the boys?' yelled Macey.

Greco shrugged his shoulders. 'They should be here any time.'

'Well, go and call them and see where the fuck they are.'

Jason heard a door being opened upstairs and hid back in the shadows of the kitchen.

Greco came down the stairs and turned right into the hallway and disappeared into another room.

Jason took a deep breath.

OK, he thought, it's now or never.

Jason left the shadows and stealthily walked up the stairway. He was halfway up when he took a step and a floorboard creaked . . . loudly. His heart seemed to skip a beat and he froze.

Fortunately for Jason, Macey hadn't heard it, unfortunately for Jane, she'd just received another slap.

He moved over to the wall and continued slowly up the stairs. He heard footsteps and then the door up the top to his left opened. Macey strode purposefully out into the corridor towards the stairway.

Oh fuck, thought Jason, turning the knife around in his hand.

Macey walked straight past the stairway, a matter of feet from where Jason was pressed up against the wall.

'I'm gonna have a shit,' Macey muttered under his breath, 'and then I'm gonna teach that bitch a lesson she will never forget.'

The gangster disappeared into the bathroom at the end of the corridor.

Jason was gripping the knife handle so tightly that his knuckles had turned white, his heart was thumping away under his T-shirt and his eyes were wide with the adrenalin coursing through his body. He proceeded up to the top of the stairs, his feet felt like they were made of lead. On the left was some sort of study, the door was open and Jane was inside with her back to him, tied to a chair and crying softly.

She could hardly see anything, her tears had blurred her vision so much that she had to blink several times before she could focus on the face in front of her. When she finally recognised Jason, she had to fight against the urge to faint.

Jason held a finger to his lips in a gesture to stay quiet, but this was really not a problem as a thick piece of silver tape covered her mouth. With the sharp kitchen knife, he easily sliced through the nylon rope that bound her and removed the tape from her mouth. As soon as she was free, Jason led her out of the room.

They could hear Macey still swearing in the toilet, Jason took Jane as quickly and quietly as he could, down the stairs, still holding the knife in his left hand and the dusters over his right.

They stepped straight onto the creaky floorboard, Jason winced. The front door was not ten yards away from them. Jason's heart was beating so strongly he was sure he could hear it.

As they reached the front door, he let go of Jane's hand and began fumbling with the locks.

'Hurry,' Jane said quietly.

'Done, let's get the fuck out of here.'

Jason reached to open the door when he felt a hard, round object push against the back of his head.

'I don't think so, mutherfucker.'

Jason froze, Jane gasped.

'Turn around.'

Jason slowly turned to face Greco with a gun, complete with silencer, pointed at his forehead. Upstairs the toilet flushed.

'Beg me not to shoot you, fuck-head.'

Jason swallowed.

'Kiss my arse, you're going to shoot me anyway.'

Greco smiled.

'Yes, I am.'

His eyes narrowed, and Jason watched as his finger began to press against the trigger.

Another second and Jason Slater's life was going to be abruptly cut short, when an arm swung around Greco's neck from behind and yanked him viciously backwards.

A shot was fired from the gun with a dull spitting sound as the gangster was dragged backwards, and the bullet hit the front door about four inches above Jason's head.

Mike had Greco in a sleeper-hold and was squeezing with all his strength.

Jason was momentarily stunned but snapped out of it as Greco began to bring his arm back down for another shot despite being throttled from behind.

Jason lunged forwards and grabbed his arm, pushing it upwards just as another shot spat out and hit the ceiling.

Jason drove his right elbow into the side of Greco's jaw. The gangster went limp in Mike's arms and fell to the floor just as Macey was leaving the bathroom upstairs.

'Now, let's get the fuck out of here,' said Mike.

Macey took one step into the hallway and saw the empty chair and the discarded rope in the room beyond.

'What the fuck, Greco . . . Greco!'

He ran to the top of the stairs to see the three desperadoes bundling through the front door.

Jason, Mike and Jane sprinted around the house towards the back garden just as a black Mercedes pulled into the driveway.

Macey ran down the stairs, pulling his gun from its holster as he went. He didn't even stop to look at Greco lying unconscious on the floor as he rushed outside, promptly colliding with his two employees.

'Round the back, get them, shoot the fuckers.'

When the gangsters opened fire, the three were only a matter of yards away from an open gate that Mike had broken through earlier with a pair of tin snips.

Bullets hit the garden wall and thudded into the ground around them, one narrowly missed Mike's head, although he didn't even realise it.

Kim, sitting in Mike's van with the engine running, watched Jane and the two boys sprint through the gate as a hail of bullets ricocheted around them.

The gangsters continued firing as they ran. They reached the gate just in time to see the van and the motorbike disappear around a corner and into the night.

One of the gangsters raised his gun but Macey stopped him. He looked into the darkness, he could still hear the engines of the two vehicles as they made their escape.

'You're dead, mutherfucker . . . dead.'

FLIGHT 763

Mike, Jason, Jane and Kim sat around the kitchen table drinking coffee. It was six-thirty and the sun had just risen. After a big teary reunion between the two girls, they each told their version of what had happened.

Mike had returned home to find Kim in his lounge room and after a brief explanation they had left for Macey's place in case Jason needed help.

'I could have handled it,' Jason said defensively. 'I was just waiting to make my move.'

'You wanker, you had a gun at your head, mate, the only move you were about to make was a trip to the morgue.'

'Well, I knocked him out.'

'Bullshit, I took him out with a sleeper-hold.'

'Oh fuck off, it was my elbow.'

'Boys,' said Kim, 'I don't think Jane really wants to relive this at the moment.'

Jason and Mike looked at Jane, the poor girl was black and blue and still trembling.

'Sorry,' they said together.

Jason put his arm around her and kissed her forehead, she winced in pain.

'So what are you going to do now?' Mike asked Jason.

'Well, the way I see it, I've got two choices. One, is to call Macey and suggest that we calmly discuss the situation over a latte at Hardie's. The second is to hide out somewhere until my flight on Tuesday and then get the fuck out of here.'

'Yeah,' said Mike. 'One sounds quite interesting, but I suggest that two would probably be better for your health.'

They laughed.

'On a more serious note,' Jason said turning to Jane sitting next to him, she hadn't let go of his hand since they'd got there. 'What are you going to do?'

Jane looked down at the floor.

'Well, there's no way I can stay in Perth. I've got some relatives on the Gold Coast, so I think I'll book a flight today and go and stay with them for a while.'

'Sounds like a good idea.'

'What about the rest of your shit at the unit, Jase?' said Mike.

'Well, I took pretty much everything I need, I mean there is some more stuff that I wouldn't mind getting but I'll be fucked if I'm going back there, not without a SWAT team, anyway.'

Even if Jason had taken the entire US Seventh Cavalry it would have been pointless to go back. After the gangsters had busted down Jason's front door and found him not there, they had gathered up everything they could find and had a little bonfire in his front room.

The four slept through the whole of Saturday, then in the evening Mike drove Kim and Jane to the home of one of Kim's incredibly square friends who had never even heard of Macey.

As Jason wasn't going to leave the house for the next seventy or so hours, the gym was definitely out so he set himself a circuit workout in Mike's backyard.

Over the next couple of hours he received several calls from the boys at Davinchi's, eager to hear first-hand what had happened the previous evening with Dominic. Jason told them of the almost sexual pleasure he had experienced as he'd thrown Dominic up against the wall.

'I had half a fat when I left the club mate, honestly,' he told Grant.

'Good on you, it's about time someone gave that little cunt a mouthful. So what are you going to do for work, go to another club or something?'

'No, I've actually got something else lined up.'

Jason told Grant and the other boys about the barbeque on Sunday, now to be held at Mike's place. He didn't, however, tell them of the chain of events with Macey. Jane, Kim, Mike and Jason had all decided that it would be best if they kept their little adventure a secret.

Jason called Caroline to invite her over to the barbeque, but when she answered the phone and heard the words, 'Hi Caroline it's Jason, please don't hang up' . . . she hung up. After trying three more times with the same result, he gave up on the idea.

He was chilling out in front of the TV with Mike when he realised that this was his first Saturday night off in over a year and he couldn't even go out.

'Typical,' he said out loud. 'Fucking typical.'

'What is?' said Mike.

'Nothing, can you grab me a video and some beers for tonight?'

'Yeah sure mate, what do you want, a dirty one?'

Jason looked at him in disgust. 'Of course.'

The Clan was due to arrive at Mike's place at around two so Jason spent an hour beforehand, repacking his suitcase.

Even in his current situation, Jason was in decidedly good spirits and was singing along loudly with the radio. He had even managed to have a look at the magazine but had to slap it shut when he came face to face with his nob.

He called Jane to see how she was doing, and apart from a few painful lumps and bruises, she said she was OK. She had managed to book a flight to the Gold Coast on Wednesday, so Jason gave her Mike and Steve's number just in case of an emergency before then. She wanted to go to the airport on Tuesday to see him off but Jason persuaded her that it probably wasn't a good idea. Instead they agreed to meet up over East as soon as things fell into place.

Steve was the first to arrive, then Chris, Eddie, Grant and Angus dribbled in soon afterwards. By three o'clock all seven of the doormen were sitting around the barbeque in Mike's garden, drinking beer and indulging in a good bout of bouncer talk.

'Yeah, I shagged her too,' said Grant.

'But she's a pig,' Chris said, pulling a face.

'Fuck off,' said Grant and Angus in unison.

'What do you reckon, Jase?' continued Chris. 'You're supposed to be the muff magnet, it's that fat tart with the tits down to her belly button.'

'Oh no, not the one that always wears that revolting tartan skirt?'

Chris nodded.

'You two shagged her?' said Jason, looking at Grant and Angus.

They both smiled and nodded.

'You fucking disgusting animals.' Jason shook his head. 'You'll get more than a dose of the clap if you carry on bonking things like that.'

'Yeah, fucking rabies,' laughed Mike.

'Well, I used a condom,' said Angus defensively.

The other doormen, including Grant, swore and threw empty beer cans at him.

'You lying bastard,' said Steve.

'Fuck off, did you use a condom?' Eddie said. 'The last time you used a dinger was when you stretched one over your head at Chris' tart's birthday party.'

'Oi, less of the tart, piss face,' said Chris.

The merry banter continued until Eddie asked, 'So

Goldilocks, what are you going to do now you've left Davinchi's?'

'Well lads,' said Jason, 'that's the reason I invited you all around here today, to tell you that I'm fucking off to Sydney.'

There was a moment's pause. Eddie was the first to break the silence.

'When?'

'Tuesday.'

'Fucking Tuesday,' exclaimed Steve. 'How come, are you in more trouble that we don't know about or something?'

'No, nothing like that,' said Jason, lying. 'Look, what I'm going to tell you is in confidence, I've even signed a contract to keep my mouth shut but . . . well you arseholes are like my family so I'm going to tell you anyway.'

'Cut the bollocks and just tell us,' said Grant.

Jason took a breath.

'I've won the Australian Centrefold of the Year, I've got a twelve-month modelling contract and I have to move over East because that's where the magazine's based.'

After another brief pause, Grant spoke.

'So let me get this straight, you flashed your cock in a dirty magazine—'

Jason corrected him. 'Women's publication.'

'Whatever, and now you've scored a modelling contract out of it in Sydney?'

'Yeah, that's about the size of it.'

Grant chose his next words carefully, as always.

'You cunt.'

'Thank you, I knew I'd have your support.'

'So what kind of stuff do you have to do?' asked Steve.

Jason told them of his duties while they listened intently.

'You dirty, lucky bastard,' said Mike.

'What are you going to do about all your shit here?' asked Angus. 'That bird you've been shagging, what's her name, Caroline, and that ugly, smelly mutt.'

'Well, Caroline hates my guts, so that one's easy.'

'What happened, I thought you two were going well?' Steve said.

'Yeah mate, we were, but you know the soapie star thing.'

Steve nodded.

'Well she found out about it.'

'Oh shit.'

'Exactly.'

'So what are you going to do about it?'

'Well, I've tried to call her about a million fucking times, all I get is Rosie telling me that she's not there, or Caroline herself hanging up on me. I'd go round there but I'd probably end up dodging crockery.'

'Have you tried the flowers and chocolates thing?'

Jason laughed. 'What for? They'd only end up in the bin. No I'll just keep trying her on the phone, I mean she doesn't even know I'm leaving yet, I'd at least like to say goodbye to the stubborn bitch.'

'Enough of the Mills & Boon bullshit,' said Grant. 'You're gonna make me puke.'

They all laughed.

'And as for the ugly, smelly mutt,' Jason continued, looking at Angus, 'you're not coming with me, so that just leaves me with Max.'

Max was lying next to Jason grinding on a T-bone, his tail wagged slightly when he heard his name.

'I was wondering if one of you boys could look after him until I get my own place organised.' Jason looked over at Steve. 'It wouldn't be more than a couple of weeks.'

'What, two weeks with that clumsy, psychotic mutherfucker.'

Max's tail wagged again, as he was used to being called by those names as well.

Steve closed his eyes and his shoulders slumped. 'OK.'

'And I've got everything else more or less sorted out.'

The doormen talked for hours as the reality that Jason, their friend, was really leaving, sank in.

They began to organise who would take him to the airport but decided to leave it until tomorrow as they'd all be going to see him off anyway. They spent the rest of Sunday evening getting totally pissed and giving various toasts to Jason's penis. Steve got so drunk that halfway through his speech, he accidentally leaned against the barbeque's hot plate and burnt his hand quite badly, much to the amusement of everyone else.

*

Seven hangovers sat around Mike's kitchen table drinking coffee. The doormen, being far too hammered to even find their cars, let alone drive them, had crashed out in various uncomfortable spots around the house. Angus had even tried to sleep in Max's bed, much to the disgust of the bull-terrier.

Just after midday, Grant and Angus very slowly rose from the table and left Mike's place, shortly followed by Eddie and Chris.

Soon afterwards, Jason's mobile phone rang loudly and Steve and Mike moaned.

Jason answered the phone in a gravelly voice.

'Jason it's Jane, you have to leave Mike's place now,' she said urgently.

He had to concentrate extremely hard, his mind, clouded by a muther of a hangover, was having difficulty absorbing her words.

'Why . . . what's going on?'

'I just got a call from a friend, I don't know how, but Macey knows where you are and they're on their way over . . . NOW.'

'OH FUCK.'

Jason slammed the phone down.

'LADS . . . EMERGENCY.'

Steve and Mike groggily attempted to listen.

'What's wrong?'

Jason was grabbing the remainder of his belongings and stuffing them into the suitcase.

'Macey.'

'What about him?'

'He's on his way here ... now.'

'Oh fuck.' Mike jumped from his chair and reached for his shoes.

'What the fuck is going on?' said Steve.

'I'll tell you on the way,' Jason said.

'On the way to where?'

'The airport, now get your shit together.'

Jason grabbed the suitcase and kicked Max out the door, followed by Steve and Mike.

'The back of the van's full of shit, you'll have to climb on top of it,' said Mike.

'Fine, I'll surf on top of the fucking thing if I have to, come on let's go.'

Shit, was an understatement. Jason and Max had to clamber over tool boxes, drills, saws and all manner of tradesman's goodies piled on the floor of the van. Jason narrowly missed putting a Phillips screwdriver through his hand.

'Mutherfucker.'

'Well I would have cleaned it out for you tomorrow.'

Steve sat in the passenger seat.

'Right step on it,' Jason said, removing a hammer from under his backside.

'No problem,' said Mike, and floored the van.

Jason immediately used his mobile and called the airport.

'Yes, Jason Slater, I've got a ticket for tomorrow but I need to fly out today, it's very important.'

'I'm sorry, Mr Slater, but all of today's flights are fully booked, oh hang on ... we do have one late cancellation.'

'Great, hold the ticket for me.'

'I'm sorry but the ticket has to remain open, it's first come first served.'

'But it's really—'

'I'm sorry, but you'll just have to keep your fingers crossed.'

Mike was driving like a madman.

'No shit, well when is the flight?'

'It's at two-thirty, Mr Slater, that's in half an hour.'

Jason slapped the phone shut.

'Step on it.'

On the way to the airport, Mike gave Steve a summarised account of what was going on, while he thrashed his van all the way to the airport. Jason and Max were thrown about in the back and every time Mike took a corner at top speed, tools would fly around dangerously.

On the second last bend before the airport, Jason had just managed to duck out the way of an airbone hacksaw that flew off its hook. Unfortunately he failed to see a small, but heavy metal nail box as it slid off a shelf and hit him heavily over his right eyebrow, knocking him onto his back and almost unconscious.

'We're nearly there, mate.'

Jason could hear Mike but was unable to answer due to the intense pain and many stars in his eyes. He sat up dizzily and put his hand up to his head where a nasty gash was bleeding heavily. He looked at his blood soaked fingers.

'Oh great.'

By the time Mike pulled into the airport the cut over Jason's eye had bled down his face and onto his clothes. He now held a handkerchief against it to stem the flow of blood.

Mike opened the back door.

'What the fuck happened to you?'

'What the fuck do you think?' said Jason motioning to the wreckage in the back of the van.

With only a matter of minutes before the plane was due to leave, Jason patted Max on his big scarred head.

'See you soon, ugly. Be good mate.'

The boys then ushered their slightly unsteady mate inside to the check-in desk.

The terminal was crowded with screaming teenagers, mostly females, who were jostling for position in front of the 'Passengers Only Entrance' holding up placards pledging allegiance to their favourite thrash band that was soon to emerge from a landing aircraft.

'Hi, my name's Jason Slater, I called earlier regarding a stand-by ticket.'

The guy at the desk punched up details on his computer. The ten second pause seemed to last a lifetime, and Jason was trying not to hold his breath.

'Yes sir, we have one ticket left, but you'll have to hurry if you're going to catch the flight.'

Jason quickly explained that he had a first-class ticket for the next day and he had no problem exchanging it for an economy seat. After another ten second lifetime had passed, Jason was issued with a boarding pass for flight 763.

He turned to make his way to the passenger entrance.

'Fuck me, look at this place, it's packed.'

As Jason, Mike and Steve approached the melee in front of them, Jason stopped in his tracks. On the other side of the crowd was Greco, with four of his 'friends' including the two who had attacked him in the carpark. One of them wore a thick, white sticking plaster across his broken nose.

They saw him at exactly the same time.

The race was on, the three boys barged through the screaming crowds towards the doorway of the metal detector. The four gangsters did the same.

Jason, Mike and Steve reached the doorway seconds before the gangsters, simply because they had a ten yard head start.

As they raced through the doorway, Jason crossed his fingers. The security beeper didn't go off. He looked momentarily skywards.

'There is a god.'

They jumped onto the ascending, moving walkway and looked back in time to see the four gangsters run through and set off the alarm.

Two burly security officers halted them and raised their hand-held scanners but the gangsters, not overly keen to open their jackets, backed away through the door.

Jason looked down at them and waved with a big smile on his face.

Greco pointed at Jason and drew his finger across

his throat, then disappeared into the large crowd of fans.

The three amigos ran to gate six where the third and final boarding call had been announced.

Still holding the blood-stained handkerchief to his head, Jason turned to face his two best mates.

'Lads, what can I say . . . I hate you both and I'm glad I'm leaving.'

They laughed and Mike and Steve shook Jason's hand and gave him a hug with a few mutual slaps on the back.

Jason walked over to the hostess with his blood-marked boarding pass.

'Jason,' called Mike.

He turned around.

'Take care, mate.'

Jason looked at his mates, waved, and then made his way down the walkway with a large lump in his throat.

Jason looked out the window and watched as Perth disappeared beneath him. His mind was swimming with thoughts of Caroline, the boys, his court appearance in six months' time and, of course, Macey.

The plane levelled out and a buxom, blonde air-hostess walked over to Jason. She was stunning.

'Are you all right, sir, I noticed you had a cut on your head when you came in so I brought you a towel and some dressing.'

Jason looked up at her, she had full red lips and big blue eyes.

'Thank you.'

'My pleasure. Is there anything else I can do for you, sir?'

He smiled cheekily.

'Please, call me Jason.'